"I know how democracies work. You won't kill me."

"I've got some bad news for you, Cusa. Officially no one has seen you. You're not in anyone's custody. This place doesn't exist and neither do we. And if we don't like your answers, pretty soon you won't exist."

The Romanian tried to gauge the expression in Mack Bolan's eyes, but couldn't. "I know what you're trying to do. You're just using psychological pressure to make me think—"

"No," the Executioner interrupted. "Don't think. Just talk. Tell us everything you can about Konrad Lorenz and his Vampyr network. His front companies. His sphere of operations. The intelligence agencies he worked with before and the ones he deals with now. I want to know every step he's taken since he fled Romania. Understand me? Talk."

"Of course I will talk. But all I can tell you is what I've told you the first time—"

Bolan stood slowly and started to drag his chair across the floor. Turning toward the shadowed faces of Sinclair and Brognola, he growled a command. "Kill him. He's had his chance."

As the warrior reached the door, Cusa called him back. "Wait! Wait! There *are* some things I can tell you."

Bolan spun around. "So tell," he said, grabbing the chair and sitting.

D0052360

DON PENDLETON's

MACK BOLAN®

Takedown

A GOLD EAGLE BOOK FROM
WORLDWIDE®

TORONTO • NEW YORK • LONDON
AMSTERDAM • PARIS • SYDNEY • HAMBURG
STOCKHOLM • ATHENS • TOKYO • MILAN
MADRID • WARSAW • BUDAPEST • AUCKLAND

First edition February 1994

ISBN 0-373-61434-9

Special thanks and acknowledgment to
Rich Rainey for his contribution to this work.

TAKEDOWN

Printed in U.S.A.

Evil is easy and has infinite forms.

> —Blaise Pascal
> 1623–1662

Evil to him who Evil thinks.

> —Edward III
> 1312–1377

I've come up against my fair share of evil,
and have rooted it out whenever possible.
We must all do our part to make sure that
atrocities committed in the past do not
reoccur in the future.

> —Mack Bolan

CHAPTER ONE

Five minutes after they checked into the restored château-hotel overlooking the Rhine River south of Koblenz, the newlyweds tossed their matching suitcases onto the bed and started to unpack. From each suitcase came neatly folded nightclothes, lightweight armored vests and his-and-hers Heckler & Koch MP-5 SD submachine guns.

The craggy-faced man with military bearing unpacked another suitcase full of sophisticated eavesdropping equipment and an Accuracy International PM sniper rifle with a Schmidt & Bender high-magnification scope.

They worked quickly and in silence, comfortable with each other.

The woman had a half-dozen different names and, according to her flawlessly reproduced ID cards and passports, was a citizen of the United States, Germany, Austria and Romania. Her leonine mane of dark red hair gave her an almost feline look. Her name for the moment was Gina Salvie.

The man had also used many aliases in the past. This time around his name was Michael Belasko, the name his "wife" knew him by. If she suspected he was Mack Bolan, the Executioner, she hadn't mentioned it. Nor had he volunteered the information.

The arranged marriage was the work of an unlikely matchmaker—Hal Brognola. The head Fed brought them together to take advantage of their mutual skills. He needed a one-man strike force, as well as a tour guide fluent in European languages, in order to unravel the maze of safehouses their quarry had set up across the continent. It helped that Gina Salvie had cultivated official and unofficial links to most of the security services across the continent.

Bolan set up his observation post by the window on the east side of the room. It had a good view of their target, a granite-and-glass building across the cobblestone road, several houses to the left.

The room also had a good escape route if they needed it, another reason why the couple had specifically requested the corner suite. Ten feet below the casement window at the rear of the building was a high-walled parapet that could serve as a stepping-stone down to the riverbank. Several shallow spider-web cracks scarred the concrete platform, but it still looked sturdy enough to support guests. Judging from the deck chairs and tables scattered about the area, it also doubled as a patio.

Depending on how long the stakeout lasted, they might spend some time down there in their role as honeymooners. It wouldn't be a hard part to play, Bolan thought as he glanced at Gina. Her faded jeans and ribbed knot top accented her slender figure.

The woman looked sure of herself and from the way she'd handled the H&K, he knew this wasn't her first time for wet work. Besides, Brognola wouldn't have put them together if she couldn't hold her own. If they couldn't trust each other, then perhaps the "until death do you part" bit might actually come true.

A cool spring breeze blew in through the open window, carrying the scent and sounds of the Rhine as Bolan picked up the Bausch & Lomb binoculars and scanned the terrain.

The honeymoon hideaway was on the crest of a small hill that looked down on a strip of houses across the road. The scene could have come straight out of a fairy tale—white-painted cottages with shuttered windows and dark, timbered beams supporting slanted roofs. Off to the right of the cottages were tourist shops and bed-and-breakfast places. Inns dotted both sides of the street.

The hamlet was accustomed to tourists—and, apparently, terrorists.

To the left of the cottages was a more recent roadside addition. It was a cathedrallike home of glass and granite. According to some of the Intelligence Gina Salvie had discreetly picked up from her contacts in the German security services, the home belonged to a reclusive artist, a sculptor named George Wagner.

At least that was the man's cover.

Brognola had reason to believe that George Wagner was actually Konrad Lorenz, the high-ranking Securitate officer who had fled Romania when the revolution toppled Nicolae Ceauşescu's regime and brought to light some of Lorenz's more gruesome activities.

Sculptor, Bolan thought. Right. Maybe the man who lived there was handy with a knife, but he wasn't an artist who worked in stone. He worked with flesh.

The Executioner settled in for the long haul. This might be the man they were looking for or it might be another false lead. Brognola and his GSG-9 counterparts had several other teams combing the countryside along Germany's western border where their quarry supposedly had been sighted. So far, most of the safehouses they'd checked out had been empty. Their target either had evaded the security net or had never been there in the first place.

Bolan put down the binoculars, then flipped down the adjustable bipod beneath the long barrel of the sniper rifle. He set it up on a narrow antique table by the window, then viewed the artist's retreat through the Schmidt & Bender cross hairs.

One more suspected site, one more stakeout, one more hit team ready to jump into the fire.

He had a feeling they were on the right track this time, although not necessarily an easy one.

"AND I THOUGHT VAMPIRES only came out at night," Salvie commented. "Take a look at this."

Bolan closed the file the Stony Man team had assembled on Vampyr, the underground railroad Konrad Lorenz had set up for ex–East Bloc secret policemen on the run, now wanted for crimes against their own people.

In return for help in evading capture and providing safehouses and false identities, the Vampyr network exacted a high price from those who used its services. Just like the victims of Romania's legendary vampire lord, once they fell under the cloak of Konrad Lorenz they, too, became "vampires"— creatures under the master's control. If they didn't do as he wanted, Lorenz would expose them without hesitation.

The Executioner dropped the file on the bed and headed back to the window where they'd been sharing the watch, one hour on, one hour off, to keep from being hypnotized by staring at the same spot for so long.

"What is it?"

"Activity on the top floor," Salvie reported. "And a couple of cars just pulled up in front of the house."

Bolan nodded and picked up the binoculars. He saw a flurry of motion on the top floor of the cathedral-styled house—a pair of quickly glimpsed faces looking through the curtains at the new arrivals before the curtains closed once again.

A half-dozen men piled out of the two cars and hurried toward the entrance. They were dressed in business suits that were tight on their bulky frames.

But none of them looked very businesslike.

"They're vampires, all right," Bolan said. "I doubt they're art lovers going to check out the latest piece of sculpture by Herr Wagner."

"Recognize any of the faces?"

"No. One of them seemed familiar, but I didn't get a long enough look for confirmation."

"Same here. But we've got a lot of time to get to know them better."

Bolan kept the binoculars trained on the heavyset men as they waited to be admitted to the house. One of them instinctively swept his overcoat back with his right hand, revealing a holstered automatic.

Old habits died hard, Bolan thought. The men looked like "legal" break-and-enter types, veteran secret police who had terrorized their own people at the point of a gun and the drop of a hat. They could be former members of Romanian Securitate, East German Stasi or Czechoslovakian STB. It was difficult to tell. Konrad Lorenz welcomed them all into his service.

The man who opened the door stayed out of sight while the visitors quickly filed into the house.

"You figure them all for vampires?" Salvie asked as the door closed behind them.

"They fit the right mold. Whatever you want to call them, they're the ones we're after. But we don't make a move until we spot Lorenz."

"You're the boss," she said, a hint of resentment in her voice.

"We're a team."

"But you give the orders."

"Depends on the situation," the Executioner replied. "Sometimes we're going to have to rely on your expertise. I don't speak all the languages you do. And maybe you'll have some of the contacts we need to carry this thing off. I won't crowd you."

"Uh-huh," she said, thoroughly unconvinced.

From the private briefing he'd had with Brognola, Bolan knew that Salvie was also used to working alone. In fact, she preferred it that way. Since this had been her theater of operations for more than a decade, in her eyes *he* was the new kid on the block.

Bolan crouched behind the sniper rifle and swept the scope across the two cars in front of the house. Next he tracked the walkway leading to the house, then up to the top-floor windows where they'd seen movement before.

It was all part of the rehearsal. When the time came, he wanted to cover as much ground as possible. The high-magnification telescopic sight would allow him to identify faces at long range—to make sure he didn't obliterate the wrong one. The bolt-action rifle had a 10-round magazine, enough for him to take care of his primary target and do some damage to the others.

Salvie sat at the other end of the table and picked up the sound-suppressed Heckler & Koch submachine gun, testing the balance in her hand.

"Anything happening yet?" she asked.

"No," Bolan replied. "Not a sign. They all must be at the back of the house."

"They're probably having a family reunion or something. Drinking blood and talking about the good old days when their word was law."

She looked around the room at some of the gadgetry Bolan had laid out by the table—directional mikes and infinity transmitters, enough to wire the vampires' roost for sound if they ever got a chance to hit it when it was empty.

"Brognola's given us everything but wooden stakes and silver bullets."

"Hal will deliver *them* if he has to," Bolan said. "He wants this guy bad."

"*Hal?*" she echoed. "I always thought his first name was 'Mister.'"

"We go way back."

"Figures."

"What do you mean?"

"I mean by all rights I should be in charge of this operation. But since you and 'Hal' are such good buddies, no wonder he makes you top dog."

Bolan looked hard at the German-born operative. It wasn't a matter of friendship or favoritism. It was a matter of need. "Think what you like," he said. "The fact is, right here and right now I'm in charge of this part of the operation."

"Yes sir," she said, tossing him a sloppy salute. "Your wish is my command."

"Good. I wish you'd keep quiet for a while."

"Some wishes don't come true."

He grinned. She was just blowing smoke, feeling the strain of waiting for a war to break out—war in which neither side cared too much about taking prisoners. And though Bolan would like the chance to interrogate a couple of the vampire operatives, when the bullets started to fly, his top priority was taking out the other guy first—and making sure he stayed down.

Two more hours passed before anyone showed himself in the loft window of the cathedral-ceilinged safehouse.

"Paydirt," Bolan said, looking at the man through the cross hairs of the sniper scope. This time he had enough time to match the man's face with the photo from the file.

It wasn't Konrad Lorenz.

But it *was* a gunman known to operate with the Vampyr network. His name was Ion Cusa, and he was a fellow Securitate refugee on the run from his own people. Cusa was in his midforties and had spent the past twenty years preying on the Romania citizenry. His graying hair was cut in a statesmanlike

Julius Caesar style that gave him a noble, almost serene look—one that people in the Securitate torture cells had never seen.

"Who is it?" Salvie asked.

"Ion Cusa."

"Oh," she said. "The butcher."

"One of Konrad Lorenz's right-hand men. Then and now."

It was tempting to pull the trigger, but Bolan didn't want to waste an opportunity to get Lorenz. They were there for the Vampyr lord. Sever the head, and the rest of the body would fall.

"What about Lorenz?"

"Nothing yet— Hold on."

Even as he spoke, two more cars pulled up in front of the safehouse, filling the rest of the driveway.

Car doors slammed, and four men hurried toward the house. They had the same look about them as the earlier arrivals. A lot of muscle was being assembled, part of a heavy mob. Something was going down soon.

"Looks like they're having a convention," Bolan observed.

"If any more of them show up, we'll have to call in reinforcements."

"No," he said.

"There's almost too many of them now," Salvie protested. "Rules of engagement call for some serious backup."

"There are no rules out here. Officially we're not even supposed to be here. Whatever goes down here is off the books."

"Brognola didn't tell me he was sending a cowboy." Salvie looked at the target across the way, then at the hard-eyed man in black, then shrugged. "You're a regular General Custer."

"You can always back out," Bolan reminded her.

"Hell, no, Belasko," she said. "I've rode this horse before. If this is our last stand, so be it."

THE MAN IN THE LONG gray coat smiled when he stepped into the high-ceilinged lobby of the château, drawn by the brightly lit chandeliers and the clinking of glasses that sounded from the rustic stone-and-timber tavern.

He had blond hair, the walk of an athlete and the look of a thirty-year-old spoiled child.

A waitress in a pseudomedieval wench costume led him to a trestle table in the back of the room. He ordered a dark beer and some sausages, but didn't really touch them. He looked around the room as if he were more interested in the people who were there.

The château catered to tourists and to newlyweds who wanted a taste of Old World elegance mixed with New World luxury.

The blond-haired man chatted idly with the waitress, who brought him a second mug of beer even though the first one was hardly finished.

Ten minutes later another man came in. This one also had a long raincoat. He glanced over at the blond-haired man, then took a table by the entrance, where he could watch everyone coming and going.

"I DON'T LIKE THIS," Bolan said, shrouded in the darkness that filled the room. "It's almost like a dog-and-pony show."

"You think they know they're being watched?"

"Hard to say," Bolan said. "But it feels almost like a pattern. One of them shows up near the window, we watch for a while, they drift away. Then, just when we're getting bored, someone else shows up. Downstairs. Almost like they're working in shifts to keep our attention."

"You sound paranoid."

"Maybe. But you know what they say. Even paranoids have enemies."

THE NINETEEN-YEAR-OLD desk clerk stared. She saw the long-barreled pistol come out from the blond man's gray coat, but it didn't make sense to her.

At first.

But when the well-oiled gun barrel swiveled in the brunette's direction, it made perfect sense. The message was coming in loud and clear. She was going to do whatever the man wanted, or she was never going to do anything again.

"Keys," he said in a cultured German voice. And there was a smile on his face as if he found her plight amusing.

"Wh-what?" she stammered.

He held out his hand, palm upward. "It's very simple," he said. "You give me the keys to the corner suite where the lovebirds are staying, or I give you *this.*" He gestured with the gun. The snout looked thick and deadly, threaded with a silencer.

"The keys," she repeated numbly, reaching behind her and fishing for the slot. She didn't want to take her eyes off the gunman, thinking that as long as they maintained some kind of contact there would be no danger.

Behind him she could see a few other men in long coats casually walk from the tavern section of the château, guns drawn. An unnatural hush filled the room, making the festive piped-in music sound eerie and lifeless.

Like puppets, the diners moved across the floor and tood against the wall with their hands up. They were guided by a man who wielded a pistol much like the one that held the desk clerk in a hypnotic trance.

"Here you are," she said, dropping the keys into his palm. "I don't want to have any trouble."

"You won't," the man said. "Ever again." He fired once. The cough of the suppressed 9 mm round sounded dully as it smacked into her forehead and punched her back against the key slots. She spread her arms out, fingers clutching at the slots. Then she drifted forward in a swan dive.

Several of the keys jangled and fell like talismans onto the girl's body spread out on the floor.

The other gunmen opened up on the rest of the guests, who had time enough to gasp out loud when they realized there would be no witnesses.

The 3-round bursts took out the civilians in economic precison. Gouts of blood erupted from their bullet-riddled bodies, staining the wall behind them as they dropped to the floor. The men who did the firing were used to shooting unarmed and innocent people. They'd spent a lifetime doing it.

While the raincoated crew silenced the staff and guests on the lower floor, another trio of gunmen spilled out of a gleaming white van that pulled up in front of the château.

They strode through the front door, unholstering their weapons as soon as they crossed the threshold. Without hesitation they followed the others up the curving stairwell that led to the rooms where the guests were quartered.

Grim four-hundred-year-old faces looked down on the hit team from their gold-framed portraits perched on the hallway walls. Painted eyes of the bearded Teutonic knights and landowners seemed to follow the progress of the intruders as they raced down a series of hallways, then gathered outside the solid oak door of the corner suite.

The hit team was oblivious to the surroundings, their minds concentrating on taking down the people behind the door.

The front man hefted a short-barreled SPAS Franchi shotgun fitted with a grenade launcher. The Special Purpose Assault Shotgun could fire up to four rounds a second and, with the launcher attached, it was a portable cannon capable of firing high-explosive shells.

The rest of the Vampyr crew were armed with an assortment of automatic weapons.

Two men stood on either side of the shotgunner, unfolding the magazine housings that had been extended forward beneath the barrels of their 9 mm MAT 49 submachine guns. The French submachine guns held 20-round magazines and were designed for this kind of in-close work, room-to-room housecleaning.

The blond man in the gray coat held his silenced 9 mm automatic pistol at the ready while his two backup men spread out along the wall behind him. They stepped back from the wall and silently slid back the wire stocks of the short-barreled 7.65 mm Czech Vz61 Skorpion machine pistols, getting ready to fire the wicked spray guns from the hip.

The shotgunner nosed the barrel of his weapon toward the heavy brass doorplate, then looked over at the blonde for the signal.

The man nodded, and the first shotgun load blew apart the wood just above the lock plate, sending a flaming sheet of sparks and splinters whipping through the air.

The second blast hit the shuddering door waist high, shredding the burnished wood.

The third one ripped off the hinges.

Even as the door fell inward, the shotgunner emptied the magazine, punching holes through wood and plaster with the 12-gauge loads. The blasts echoed in the hallway, the ferocious roar drowning out the sounds of the full-auto submachine guns and pistols that opened up and spit flame.

The small group of hard-faced men moved like a precision team. They shot through the walls in rapid-fire sweeps about waist high, then fired another volley of bursts at foot level to catch anyone diving to the floor.

They stood there like firemen hosing down a fire. But instead of putting out the flames, they were pouring streams of fire into the room.

Bullets chomped through the outside walls in crazy zigzag patterns that blew shards of plaster into the air and stirred up whirling clouds of smoke and dust.

From inside the room came the sound of breaking glass and falling mirrors, chandeliers clinking and crashing to the floor, the bed frame caving in with a loud thunk and the whip and whine of full-auto fire streaking through the air and chipping into the far walls.

"Reload," the shotgunner shouted, advancing across the fallen door into the room.

Empty clips clattered onto the hallway floor while the hit team advanced, some of them bursting through homemade doors bashed out of the bullet-shredded plasterboard.

And then they stood there in the cordite fumes and clouds of smoke swirling around the room that had been suddenly turned into a battlefield.

But only one army occupied the field.

"Where are they?" the shotgunner cried out in his native Romanian tongue.

"There's nobody here," said the countryman who joined him.

Cursing roundly, the heavily armed men spread out slowly through the room, stepping carefully over the splintered debris as if they expected to find their prey at any moment.

"They've got to be here," the blond-haired German growled. "No one saw them leave—"

"Ghosts," said one of the Skorpion-wielding Germans, his eyes full of amazement as his machine pistol tracked nothing but air.

The sudden absence of deafening sound was overwhelming. One moment it had been World War III. The next moment it was eerily quiet. The silence fell over them like a shroud.

The entire crew was caught in a hypnotic state of mind. They'd been expecting to find bullet-riddled, blood-spattered bodies of the man and woman who'd fallen into their trap.

They looked from one face to another, hoping to find the answers written there.

But no one had the answer.

Not yet.

Then gradually their eyes picked out the signs that told them this indeed *had* been the right room.

In tandem the trained security operatives scanned the shattered room, searching for clues to the whereabouts of the former occupants.

Surveillance equipment sat on the table by the window facing the cathedral-shaped building that the first vampire unit had set up as a lure for the hunters.

And there was the sniper rifle set up on a bipod, its long barrel aimed at the building.

More weapons and gadgetry were scattered about, as if the couple had left in a hurry.

A collection of files and photographs were sprawled out on top of a small desk in one corner of the room, totally untouched by the barrage that had ripped apart the walls.

One by one, like dreamers waking from a shared dream, they caught sight of the black rubber-tinted tines clutching at the sill of the window at the back of the room.

The tines belonged to grappling hooks, their sharp metal fingers grasping on to the sill from outside the window.

"Over there," the shotgunner said, starting to move the barrel of the SPAS Franchi assault weapon toward the escape hatch.

But he only made it halfway before the world ended right in front of his eyes with a bang and a flash.

The shotgunner's teeth clicked together when a piece of the sun exploded right before his eyes.

Another sun followed it, with streams of bright light flooding his eyes and making him dance backward, riveting his body in place.

The rest of the hit team followed suit, suddenly finding themselves frozen in shock as if they'd been run over by a freight train.

The multiburst stun grenades rocked the room with thunderous echoes that seemed to pierce every last fiber of their bodies.

MACK BOLAN HUNG from the grappling hook's thin black nylon cord stretched taut outside the window.

After pulling the ring of the multiburst stun grenade and tossing the bomb through the window, he had a few crucial seconds to follow up the light show.

Fighting for balance, the Executioner looped the cord around his black-gloved hand and dug the treads of both feet into the rough surface of the stone wall. His feet tensed as he got ready to spring out and up.

It was a precarious position, but judging from the barrage of ammo that had ripped through the room just moments earlier, they were a thousand times better off.

Salvie held a similar position off to the right. Like him, she had scaled from the window and maintained a delicate balance in order to toss in a flashbang when the wrecking crew paid them a visit.

Bolan plucked the Heckler & Koch MP-5 SD from the Velcro harness across his chest, flicked the selector to 3-round burst, then signaled to his companion that it was time to deliver the knockout punch.

He pushed off from the wall and, like a man casting a line into the water, he swung his right arm up and over the window casement, scanning the positions of the attackers. Then he raised the subgun, triggering a burst that whipped into the heavyset shotgunner, stitching him from his gut to his throat, then kicking him off his feet. His thick forearms flapped straight as the heavy shotgun pinwheeled from his hands and clattered to the floor.

From the periphery of his vision Bolan saw a flash of metal bearing his way. His gun hand skirted past the blond man, who was still caught up in the stunflash dash, staggering around like a man lost in the desert. Then Bolan settled on his more immediate target, the screaming guman whose Skorpion machine pistol was moving his way.

Some men could recover quickly from the stun blasts. It was all a matter of training.

Bolan triggered the MP-5, and the guy was dead where he stood, a triplet of 9 mm slugs carrying part of his forehead through the back of his skill. The Skorpion fired a harmless burst into the floor as the man's finger instinctively clutched the trigger.

Bolan rode the recoil of the Heckler & Koch and squeezed off a series of bursts that clotheslined the room, catching two more targets before he swung out of sight.

"Take it," Bolan said.

Salvie was already in motion, pushing off the wall and firing into the room. Her feet scrambled against the stone for balance while she burned off several 3-round bursts.

A few wild shots of return fire poured from the top of the window and harmlessly buzzed the air overhead.

Thumping hard against the wall, the Executioner maintained his grip on the cord while he took out a fresh clip and slapped it into his subgun.

Salvie emptied her clip, then dropped back from the window.

Once again Bolan swung himself up into firing position. Two figures were darting out of the room— one of them the blond-haired man, the other a gray-haired man wildly firing a Skorpion behind his back.

Bolan squeezed off a round and sent the running man headfirst into the wall.

The other man got away.

The warrior clambered through the window and rolled onto the floor, then ran across the room, picking up the shotgun on the way.

The hallway was empty.

The room was full of the dead.

The honeymoon was over.

CHAPTER TWO

The Executioner leaped down the ornate steps of the château and landed hard on the cobblestone street, the soles of his shoes skidding as he fought for balance.

He waved the nose of the subgun toward the white van screeching away from the curb, enveloped in an acrid, billowing cloud of burning rubber. The rear doors of the van flapped open from the sudden takeoff, exposing a crouching gunman with a 9 mm submachine gun pointed Bolan's way.

As the getaway vehicle swerved to the other side of the street, the gunman in the back of the van shot forward. He landed gut first on the floor of the van with both arms extended over the edge. He was trying to aim at Bolan and at the same time keep from falling out of the van.

His body swerved like a pendulum, but he managed to hook his feet on the wheel wells inside the van and gain enough balance to keep from dropping onto the cobblestones.

Bolan was still in motion, gauging the time it would take to squeeze off a burst and hit an erratically moving target, versus the time it would take to catch a few rounds in the chest.

It was no contest.

The other man had the advantage.

Bolan kept moving.

He launched himself into the air and dived sideways while keeping his eye on the gunman who'd let loose with his 9 mm autopistol. A spray of bullets bit into the ground below him and kicked up shattered stone that chewed into his ribs.

Bolan landed hard on his shoulder and tucked himself in for the inevitable roll. While the world spun around him end over end, he did all he could to hang on to the MP-5.

The Executioner came up in a crouch, ready to trigger a retaliatory burst, but held his fire.

Suddenly a woman was dancing in front of him, hysterically shouting in English. She was in high heels and a black dress, her eyes wide with fear and shock.

And she was standing right in the line of fire.

"They've killed everybody, they've—" She stopped speaking in midsentence when she suddenly noticed the weapon in his hand. She'd seen the man in the van firing and correctly assumed Bolan wasn't with them. But now that the gun was evident, she wasn't sure where he stood in the scheme of things.

So much had happened to her in such a brief span of time that the frightened woman was no longer in the right frame of mind to think. Or to act.

She stood there in the middle of a cobblestoned battlefield, shaking her head, unsure which way to go.

Then she looked down at her wrist where Bolan had grabbed her and she realized she was either about to be rescued or become a hostage.

Bolan flung her back toward the stone steps of the château, pinwheeling the two of them up the stairs, while another burst of wildly aimed autofire flashed from the retreating van.

"What can I do—they're all dead! We were just stopping here for the atmosphere, you know, candlelight, music, before we went on to Koblenz. But they're all against the wall now, all *bloody* and—now what am I supposed to do? I was in the rest room when I heard them so I stayed hidden but now there's nowhere to go...."

Bolan scanned the street, looking past her at the van as it roared toward the cathedral-shaped safehouse.

"If you want to stay alive, get yourself across the street when I tell you to move. Go into the inn and don't come out until the authorities get here. This thing isn't over yet. They might be coming back for a second round."

She was shivering and running her hands over her shoulders while she looked at the brightly lit windows of the inn across the street from them. Some shadowy watchers could be seen moving in the windows, peering out at the eerie tableau. Her fairy-tale tourist trip had just turned into a nightmare.

"Go!" Bolan shouted. "Now!" He steered her toward the road and gave her a gentle push so she'd move while it was still safe. Before the vampires came back.

Then he hurried back inside.

It was like stepping into a slaughterhouse.

They'd taken no chances, wiping out every potential witness who'd had the bad luck to get in the way of their strike.

If Bolan and Salvie hadn't gone out the window moments before the killing crew trooped down the upstairs hallway, they'd be just as dead as everyone else.

The desk clerk, a bright young teenage girl, had been cut down without a second thought.

It was the same with the men and women who'd been herded up against a wall. The last things they'd seen were the cold barrels of submachine guns.

Their broken bodies lay side by side, covered with shards of glass from shattered wine bottles and crystal goblets, the pulverized glass glittering in the dim halo of light from the overhead chandelier.

Bloody red footprints were still slick and glistening on the stone-tiled floor, forming a trail to and from the bodies, almost as if the gunmen had moved in close to check on their handiwork.

War had come back to the château, just as it had hundreds of years ago, striking suddenly out of the night. And it was carried out by an army of modern-day vampires who'd sold their souls to Konrad Lorenz.

As he hurried through the bloodstained trail of carnage, Bolan swore that he'd show the vampires just how quickly they could die. When he reached the top floor and thundered down the hallway leading to the corner suite, the Executioner called to Gina Salvie so that he wouldn't be met with a burst of automatic fire.

"Belasko!" she shouted in return, glancing at the doorway from her post by the window when he burst into the room. "Hurry up. They're on the move."

Bolan took up his position by the table where the sniper rifle awaited him. It had remained in position, its metallic finish shining in the moonlight that splashed in through the window.

Things were moving too fast. This was supposed to have been a take-out service assignment. Simple and silent. He and Salvie were supposed to come in quietly, wait until the Vampyr chief showed his face, then take him out before he knew what hit him. Simple.

But now it was turning into an Alamo operation, with Bolan and Gina stuck behind the crumbling walls waiting for the next and maybe final attack.

The backup team would be coming for them any time—unless the threat was nullified now.

Scanning the safehouse through the night scope on the sniper rifle, Bolan quickly took in the layout to calculate the geometric equations of death. The white van had come to a stop behind the cars in the driveway of the safehouse, creating a temporary bottleneck while the driver and passenger ran toward the entrance to consult with the rest of the crew.

It was fight-or-flight time.

While the Vampyr gunmen were making up their minds, precious time had been lost.

Time taken by the Executioner.

He swept the cross hairs over the backup men as they moved through the front door in single file, looking like plainclothes troopers on an urban exercise. This time they made no effort to disguise the weaponry they were carrying.

Bolan zeroed in on one of the men who seemed to be giving the directions. He carried a micro-Uzi in his right hand and was gesturing toward the château.

The Executioner squeezed the trigger.

A fountain of blood sprayed in the air like a burst balloon. The micro-Uzi went flying end over end in the air while the gunman went flying off into eternity with a piece of his temple missing.

Bolan worked the bolt, following the stare of a second man who was running for his car and looking for the source of the gunshot. A 7.62 mm bullet ripped through the man's chest, kicking him back off his feet.

The Model PM was designed for rapid firing without having to look away from the scope while working the bolt between rounds. Bolan had used it several times before, both on the firing range and in the killing fields. With practiced ease he fired several more shots toward the tightly grouped wrecking crew before they spread out to improve their chances of survival.

There was no sign of Ion Cusa, the biggest catch in the pack of hunters Konrad Lorenz had dispatched to the safehouse.

Cusa was probably holed up inside, Bolan thought, waiting to see which way the fight was going.

The Executioner knew the type well. If the operation was a success, Cusa would come out to take all of the credit. If it was a rout, he'd be the first one to cast blame on the others.

The blond-haired man and the one who'd fired at Bolan down in the street were both crouching low, heading for the van and escape. The warrior drilled the gunman in the center of his forehead, the 7.62 mm bullet knocking him straight down to the ground as if a hammer had cracked the top of his skull.

And then there were no targets. The hardmen had taken cover behind the cars or the side of the house. Now it was time for them to make a run for it, or a run toward Bolan.

"I think we took some of the wind out of their sails," the Executioner said. "But it's hard to say for sure. They still might come after us. Let's be ready either way."

Salvie nodded. She was already inspecting the SPAS Franchi shotgun that had been dropped to the floor.

"The SPAS door knocker's still ready to go," she reported. With a flash of her sharp blade, she cut the strap of the compact bandolier the downed shotgunner had been wearing. "We've got high-explosive grenades and armor piercers, take your pick."

Bolan nodded, still looking through the sight of the rifle, waiting for one of the hardmen to make a wrong move. Then he glanced briefly back at his companion.

"Sanitize the room," he said, "the files, the gear, then get the hell out. I'll meet you down at the car. We've got about five, maybe ten minutes before this place is swarming with police."

Salvie swept the Vampyr files provided by Brognola off the desktop and into a wide-open carryall. Then, like a mad shopper on a spree, she hurried through the debris of the room, uncovering the electronic gear that would have linked their presence to an investigation.

Bolan gently swiveled the sniper rifle, pressing the stock into his shoulder while he squeezed off another round just to remind his targets of his presence.

Finally the gunmen made their break, moving all at once like ants swarming from a hill.

Bolan fired two shots as the van roared away.

He took another shot.

One of the cars backed up with a loud metal thump, smashing another car out of the way before it screeched down the road.

Bolan grabbed the sniper rifle, took one quick glance around the room, then hurried down to the front entrance.

Salvie was already waiting for him, sitting behind the driver's wheel of the customized Mercedes with the rear door wide open for the Executioner.

The warrior dived into the back seat, thrown against the cushion as she stomped on the gas pedal and headed for the safehouse.

"We go after them?" she shouted over her shoulder.

"Damn right. See what we can find before every cop in Koblenz gets on the scene."

She raced over the cobblestone street, lights out, engine whining as she bore down on the safehouse. One car had remained in the driveway, a bright red Volkswagen with the door hanging open like a broken wing and the dead would-be driver stretched out on the ground.

Salvie skidded to a diagonal stop behind the Volkswagen, giving Bolan some cover while he got out of the back seat of the Mercedes. With the Heckler & Koch submachine gun back in its chest harness and the SPAS Franchi shotgun and grenade launcher cradled under his arm, the warrior skirted alongside the Volkswagen in a low crouch that brought him almost to the front of the house.

There was movement from the bottom floor where the trapped gunmen had holed up.

Bolan stopped, planted his feet for a split second, then fired the grenade launcher.

The high-explosive shell thundered through the glass wall to the right of the door, blasting it to pieces. Panel after panel of brittle glass cascaded to the ground in guillotine-sharp wedges.

Bolan dropped the shotgun and burst through the freshly made opening in the front wall. The more controllable Heckler & Koch subgun was in his hands, sweeping across the interior of the safehouse in cadence with his gaze.

There was nothing left alive.

Then he heard a groan and saw a thick forearm sticking out from under wreckage in the corner of the room nearest a fireplace. It was the scorched remains of a long wooden table. The man had either sought shelter before the wall caved in, or the blast had thrown it on top of him.

As Bolan stepped around to view the survivor from a better angle, he saw that the man was bruised and bloody but conscious.

He also saw that it was the heavy-jowled Ion Cusa.

Bolan pulled back the remains of the table with one hand while aiming the barrel of the H&K submachine gun an inch from Cusa's broad forehead.

"Can you walk?"

The man shook his head. He was groggy, but there was a cagy look in his eyes that shone through his feined confusion. Cusa was in better shape than he was letting on.

"Too bad," Bolan said. "I'm not about to carry you out of here."

Cusa sat back against the wall, looking for a moment like a tired old man. His eyes raised heavenward while his hands raised in a surrendering position. He was also speaking a stream of Romanian.

Bolan backed away from him, taking a quick look at the carnage around the room. Nothing else moved.

"Can't walk," the warrior growled. "Can't talk English..." He aimed his weapon at Cusa's head. "Then I guess that means you can't live, either. You're no use to me."

"Wait! Don't shoot me...." He spoke in heavily accented English but obviously knew enough of the language to get by. At least enough to live for a while longer.

"Get up!" Bolan ordered, gesturing with the submachine gun.

Cusa pushed himself up from the floor.

"It's a miracle. You *can* walk. Go out to the car with your head down and your hands up. And start thinking how you can be of use to us. Otherwise, you're out of the game."

The burly Romanian nodded and walked unevenly toward the huge gap in the shattered glass wall, still playing up the walking-wounded angle.

Bolan poked the barrel of the H&K into his back and pushed hard, making Cusa quick-step through the opening.

"Don't look back," the warrior cautioned. "If you do, you're dead. Got it?"

"Yes!" Cusa said. "Got it. I'm no fool."

"That's what we're going to find out," Bolan said, hurrying him down to the car, then tipping him forward and knocking him onto the floor in front of the rear seat.

"Let's get out of here," he said to Salvie, slamming the door behind him.

The woman spun the wheel and raced the Mercedes back down the road toward the château.

As they headed south, Bolan leaned forward and spoke softly to the Romanian. "Let's get something straight right now. She speaks Romanian. I speak English. There's no reason you can't communicate with us. If you don't answer all our questions, you won't have a future."

CHAPTER THREE

Dracula never died, Simona Lascue thought. He simply went underground for a few hundred years before surfacing once again in the form of Konrad Lorenz.

From her leather-cushioned perch on the contoured sofa, the long-legged former actress and Lorenz's current mistress watched the muscled shoulders of the Romanian exile expand and contract in a slow, graceful motion.

It looked almost as if he were conducting an orchestra as his outstretched hands slowly drifted downward. The rituallike movements were part of the t'ai chi or aikido or yoga exercises Konrad always practiced after a weight-lifting workout.

Simona could never get them straight. The movements were always too complicated or too slow for her to watch.

But she had no choice in the matter.

Konrad had a godlike hold over every aspect of her life, and gods had to be worshiped twenty-four hours a day.

She couldn't go anywhere or speak to anyone without first clearing it with him. And then he would coach her in how to act and what to say. Everything she was permitted to do had to have a purpose—and the ultimate purpose was the greater glory of Konrad Lorenz.

Even her looks came under his control. The plunging bodice of her black dress showed too much rounded flesh for her taste, but it had been personally selected by him. So were the shoes. So was the style of her hair, swept back in a braided Viking-vixen look that appealed to his warrior fantasies.

Simona had also dyed her hair platinum on his orders. True, part of it was the need for disguise. Part of it was simply his desire. He'd said the color reminded him of the treasure that he'd amassed in Romania, bullion that was secreted away where only he could get at it. One day he would cash it all in.

And perhaps one day he would decide to cash *her* in.

Such was life with Konrad Lorenz.

The exercise session was almost over. Ever the actress, she manufactured another worshipful and seductive smile while she followed his hands craning high over his head before drifting down slowly, the fingers coming together in a pinching motion. *What was this movement called?* she wondered.

Bird catches worm?

Eagle has snack?

Vampyr flexes claws?

Whatever it was called, she was sure Konrad performed it with mastery. The man was always conquering new territory, even while he was on the run, always combining as many activities as he could at one time.

Right now, as he carried out the intricate movements of his exercises, he was enveloped by an electronic wall of voice and vision, a hissing and static-filled babble that streamed from the banks of television monitors, speakers and multiband radios that dominated this part of the penthouse complex of the Europa-Musikorps Tower.

Animated faces of newscasters from around the globe murmured in discordant harmony, their camera-hardened eyes full of urgency that looked studied and pretentious when viewed as part of a pack. The satellite news feeds brought an unending influx of crises and confusion from around the world, entertaining and frightening the public like a good horror show.

From one of the multiband radios came the hushed and refined voice of a BBC broadcaster. It was accompanied by an Austrian counterpart whose voice boomed from a radio next to it. And filtering through an ocean of static from one of the other stacks of slim-framed high-tech radios was an Asian voice, chatting calmly and rapidly.

Amid the gentle tumult Simona heard an American accent identifying itself as the Voice of America. From another station came a musical interlude, classical piano notes that swirled in counterpoint to the chorus of voices.

The controlled chaos was part of Konrad's routine. It was a holdover from his days and nights spent in the underground rooms beneath the Romania Communist Party Central Committee building in Bucharest. He and his kind used to listen to the conversations of dissidents and political rivals, of criminals and Intelligence operations, of men and women thinking they were sharing private moments.

The voices from the television screens and radio banks were just loud enough to be heard, but low enough to blend into a subliminal curtain of sound that Konrad could raise or lower with a small remote-cotrol unit if anything deserving of his attention came on-screen.

"Almost finished," Konrad said as he turned in her direction once again, his hands still rising and falling like those of a puppeteer.

Simona nodded and summoned up a glassy-eyed gaze to cover her unease at the serene look upon his face. He looked totally at peace now, and that was one of the most frightening things she found about Konrad, this chameleonlike ability to project so many different moods.

Could sadists like him find satori?

For a man so skilled in inflicting pain on his fellow man, it was quite a Zen-like accomplishment, as if the strength of his meditative image could override the years of terror she'd felt at his hands.

It was so convincing that for a moment Simona almost found herself believing in the cover he'd established as the CEO of an international entertainment group devoted to preserving and promoting the music and culture of emerging Eastern European countries. Maybe the part of her life that was anchored in Romania was all a dream, a part of the madness she felt within her night and day. And this was the permanent reality.

Sometimes it was hard to tell. After all, a man like Konrad Lorenz could make you think anything he wanted to, given enough time and enough rope.

It was easier to accept this image of Konrad, this noble man making his way in the cultural capital of Germany.

Konrad had trimmed down some of his bulk and looked like an entirely different man. His hair was cut shorter, well trimmed, well dyed. No longer was he one of the gray-haired old men of the Securitate. Now he resembled a vibrant entrepreneur, a spokesman for the arts, not for the state.

The refined look couldn't totally disguise the Old World cold warrior that resided in his challenging gaze. Konrad kept himself in fighting shape, sometimes spending hours a day conditioning himself by running, working with weights or slashing the air with some of the wicked bladed weapons with which he was so proficient. Though he was in his fifties, Konrad had the body of a much younger man. His profession demanded it.

He saw himself as an Iron Guard man with an iron will. Konrad wasn't content merely ordering his subordinates into combat. By staying in fighting trim, he could physically enforce his will on others. He could kill when necessary, just as he had done in their native country.

Konrad was nostalgic for those days. Not necessarily for the land or the people, but for the power he'd wielded as one of the dictator's chosen ones—a Securitate colonel.

The Securitate had been the privileged elite of the secret police who ruled Romania, a private guard nearly twenty thousand strong devoted to protecting Nicolae Ceauşescu from his own people, who loathed the very sight of the dictator or the sound of his name. Much as their ancestors in the Transylvanian province had feared the medieval warlord known as Vlad Dracul, the Romanians feared Nicolae Ceauşescu and his shadowy Securitate agents whose late-night visits often resulted in the "vanishing" of dissidents or those who spoke their minds at the wrong time.

There was a crucial difference between the two leaders, Simona thought. Vlad Dracul had been a warlord, a soldier who'd fought to keep his people free. There was no denying his cruelty. That was legend and that was what kept his name alive even today. But there was also no denying his accomplishments. The medieval warlord had fought the Turks and the Hungarians, emerging victorious from battles with armies that dwarfed his many times over.

And Ceaușescu?

He warred only against his own people, carrying out incessant purges with such ferocity that finally the people couldn't take it anymore, rising as one and risking everything until the tyrant was overthrown and executed.

It had simply grown too much for the people to bear.

While the lights in the houses of common people stayed dark and their furnaces stayed cold, Ceaușescu's minions lived in luxury. Whatever money the dictator didn't squander on building monuments to himself had been spent on the secret police apparatus. They'd drained the pitiful resources of Romania to keep themselves in the style they were accustomed to: bugging devices, hidden cameras, armored cars, weaponry, private stores for them to shop at, private mistresses for them to keep on their own. The litany of privilege was as inventive and endless as the number of Securitate agents.

The thought of it all made Simona sick.

It made Konrad Lorenz sentimental, longing for the days when his word was law, so much so that he was trying to create a little bit of his homeland right here in Germany.

Using money he'd sifoned off from the treasury and from foreign aid that poured into the country, Lorenz had created a number of dummy corporations across Europe. That was where the funding for the Europa-Musikorps came from.

In its guise as a music recording and reissuing company, Europa-Musikorps sent representatives all across Europe. While they always had some form of business to transact as a cover—a recording session or just a preliminary meeting with managers or musicians—the representatives were really taking care of another kind of business. Along with its interest in saving the music of the continent, Europa-Musikorps was also devoted to saving lives—those of the hunted men and women who used to wield the secret reins of power.

The music company was just one more hidden piece of the Vampyr jigsaw puzzle that Konrad used to move men and money around. The logistics were perfect for moving "recording crews" and "artists" across borders. The corporation also had film specialists to make documentaries—and now and then documents.

It was all too perfect. Simona Lascue had never really escaped from Romania. Konrad Lorenz had brought his apparatus with him, tyranny and all.

"A drink," Konrad said, his voice suddenly snapping the spell she'd fallen into.

"Of course. What do you want?"

"Something healthy," he replied. "But something with a kick."

Simona bowed sharply, the perfect servant and seductress as she swept her feet off the couch and drifted over to the richly appointed bar near the window that looked down on Turkenstrasse. She poured him a healthy shot of orange juice, then added a splash of vodka, wishing she had a bit of odorless poison to add to the mix as a final kicker.

It was just another fantasy.

She often amused herself by thinking of ways she could get rid of him. But so far, she was stuck in the fantasy stage, too conditioned by her fear to act. Too many times she'd seen what happened to those he even suspected of plotting against him.

If only she could do it. If only she could find a way to rid the world of this modern-day vampire, then she could slip away to the countryside and live out a new life under a new name.

Simona dismissed the thought. Konrad wasn't an easy man to surprise. He watched everything she did. Even now, as she poured the drink, he was studying her every move.

"Make one for yourself," he said.

She nodded, grabbed another glass and poured a splash of orange juice and a splash of vodka into it, thinking that all he needed to make his life complete was a poison tester to take the first sip.

Simona carried the drinks across the room, handed him his, and then waited for his customary toast.

They clinked glasses.

Then in unison they sipped the drinks.

He smiled and wiped the back of his hand across his lips.

She stared at him with a sultry gaze, dreaming of the day she could make that smile freeze in rictal agony.

One day she might serve them both a final drink.

It would almost be worth it, she thought. But then an even worse thought crossed her mind. If they both went at the same time, they might end up sharing an eternal berth in hell.

Simona carried her drink over to the windows. The vertical blinds were closed now, just as they were closed every night. Konrad had an almost psychotic obsession about his privacy.

After all, he was the one who was supposed to do all the watching, and with the blinds open it was like swimming in an aquarium for all the world to see.

Not that too many people in the Schwabing district would be looking up at the top floor.

The streets below were the center of Munich's nightlife, filled with tourists, students and club crawlers who moved up and down the wide boulevards in an endless search for pleasure and diversion.

Beer gardens and dance halls, nightclubs and theaters, stately old homes and neomodern cinemas, all were part of the parade in the Schwabing district.

Simona hooked her finger into one of the blinds and pulled it off to the side as she looked down at the street below.

If only she were with them, she thought. Lost in the crowds, going where she wanted to go, saying whatever she wanted to whomever she wanted. To be free . . .

It seemed impossible. The vertical blinds felt like prison bars, holding her aloft in some high-tech dungeon.

But there were no knights left in this world, she thought. No one would come to the rescue. Not when there were warlords like Konrad Lorenz around.

She turned away from the window, ready to gauge his needs for the rest of the evening.

Then she saw the flashing light on the phone bank on the onyx stand by the couch. The call was coming in on one of his private lines. Good, she thought. It meant a reprieve.

The shrill ringing of the telephone pierced the electronic wall of sound from the opposite side of the room. Konrad always kept the volume on the phone turned up at its loudest level. Like the big-time producer he pretended to be, the phone was his lifeline to his empire.

"Yes?" Konrad said.

He nodded, then turned toward Simona, instinctively covering the mouthpiece of the phone. With a toss of his head he gestured for her to leave the room.

As she walked past him she tried to listen to his part of the conversation. He spoke in his customarily flawless German, yet another skill the Vampyr chief had acquired. For several years he'd cultivated solid relations with his former East German secret-police counterparts, the Stasi, who had been convenient partners in black market and Intelligence operations.

Konrad Lorenz had planned his exile well. From the beginning of his career in the Securitate he'd known that his corrupt ways might someday bring about his downfall.

Or at least a temporary relocation.

As Simona reached the hallway leading to her bedroom, she took one last look behind her. Though his voice hadn't risen or lost its calm tone, his face was getting red.

And sweat was starting to bead on his forehead.

Wonderful, she thought. When Konrad Lorenz was in trouble, angels were loose in the world.

Maybe avenging angels.

"IT'S NOT POSSIBLE," Konrad Lorenz said, straining to keep his voice even and in control. But his hand was gripping the phone receiver so tightly that his knuckles were white.

The man on the other end of the line repeated that not only was it possible, but it was fact. Using a long-established code, he explained that the siege of the château had turned into a rout.

Subconsciously Lorenz had already accepted the news. For the first man reporting on the Koblenz operation wasn't Ion Cusa. It was Axel Erhard, the ex-Stasi man who had helped him set up the network in Germany—for a handsome fee.

"Why didn't Ion call in to his control officer?" Lorenz demanded. "I've checked twice. There's no record of his call."

There was a long pause on the other end of the line before Erhard cleared his throat and said, "I don't believe he will be calling anymore."

"But he has to—"

"Ion left suddenly. He won't be back."

Lorenz stood there in shock.

Ion Cusa had been with him for decades. They had risen through the ranks together, standing side by side through all the midnight plotting, scheming and killing.

Since they'd left Romania, Cusa was the one he trusted to carry out any order. No questions asked. The man was a fighter, not a thinker.

But now Erhard was telling him that Cusa was dead. "How did it happen? Did you see him go? Did he say anything to you?"

"I spoke to him just before I left. We were all in a hurry. He was about to leave also, but, uh, not with us."

They spoke for several more minutes, sounding as if it were a regular business conference. As much as possible through coded words, Lorenz learned what had happened to the Vampyr crew.

They had laid the perfect trap.

Their contacts in the German Intelligence services had indicated that a special operation was under way, designed to root out the underground network that Lorenz had set up.

Lorenz had set the lure himself, giving overall command of the operation to Ion Cusa.

Cusa had then designated Erhard as the leader of the action team.

Erhard was returning.

Cusa was not.

That meant Axel Erhard was moving up in the ranks a lot quicker than anticipated.

As Lorenz set up terms for their next meeting, where he would get a fuller briefing, he couldn't help wondering if Erhard had anything to do with Ion Cusa's sudden retirement.

"Very well," the Vampyr chief said. "It's settled, then. You'll assemble the rest of the people working on the account. After you assign them their resposibilities, come back to headquarters where you and I can have a friendly chat to discuss the rest of the campaign."

"It's already in the works," Erhard said. "The others know what to do and where to go. And I'll see you as soon as I get in—"

"One more thing. I thought you should know that our business affairs aren't suffering on all fronts. In fact, one of your competitors completed a quite successful contract. Completely on our terms."

"I understand," Erhard replied. "And naturally I was hoping to report the same. But, uh, some matters were simply out of my control."

"Just so you know where you stand," Lorenz said. "You'll always have a place in the organization."

As he hung up the phone, he added, "Right up until the day you die."

Lorenz picked up the remote-control unit and turned up the volume on the satellite news feeds.

He had a feeling that very soon the results of Ion Cusa's failed business would be splashed on the air in living, bloody color.

CHAPTER FOUR

Headlights from the Mercedes 280SE swept out into space as it rounded the curving stretch of road high above the Rhine River. Gina Salvie spun the wheel quickly in the opposite direction as the road dipped into yet another serpentine pocket.

They were traveling the River Road on the breath-taking, and, at high speed, killer strip that was known as the Rheingoldstrasse.

Dense woods and sheer cliffs flanked the road as it followed the gorge carved out by the Rhine through the ages. Jagged fingers of stone and iron steeples sprouted out from the treetops, marking the moon-splashed ruins and crumbling burgs perched on distant clifftops.

Any other time the rich wineland and castle-studded stretch of land would have been a fairy-tale setting. But this night it was a grim one.

Unless they evaded the net that was surely being cast for them by the authorities, and maybe even another Vampyr crew in the area, the mission would be over before it started.

If the police caught them, it would be hard to explain the presence of Ion Cusa, who was still crouched on the floor between the seats. Bolan could always call on Brognola to pull a few strings, but that would expose the whole operation that was being mounted by the big Fed and his German counterparts.

The newspapers might get hold of the story and wring it for everything they could, jeopardizing many of the ongoing operations in Germany and the rest of Europe.

And Ion Cusa would be taken out of Bolan's hands before he could get all of his questions answered. So far, Cusa was the biggest catch yet in the covert war going on between Vampyr network and the Intelligence services.

The captive Romanian groaned loudly each time the Mercedes rounded a turn. As the Mercedes hugged another curve, Cusa shuffled his body and manufactured a pitiful cry.

"Quiet," Salvie told him. "This isn't the local chapter of the Red Cross. Your comfort isn't our top priority."

Cusa muttered something in Romanian, then switched to English and began to describe his injuries.

"I looked you over close enough," Bolan said. "You're hurt, but you'll live."

The Romanian swore, then started to turn his head so he could look up at Bolan to plead his case.

The Executioner changed Cusa's mind with a quick tap with the barrel of the H&K subgun.

"As long as you can walk and talk, you've got nothing to fear from us," Bolan said.

"I've told you already, I will give you my fullest cooperation." His voice was muffled. Once again he put on his wounded act. "I've already demonstrated that. After all, you and I have made a bargain. We have an understanding."

Bolan shook his head. The man was falling into the lingo of a typical bureaucrat, which was exactly what he'd been during his years with the Securitate. But Ion Cusa had also been a lot more than just a bureaucrat. Despite his bulk and his apparent vulnerable state, the man was a trained agent and assassin.

Even now, while he feigned suffering, Cusa was twisting his hands out of sight, trying to work them free from the nylon cord that bound them.

It didn't matter.

Bolan didn't need to have a risk like Cusa around. Nor did he want him overhearing any of their conversation. There was little chance that the Romanian would walk away from this, but even so the Executioner didn't want to play the odds.

The warrior folded down the armrest that was built into the back seat, then flipped open a small compartment on the side. Inside were a few devices provided by Brognola's spook shop.

Bolan took out the small black pistol, then held the nose of it to Cusa's neck.

"Wait! What are you doing?"

"A favor," Bolan explained. "To you and us."

The Executioner squeezed the trigger of the compact weapon. There was a slight flicking noise as it fired, followed by a loud whapping sound of a tiny projectile piercing skin.

And then Cusa went rigid.

The Romanian's head tilted backward as he craned his neck as far as it could go. His thick eyebrows were rasied high, his eyes rolled in his head and his mouth gasped like a fish suddenly pulled out of the water.

Then his face smacked down hard on the floor of the car, his head rolling from side to side.

"What happened?" Salvie asked.

"Nothing much. Cusa's gone down for the count."

Bolan replaced the small black pistol in its compartment. The technical-service spooks called it a microbioinoculator, an electric-powered pistol that fired a variety of narcotic fléchettes. The one that had pierced Cusa's neck flooded his bloodstream with a minute concentration of some potent CIA alchemy that would keep him out of action for a while.

Of course, there was always the chance that Cusa would have a reaction to the narcotic, but it was a lot better off than using chloroform.

Despite all the shows on television that portrayed it as an easy, foolproof way of knocking someone out with a chemical-laced cloth, chloroform proved fatal more often than not when amateurs tried to use it.

No, the warrior thought, Cusa would live. At least he would live long enough to tell his tale. What happened after that was up to him and his permanent captors. Bolan wasn't a diplomat. He'd promised the man he would live and so he would. But he promised nothing beyond that.

When the Mercedes came out of another curve and began to accelerate down a long straightaway, Salvie glanced over her shoulder at Bolan. "We're getting close."

"Yeah. I recognize the terrain from our ride up. I got a fairly good fix on our location, but thanks for cluing me in."

The woman nodded, her eyes momentarily drawn back to the road by a snakelike series of curves, flanked by deep, thick walls of forest that stretched far back into the mountains.

"We're close enough to call up the welcoming committee," Salvie continued, gesturing toward one of the three phone sets mounted in the customized dashboard of the Mercedes.

Bolan leaned forward in the seat, scanning the communications equipment loaded into the console.

It was the typical setup favored by Grenschutzgruppe 9. In fact, the Mercedes had been a GSG-9 vehicle before its current incarnation as one of Brognola's rolling command posts. With all the gauges and buttons, it looked like the cockpit of a rocket.

The maze of phones and scramblers was designed to handle separate and simultaneous communications with all the teams involved in an undercover operation. Once the mission got into motion, a fleet of these special-purpose vehicles could be put into the field, all of them equipped with the same kind of gadgetry.

The Mercedes 280SE also had a satcom unit built into the dash to provide instant location fixing, as well as communication with any point in the world.

Not a bad touring car, Bolan thought. But then again, against the Vampyr network they needed everything they could muster. Konrad Lorenz controlled a large enough fortune to fund his own Intelligence empire. With a lifelong career as a spook, there was no telling what the man would throw at them.

"How long before we reach the turnoff?" Bolan asked.

"Twenty minutes," Salvie ventured. "Maybe a half hour."

"Make it twenty."

"You got it," she said. And once again the Mercedes surged forward, slingshotting around a curve and racing down a relatively straight stretch of road.

They drove on in silence for another few minutes before Salvie said, "Well?"

"What?"

"You going to make the call? They might want to know we're coming in kind of fast, and that we're bringing in at least one unexpected guest."

"Might be a whole lot more on our tail by the time we get there. Let's wait until we're closer. Just in case."

"The com units are secure," Salvie insisted.

"Right. But let's wait until we're closer. They won't mind."

There was no sense in taking risks, Bolan thought. The farmhouse staff would be ready to go on a moment's notice. He wasn't going to bring them out of hiding unless absolutely necessary.

"You don't trust anything that goes out over the airwaves," she said, "do you?"

"As a rule, no. Less chance of getting burned or betrayed that way."

"What about people?"

"People, yeah," Bolan said. "That's different. With people it doesn't take so long to figure out where you stand."

"Or where you might fall," she said, finishing the thought for him. "If you don't put your trust in the right people."

"You're reading my mind. And now we know we're the right people." They were on the same wavelength. She'd handled herself well back at the château and its aftermath. That took away one of his concerns.

Even though he knew before going into the operation that Gina Salvie was a vetted operative—otherwise Hal Brognola never would have risked her on this assignment—Bolan had still felt a bit uncertain of her. It was all a matter of chemistry. Fortunately she'd passed the test when the lead had started to fly back on the cobblestoned battlefield.

Next time he wouldn't have to worry about her. He could count on her even more.

If they made it to the next time.

Once they made the turnoff road there was still a good distance to travel before they reached the farmhouse, which was twenty miles from Germany's western border with France and Luxembourg.

It was one of the safehouses left over from the days when the United States and Germany had cooperated in conjuring up and then countering coldwar scenarios. A lot of these places had been phased out when the United States had cut back on its European presence. But a few such places remained out of necessity. Even during peacetime a lot of private and nasty little wars broke out.

If need be, Bolan and Salvie could get lost for a while at the farmhouse. Brognola had staff and equipment waiting to shield or outfit them for the next part of the operation.

As the Mercedes roared up a steep mountain road, Bolan looked out through the windshield at the starlit sky. The blanket of night was so close that it felt as if they were on top of the world. But he was more interested in the height than he was the view. When it came time to use the satcom unit, he wanted a quick and clean line of communication. No interference. No unnecessary information. Just the vital stats. They were in trouble, and they were bringing one in.

The car drove on into the night, a sleek and fast-moving Mercedes with a strangely quiet crew. With the Romanian at his feet and Salvie at the wheel, Bolan felt strangely calm, almost as if they were out for a night on the town.

But he'd experienced many nights such as this before. The trick was to maintain the illusion of calm. If you did it just right, remaining poised and prepared, your mind would fall for it. And then when the time came, you'd be ready for whatever the world threw at you.

Ten minutes later Bolan leaned over the front seat and detched the black box satcom unit from its slot in the dashboard console, pulling it into the back seat with him. He picked up the satcom phone and pressed several numbers on the soft-touch keypad. His scrambled voice bounced off a satellite in geosynchronous orbit, then streamed down into the farmhouse that was no less than ten minutes away.

As soon as the farm team responded, Bolan identified himself as Striker.

The man at the farmhouse identified himself as Old MacDonald, and he did it without laughing.

Despite the complicated code names and countersigns that appeared in the movies, people in the field usually relied on the traditional code system KISS—Keep it Simple, Stupid. It was best to use words related to the mission but not too esoteric. Besides, the "Old MacDonald" bit added a distinctly American touch to it.

"We're coming in with an extra passenger," Bolan said into the narrow black satcom transceiver.

"Lorenz?"

"Negative. But we've got someone who might lead us to him. He's got fangs, too. Reserve a private room for him."

"Injuries?"

"Minor for us," Bolan replied. "Possibly major concussion for him. At the moment he's out cold, and he should stay that way for some time."

"Do you need help finding our location?"

Bolan looked over at Salvie. "You need a map to get there? Some landmarks to help you out?"

"No," she said. "I'm the guide, remember. I know the area we'll be driving through."

"It's dark out. It might be harder to spot at night. If we can use some help—"

"Trust me," she stated.

"We're doing just fine," the Executioner said into the transceiver. "If the situation changes, we'll let you know."

"Same here, Striker. In the meantime, do you have any special requests?"

"Yeah," Bolan replied. "A change of clothes. And a change of address ready for us in case we have to move real fast."

"It's all taken care of."

"Right. That only leaves us one more thing."

"What's that?"

"This is a lot bigger than we thought. Konrad Lorenz is fielding a regular army out there. Start stocking up on silver bullets and wooden stakes."

CHAPTER FIVE

"This is it," Gina Salvie said, jerking the wheel of the Mercedes hard to the left, making a sharp turn off the main road and heading down one of the narrow arteries that bisected fence-bound farmland and vineyards.

On some stretches the trees had grown so close that their upper branches leaned across the road, intertwining in a bark-lined halo that masked the moonlight.

Salvie maintained a steady speed, looking straight ahead as they hurtled down the tree-lined tunnels.

A perfect spot for an ambush, Bolan thought, but they'd made it this far without trouble, and there was no reason to think that the site was compromised.

Out of habit he glanced back through the rear window to look for any sign of pursuit while the Mercedes swallowed up the road. But all he saw was the darkness. There'd been little traffic on the roads, and now anyone following them would have been especially noticeable on the back-country route they'd taken.

In the back of his mind, Bolan felt they were home free, which, he knew, was a dangerous state of mind at any time.

Now that he was starting to wind down he realized how tired he was from the long stakeout and the sudden firefight. The minor injuries that his sense had numbed during the battle and its immediate aftermath now painfuly reminded him of their existence.

The pain could only be put off for so long.

Sharp spearpoints of stone had shredded a patch of skin along his ribs where the bullets had kicked up a spray of cobblestone chips. His right shoulder was bruised from the fall onto the road in front of the château. Something felt twisted or torn inside—an echo of an old injury coming in loud and clear. In order to heal properly the shoulder had to be wrapped and rested. But time was a luxury he didn't have.

The Executioner was damn sure the Vampyr network wouldn't be going on a sabbatical while he took some time off to mend.

There were other injuries not so drastic as the shoulder. His face and hands were cut with minute splinters of glass from the shattering explosion at the Vampyr safehouse where they'd captured Ion Cusa.

Yeah, Bolan thought, he was hurting, all right. But it was nothing compared to what had happened to the civilians who were cut down at the château.

They would never hurt again.

The image of their tattered bodies came back to him, their innocent lives ended in a splash of blood. And then he saw the face of the hysterical woman survivor who'd run up to him in the middle of the street. She'd never be the same again. For the rest of her life she'd be wondering what was going to come out of the shadows for her.

Bolan was damaged in body. She was damaged in spirit.

The warrior glanced down at Cusa's unconscious form. Thousands of civilians would be happy to put a bullet into the back of the man's head. One shot and it would be all over. But it wasn't an option that the Executioner had. The Vampyr chieftain who'd orchestrated the massacre would get his punishment eventually.

But not now. No matter how much he deserved death, his fate would have to be postponed so they could get at Konrad Lorenz.

They passed a gray church that stood close to the road, its cross-capped spire glinting in the moonlight. That was one of the landmarks Bolan remembered from his earlier briefing with Brogola. In case Salvie hadn't made it through the mission, the warrior would have had to find this place himself.

Next to the church was a cemetery of crumbling white stone markers laid out in a sprawling circle. The weathered gravestones were watched over by ancient oaks while their long-departed souls seeded the afterlife.

Salvie braked suddenly as two whitewashed stone gateposts leaped out from the darkness on the left side of the road. The gates were partially open.

The Mercedes rolled to a stop on the shoulder of the road. "Here we are," Salvie announced. "Looks like they're expecting company."

"Yeah," Bolan said. "But go in slow until we see what kind of welcome we get."

Salvie backed up the Mercedes, then nosed through the narrow opening and slowly drove up the wide clay driveway toward the farmhouse.

Halfway there she flicked the headlights on and off twice to signal their arrival.

"Old MacDonald, here we come," she said.

"Gift wrapped. Just like sitting ducks."

"If you think this is a trap," Salvie told him, "then let's just haul ass here and now. We can find our way out of here."

"I'm not saying it *is* a trap. I'm saying it could be. Just keep your eyes open." He raised his subgun. "And until we're absolutely certain of our reception, make sure you keep your invitation cocked and ready to go."

"Dammit, Belasko, you checked in with them two times since we left the turnoff. Did they say anything that made you even think there's something wrong?"

"No," Bolan replied, sitting back against the cushion. "But that was just voice contact. It could have been anyone on the other end of the line."

"You think maybe some of those vampires flew here ahead of us and took the place over?"

"I wouldn't count it out," Bolan said. "It's hard not to suspect something after what we've been through."

Salvie stopped the car and put it into park. Then she leaned back over the seat and studied the craggy-faced warrior. "Look, I go by intuition. Just like everyone else in this business. If there's something bothering you about this setup, then let's just play it safe and go."

Bolan met her gaze. "Let's play that intuition. Everything look all right to you?"

"I know the place, not the people," Salvie said. "And believe me, this is the right place. As far as the people inside, your guess is as good as mine."

"Feels right to me," Bolan said, looking on both sides of the road to get the layout of the farm. But he'd been in too many "right" places before that suddenly turned into hellgrounds to put blind faith in anything.

There wasn't anything concrete that made him feel the area wasn't secure. Something else was weighing on his mind, which he couldn't afford to dwell on— the civilian casualties at the château. They were more than numbers tallied up in body bags, more than bystanders. The Executioner's conscience had acquired a whole new family of ghostly passengers, and there was damn little room for them. Especially now.

He could almost sense their presence. They might still be alive if he hadn't fallen for the lure, the apparent easy setup for Bolan and Salvie to take out the Vampyr chief.

They should have realized it seemed too good to be true. Too much Intelligence on the Vampyr team had fallen into their laps, placed by a professional who knew how to make sure it filtered through the ranks until it reached the right people—the people who were gunning for him.

"Start rolling again," Bolan said. "If we stand still any longer, they might think there's something wrong."

"Or that we don't trust them," Salvie added.

Crisp spring air swept through the slightly lowered windows of the Mercedes as it proceeded down the road. Mingled with the air was the pungent scent of burning wood from the chimney spewing smoke from the side of the farmhouse.

It was a two-story blockhouse structure with a gray shaled roof and a half-dozen narrow and thick-framed windows on the top floor. A wraparound porch braced the side of the house closest to the driveway. The sturdy old dwelling had obviously been reinforced to withstand a lot more than the Rhineland weather.

An eight-foot-wide stream studded with stepping-stones cut a meandering path down the right side of the farmhouse. In the back was a wide and still pond, its shimmering surface carpeted with reflected stars.

The driveway continued straight to a huge barn and garage, where several vehicles were parked next to heavy farm equipment.

It looked exactly as it was supposed to—a working farm. But to someone in the field, there were a number of other touches that hinted at what the real work of the place was, such as the stone walls and strips of brush that had been laid out to provide a regular obstacle course in case the place had to be turned into a hardsite.

Salvie drove toward the barn, coming to a stop just in front of one of the entrances.

"No," Bolan said.

"What now?"

"Just back it up a bit and turn us around so the front is facing the road."

"I thought you decided we were among friends."

"If friendship means so much to you," the warrior said, "then consider this a favor to a friend and turn the vehicle around."

She swore under her breath, but did as he said and slowly wheeled the Mercedes around. "I don't see why we have to go through all of this. If they were going to take us down, they would have done it by now."

"Maybe they want to see who it is before they shoot," Bolan suggested. "Ever think of that?"

"No, but I'm sure you have. You've thought of just about everything that could go wrong."

"Yeah. That's how you make sure it goes right."

"Okay, okay." Salvie turned off the headlights but kept the parking lights on, casting a dim halo around the Mercedes. Then she dropped her hand to the ignition key, pausing for a moment before she looked over her shoulder at Bolan. "I suppose you want me to keep the engine running."

"You suppose right," the Executioner replied, watching the shapes that came from both sides of the farmhouse. "If I say hit it, step on the gas and get us the hell out of here."

"You're the boss."

A half-dozen figures emerged from the darkness, moving quickly from both sides of the road. There was activity down at the porch where the light from the inside briefly splashed on the figure of a tall man with a rifle.

"Dammit," Salvie muttered, reaching across the seat for her weapon. "Now you've got me thinking the same way. This paranoia of yours is contagious, Belasko."

"Get used to it. It lasts a lifetime."

The air was thick with tension as they waited for the "farmhands" to reach them. Bolan sat in the back seat with one hand on the H&K subgun and one hand on the door.

The team that was approaching had to be feeling the same thing, Bolan thought. After all, the only reason he and Gina had come here was that something had gone wrong and the operation had blown up in their faces. The farm team had to be wondering if its position was compromised.

With a glint of black metal in the moonlight, the rifle team split up on both sides of the car.

The tall man came at them head-on, carrying a Bernadelli Roma side-by-side shotgun with a chromed barrel and a silver-engraved frame. The barrel was casually aimed in their direction.

The man stamped on the front bumper with his right foot, rocking the nose of the Mercedes while he peered through the windshield.

The man definitely wasn't a farmer type.

He wore a faded denim jacket and a scuffed biker's cap, with a coil of longish hair hanging over his forehead. His face looked sunburned, as if he'd just come from a much harsher climate.

His eyes burned with a hard, cold intelligence as he studied the new arrivals. Suddenly he lowered the shotgun and cradled it in a sportsman's carry. Then a half smile appeared on his face.

"I know him," Bolan stated.

"Exactly which 'him' are we talking about here?"

"You can relax."

Salvie let out her breath and switched off the ignition. "I guess I recognize him, too. Sort of. But I don't know from where."

Bolan pushed open the door and stepped out into the soft earth, his foot sinking slightly in the rut of the dirt track. He was still holding on to the subgun, but it was at rest now.

"Welcome to the party, Striker," the man said, coming around to Bolan's side of the car and holding out his hand.

"Herr MacDonald, I presume?" Bolan said, gripping his hand.

"Don't look so surprised."

"Guess I'm not used to seeing you without a trench coat or a flight jacket."

"You and a few million other viewers."

August Sinclair's face had been seen around the world quite a bit in the past few years. He was part of a free-lance news crew that hopped around the world from battle zone to battle zone, often setting up shop one step ahead of the battles.

He and his fly-by-night crew had a well-deserved reputation for getting into and out of any area that had been marked off-limits to the press. It was his Special Forces training that helped him infiltrate the restricted areas and his special contacts with the community that helped him bail out.

His televised "bits and pieces," as he called them, appeared on American networks, as well as European news services, many of whom claimed Sinclair as one of their own. He was the proverbial man on the scene.

The boyish but weathered face of Gus Sinclair had nightly haunted television screens around the world during the Desert Storm conflict, making him something of a minor celebrity. His trademark cocky grin and his raspy, deep voice had made him a regular part of the global electronic family.

Desert Storm wasn't his first exposure. He'd been in South America, Central America, Asia and Africa, a combat junkie who was always nearest the fighting and bringing it into the living room.

"Now I recognize you," Salvie said, coming around from the other side of the car. "You're awful far from the front, aren't you?"

"Not really," Sinclair replied, his eyes widening in appreciation at the red-haired agent. Despite the streaks of sweat and the signs of fatigue and battle that showed in her face, she still exuded an almost overpowering aura of sensuality.

Sinclair gave her one of his best trademarked smiles—the half smile that had captured huge demographics among the American female viewing audience.

Salvie didn't melt at the look. So far, the sparks were only flying one way. From Gus Sinclair.

The legendary womanizer and combat correspondent looked at Bolan and shook his head as he said, "Are you going to introduce us, or were you planning on keeping her for yourself?"

"Her name's Gina," Bolan said. "At the moment."

"A beautiful name for a beautiful lady."

"Save it for the cameras, Gus," the woman replied.

He shrugged off the rebuff with a genuine smile this time. Then, all business, he looked into the back of the Mercedes. "This is someone else I must get to know."

He motioned to two of his men, who opened the door on the far side, then lugged out the unconscious cargo. Hauling his arms and legs like an unsightly stretcher, they carried Ion Cusa toward the farmhouse.

Bolan and Salvie fell in behind them, flanking Gus Sinclair. As they neared the farmhouse several other shapes shadowed them in the darkness. One of the men approached Sinclair and had a hushed conversation with him before fading back into the darkness.

The newsman hadn't been too far off the mark earlier when he'd told Salvie they really weren't far from the front. The site was gearing up for war.

Bolan knew the routine. There would be a good number of men on-site to carry out enough farming duties to make it look like a real working farm. But there would also be another well-armed contingent with specialized training working in shifts, ready to deal with anything that came along.

Despite his cover as an independent news packager and producer, Sinclair had been a long-time associate of Hal Brognola. He'd built up a good cover for his activities, and now that cover was being put to use on a major operation. If the cover was blown, everything would be denied and Gus Sinclair would be portrayed as just another cowboy.

But until that happened, he was in a great position to strike at the heart of the Vampyr network.

"What about our prisoner?" Sinclair asked as they neared the house. "What's his condition?"

"Out like a light," Bolan replied. "He'll be good for a few more hours. You got a place to put him in storage?"

"There's a cold cellar beneath the house. We'll plant him there for a while."

The warrior nodded. "Keep an armed watch on him. He's got a lot of notches on his gun and he might try to get a few more before he goes down for good."

"Done. Now let's go in and you can give me a quick briefing on tonight's... misfire."

"Real brief. My friend and I could both use a few hours' sleep—until it's time to question Ion Cusa. Then we'll go into details with the whole crew so we only have to go over it once. Hal should be here by then, right?"

A worried look crossed Sinclair's face. "He should have been here by now, but there's been an incident. He'll have a lot to tell you when he arrives."

Bolan nodded. From the looks of things, the "incidents" had only just begun.

As soon as they stepped into the farmhouse, the dry heat from the fireplace washed over him, weighing him down with a tiredness that he'd held off for longer than he could remember.

About eight or nine people were scattered about the front room. Some of them looked their way briefly, then resumed their positions at the windows.

Bolan and Salvie followed Sinclair past a wide wooden staircase toward a room at the back of the house. The lights were dim, and the center of the room was occupied by a long bare wooden table scarred with bottle marks, coffee stains and scorched scars from many a cigarette or cigar.

Off to the side of the room was a glass-tiered liquor cabinet. Beneath a long and narrow window that looked out to the back of the pond was a cache of electronic gear—VCRs, television screens, cameras and microphones.

A home-entertainment center for spooks, Bolan thought as he took a seat across the table from Salvie. She looked as tired as he did.

"Now that we're all here," Sinclair said, "let's have a damage report."

"It's a good thing our friend Striker recognized you right off," Salvie stated. "Otherwise *you* might have been on the list of the damaged."

"Why's that?"

"Because Striker here was about to open up on anyone who looked cross-eyed at him."

"Is that right?" Sinclair said. He nodded, the smile once again beaming for his audience. "Well,

I've been on both sides of that equation myself. As a matter of fact, I had about ten men aiming at the two of you ever since you crossed the threshold."

Salvie shared a look with Bolan. "That must have been what you picked up on."

"Must be. I guess it wasn't my imagination after all."

"No," she agreed. "Guess not."

Then she looked from one face to the other— Bolan's hard and grim, weathered visage, and Gus Sinclair's smooth, handsome complexion. Despite the good looks, he had the air of a predator about him.

"You guys must be related," she said. "One wrong move and *boom*. Out go the lights. It's a wonder we aren't all killing ourselves here."

"Don't worry about that," Sinclair told her. "From the Intel Brognola sent along, it might not be too long before Lorenz's people are standing in line to take a shot at us."

CHAPTER SIX

At midnight the streets of Munich took on a darker and wilder hue, especially in the Schwabing district.

The hard-core revelers who drifted through the beer gardens and nightclubs of the red-light district were on an endless search for excitement, always certain that something wilder could be found around the next corner.

Clattering high heels, druken boasts and liquor-laced laughter all blended into a loud parade that could go on until the dawn.

Leading that parade was a horde of university students. Their trendy clothes hinted at upper-class upbringings, while their boozy bravado hinted at their more recent past in one of the beer halls.

They were oblivious to the predators who were also on the street at that hour.

Axel Erhard was not. The blond-haired ex-Stasi officer had sensed the black-leather wolf pack running the streets on the prowl ever since he was dropped off three blocks from the Europa-Musikorps Tower.

He'd wanted the time to think before dealing face-to-face with Konrad Lorenz. Their lives in the underground—and their masks in the aboveground world—had hopelessly wedded them.

Each man needed the other to survive.

Each man could tear the other down.

He wasn't exactly afraid of the Vampyr lord. He was just uncertain. Despite the wealth and power Lorenz craved, there was still a touch of the bully about him, a sense that he could risk his empire for the immediate satisfaction of punishing a subordinate, which he considered Erhard to be.

It didn't bother the German at all. What other people thought of him was their province. He knew what he could do.

And as he walked down the street behind the bar-hopping bravos he knew he could surprise the hell out of the band of thieves who'd marked him as easy prey.

Maybe even surprise the life out of them.

He knew he fit their image of a perfect victim, resembling one more naive and lonely businessman walking the late-night streets in search of some illicit female company.

His blond hair, slicked down and immaculately parted, presented a conservative and vulnerable image to anyone who bothered to give him a second look.

It was a pose he'd mastered long ago, looking harmless and timid like a man just asking to be relieved of his wallet.

As he passed by a noisy beer hall that was literally packed to the windows with red-faced revelers, he pretended not to notice in the window the reflection of the two men who had moved up close behind him.

The wolves were ready to cut him from the herd.

They were part of a much larger pack that was trolling the district for suckers like him—Goths, Vandals, barbarians, Hitlerian youths.

Whatever they were calling themselves these days, Axel Erhard thought, they were certainly out and about in large numbers. And though they tried to look intimidating with their studded leather jackets and stomping boots, they were also advertising their intent—Mongol locks, skinhead scalps, long, unwashed greasy hair hanging down to their collars. No matter what style they affected, they stood out so drastically from the crowd that their threat was easily discerned.

And neutralized.

The youths headed toward a shadow-filled alley between an upscale nightclub with an Old World stone facade and a beer hall.

It was a gulf of darkness, the usual spot where they ran their prey to ground.

Footsteps suddenly clattered on the sidewalk as the pair rushed him.

But Erhard had picked up on their plan even before they went into action. He stopped in his tracks halfway past the alley, stepping back as his attackers' momentum carried them a foot past him.

The man on his right who'd grabbed him had a bulldog mouth with a jutting lower jaw that showed mishapen teeth. His beefy hand had circled around Erhard's right bicep and was tugging downward with a crushing grip.

The man on his left was a bit too boozy to be in top mugging condition and had stumbled as he passed, his hand sliding harmlessly off his intended victim's coat.

Erhard went with the motion of the ham-fisted Goth who'd managed to latch on to him and let himself be dragged, apparently off balance, into the alley.

But Erhard's balance was perfect.

He bent his elbow slightly and swept his right arm in an inside circular block that broke the man's grip. He continued with the motion and jabbed his hand straight out until it clasped the man's shoulder, the impact knocking him back a few steps.

Erhard's closed fist pulled slightly to the right on the silver-studded leather strap on the shoulder of the man's jacket, tilting him in a leaning position, while he swept-kicked the man's feet out from under him.

He landed flat on his back in the debris-filled alley, puffing from the impact as the wind was knocked out of him.

In an instinctual fluid and practiced motion, Erhard cocked his left knee, then extended his heel straight out in a rapid snap until the kick conected with the fallen man's jaw.

The man's teeth came together in a resounding crack. In a split-second follow-up move, Erhard stepped hard on the man's face, breaking his nose as he moved past him deeper into the alley.

By now the other assailant knew something was wrong but wasn't quite sure what. When his numbed senses decoded the trashed face of his friend, he stopped in his tracks. Then he took one step backward out of the alley.

"No," Erhard growled.

The savage voice alone might have been enough to stop him from retreating. But when he saw the gleaming black barrel of an automatic pistol slide out from Erhard's shoulder harness and zero in on his forehead, he froze.

He slowly raised his hands over his head while he took in the bloodied, groaning heap that was his friend.

"He's bleeding. Look at him. What the hell did you do to him?"

"Not enough," Erhard replied.

Suddenly the Mongol-locked street fighter didn't look so eager for battle. Not when he realized it was a two-way street. His eyes looked from his fallen friend to the calm blond-haired man.

"Look, we weren't going to do anything—"

"Not to me, you weren't," Erhard said pleasantly. "Not ever. But don't tell me you weren't going to try."

Erhard stepped closer, bridging the gap between them with the outstretched pistol until it was only an inch away from the mugger's face. Close enough to look like a cannon.

"Finish what you started," Erhard said.

He shook his head.

"Finish."

"You've got a gun."

Erhard nodded. "You're right," he said, sliding the automatic back into its harness.

As soon as the barrel was out of sight, the street tough made his move, swinging a wild roundhouse punch for Erhard's head.

To a man like Erhard, the clumsy swing appeared to be in slow motion. Instead of a straight punch, the man had given his adversary a lot of room to work with.

Erhard stepped back while his left hand shot out in a palm-heel strike that pushed the roundhouse harmlessly out of the way. The ex-Stasi officer whirled so his back was to his assailant and gave him a sharp elbow to the spine. It was one of his favorite moves, a graceful and powerful strike with little movement but maximum results.

The man cried out as the surprising jolt of pain stunned his nerve endings. He staggered away with his neck tilted and his feet shuffling on the pavement as if he were suddenly a hundred years old.

Erhard spun and grabbed the back of his adversary's neck. Then he stiff-armed him forward, smashing his face into the brick wall.

"You are not a very subtle pair," he said in the voice he used when he was a hand-to-hand combat instructor.

A gash on the mugger's forehead opened up a river of blood that seeped down over his eyes.

"Any good hunter knows when he is being hunted. It was almost an insult the way you tried to take me down."

The man groaned as Erhard pushed his face against the bricks and moved it from side to side, as if he were stone-washing the man's skin.

"Next time don't waste yourself in stalking your opponent. Seize the opportunity the moment it presents itself."

With an almost gentle throw, he pushed the bleeding would-be assailant off to the right, letting him crash to the ground like a falling tree.

"You see," Erhard said, continuing the measured tone of an instructor, "you must make your move before the other man even suspects you are there. Otherwise..."

He laughed and looked down at the broken and bloody pair. "Otherwise, you see what can happen."

Erhard walked toward the mouth of the alley, stopping near the end under a splash of light to look at the cuffs of his coat for specks of blood. Not enough to be noticed at this hour.

He glanced over his shoulder one more time. The two men were slowly moving, their groans rising in volume. He probably could have avoided the situation if he had wanted to. But in a way he'd been looking for the incident as much as they were. After what he'd gone through, it was nice to have an easy victory drop into his lap out of the blue.

Erhard turned and stepped out of the alley.

After he rounded the corner and walked another block, the purring throb of a sleek black Porsche sounded behind him. The vehicle rolled over to the curb and started to pace him.

The headlights flashed on and off quickly when he turned to check out the driver.

He smiled.

The woman didn't even look old enough to drive, let alone own such a car. Her hair was piled in an impossible crown of blond curls in an attempt to make her look elegant and ladylike.

But the prostitutes who patrolled the streets of the Schwabing district flashing their headlights at prospective customers were not exactly ladies, he thought. Thank God.

As the car rolled parallel to him he leaned over for a better view. She had a black satin wrap over her shoulders that formed an X just below her bountiful cleavage. She made an exaggerated shrug that on another night would have pulled him into the car.

But he shook his head and said, "Sorry. But no thanks. I've had my fun for tonight."

She bowed, shifted gears, then roared away in search of someone else who looked as if they had the right price to play.

Fifteen minutes later, feeling perfectly at peace with himself, he used his key and a coded entry card to buzz himself through the electronically locked private entrance at the Europa-Musikorps Tower.

Once he was inside the outer entrance, there was yet another set of doors to pass through before gaining access to the small lobby. He slid his computer-coded access card through the metal slot and once again had about ten seconds after the buzz to push through the inner doors.

As the doors snicked shut behind him, Erhard avoided glancing up at the miniature cameras mounted in the corner of the ceiling, following his every move. Acting as casually as if he were here for a pleasant get-together with an old business partner, he pressed the button on one of the two private elevators that would take him to the top floor.

He knew that before any of the elevators would come down, someone from above would look him over through the monitors. Only then was access to the top granted.

Erhard waited patiently.

He was used to the routine surveillance.

A life spent growing up behind the Iron Curtain had made him accustomed to a lot of bizarre practices. And his career as a prime mover in the Intelligence world had reinforced the feeling that surveillance was natural.

It was odd—but not odd enough to remain a hindrance. Everyone everywhere was watched by somebody.

It was a kill-or-be-killed world.

Watch or be watched.

Ever since he was a child, the scion of the privileged class in a so-called classless society, Erhard had decided to be one of the watchers, to be just like his father, a high-ranking officer in the SSD.

It was his father who brought home delicacies when the rest of the population couldn't find meat.

It was his father who took the family to the resorts set aside for the privileged party members.

It was his father who took him into his confidence at a young age and told him what the world was really like. That at any given time inside the iron-curtained German Democratic Republic, fifty percent of the population was considered to be security risks. And the other fifty percent was watching them.

The lines were clearly drawn. You were a winner or loser. There was no in between.

Erhard had decided to be one of the winners. He'd found his natural calling in the ranks of the Stasi—the elite spy service that even spied on all the other spies.

It had been a good world until fate came along and tore the wall down. The Iron Curtain was no more, but a different curtain had been raised, by men like Konrad Lorenz.

The elevator arrived with a soft hiss.

He climbed inside, pressed the top-floor button, then stepped to the back of the elevator car. He held tightly on to the guardrails, his stomach plummeting while the car rocketed upward.

He gritted his teeth on the ride up and forced himself to maintain a mask of calm.

Elevators were one of his weaknesses. He never got used to them. Despite all of his training and all of the dangers he faced, a cold hand of fear still clutched his insides whenever an elevator was in motion.

The ride was no better at the top when the elevator came to a sudden jarring stop. While his stomach was still lurching upward, the doors hissed open.

And Axel Erhard looked into the barrel of a gun wielded by a bullnecked guard in a brown shirt and drab brown pants.

It was a sportman's gun, an engraved and damascened Hammerli 208—but the man who fisted it was no sportsman. The bald and bearded Christov Gudru looked as if he'd been an original member of the Iron Guard who'd died and come back to life just to haunt anyone who dealt with Konrad Lorenz.

"Christov," Erhard said. "Always a pleasure to see you." He clicked his heels together and bowed facetiously at Konrad Lorenz's personal bodyguard.

The man grunted and grudgingly holstered his weapon as he leaned back against the wall facing the elevator.

It was absurd, Erhard thought. Gudru had obviously seen him through the monitors and knew him from several past meetings. Yet he'd still held a gun on the elevator doors when they opened—as if Axel Erhard was some kind of shapeshifter who could change from an ally to an enemy in the space of a second.

But then again, in the world of the Vampyr chief, anything was possible.

And, Erhard admitted to himself, he *would* like to get rid of Konrad Lorez. But his own need for survival wouldn't permit it. Not now.

"Go on in," the bodyguard grunted, jerking his head toward the formidable dark wood doors that led into the penthouse.

"Thank you, Christov," Erhard said, nodding politely. "We'll resume our chat some other time."

The man glared at him, his arching gray eyebrows looking like steel wool etched into his prominent forehead.

Erhard paused at the doors and waited for Konrad Lorenz to look him over yet again before admitting him to the inner sanctum. The doors were reinforced with steel bars that made it as hard to get in as it was to get out.

Despite all of his outward changes and his guise as an international captain of industry, Lorenz couldn't shed his bunker mentality. He was like a doomed Hitler awaiting his final assault. And Simona Lascue was his Eva Braun, a peroxided parakeet in a vampire's cage.

With the loud thunking of steel bars recessing into their slots, the doors opened inward and there stood Konrad Lorenz, a thin smile on his face and murder in his eyes.

He waved Erhard inside and led him to his electronically walled-off cocoon, the incessant hiss and murmur of the radios and televisions filling the air with a crackling live-wire sensation.

"I am not happy," Lorenz said, sitting down in a wide-armed chair across from his guest, his thick palms spreading out on the leathery throne. He leaned forward with a patrician look on his face, like the head of some underworld family.

"You hide it well," Erhard replied, crossing his legs as he leaned back into the leather couch.

"And *you* have wasted several of our best men," Lorenz stated. "And you've done it in a high-profile operation that will make the public scream for our heads."

"Since when have you listened to the public?" Erhard demanded. "Your own or anyone else's?"

Lorenz frowned. "This is a serious matter," he said. "Several deaths resulted from—"

"I know. I was there, remember. I risked my life and almost lost it. But we are agreed on one thing," he said. "It was a poorly planned operation. Cusa didn't have a clue about what we were facing there."

"Cusa was following my orders," Lorenz snapped.

"And I was following Cusa's. At least until we went in. Once the shooting started, I called the shots. But we went in on Cusa's say-so. He managed to set the lure all right, but his countersurveillance was too slipshod to identify what we were facing at the château. That marksman had set up an armory there. And the woman who was with him wasn't just a piece of fluff to make it easier for him to sleep at night. She was formidable."

"Too many of my people died."

"And mine," Erhard said. "We are obviously facing someone of a much higher caliber than you initially guessed."

Lorenz exhaled loudly, a mixture of grief and anger sailing on his breath. "Your Intelligence and mine indicated a specialist was coming after our group. But at the time there was nothing to indicate who that specialist was."

"And now you have a name for him?" Erhard asked.

"The Executioner."

Erhard's eyes widened, making him look almost pleased at the news. Everyone had heard of the Executioner. But few who faced him survived. "Perhaps it was him. It was hard to tell under the circumstances, with bullets flying and grenades flashing all around us. What makes you so sure?"

"The fact that he killed Cusa—one of my most trusted and capable men—is reason enough."

"So trusted you didn't even let him know this is where you really live?" Erhard demanded. "Or about this cover identity we established for you? How trusted is that?"

Lorenz sat back a bit, looking preposterously like a schoolteacher with an errant pupil. "Cusa was a simple man," he admitted. "He was expert at getting secrets, but not keeping them. I couldn't afford to expose him to this part of the operation."

Erhard shrugged. He had already relegated Cusa to the past without feeling any need for sorrow. So he was dead. That was what he deserved after causing such a debacle.

"It took an extraordinary man to kill Cusa," Lorenz said. "But there are other reasons to believe the Executioner is involved. Information from other sources point to his presence. Apparently he's working with a joint task force assembled from German, Austrian, American and British counterterrorist units."

Erhard nodded. Germany, Austria, England and America were the most frequent destinations of the riders on the underground express, so it was natural their covert units were the key players in the struggle with the Vampyr network. And they had a long history of cooperation in Intelligence matters.

There was also a solid Vampyr presence in Switzerland and France, but fortunately the services of those countries preferred to keep their covert operations independent.

"My people have encountered the Executioner in the past," Erhard said.

"With what result?"

"We had fewer people when the encounters were over.

"Whoever he was," Erhard went on, "he was very good. He had only a few moments' notice to evade our assault and prepare his counterattack. But he took us down one by one, like we were leading the charge of the Light Brigade. It was a massacre."

"And that brings us back to Cusa," Lorenz said. "Tell me how he died."

Erhard clasped his hands together and leaned forward on the couch, facing down Lorenz. "I would like to tell you he died like a hero. And I know that is what you'd like me to say. But to tell you the truth, Ion Cusa died when a wall fell on him. He didn't have a chance."

"Did you see it personally?"

"No."

"Where were you?"

"I was busy saving my life."

"Then who saw him die?" Lorenz pressed.

"One of my people was there when it all came tumbling down on top of him."

"But is he sure? Did he actually see him perish?"

"He saw him fall," Erhard replied. "Crushed beneath wood and concrete...and then the entire building went up in flames. You should know that by now." He gestured at the talking heads on the television screens, watching over them like omnipotent gods. "I trust you've been following the news reports."

Lorenz nodded. "I saw what the media wanted us to see. Bodies being carried out. There was no way of recognizing any of those charred bodies as Cusa."

"We were in the same position." Erhard nodded. Then he gave Lorenz a detailed briefing of what had gone wrong with the attack on the château until Lorenz was satisfied he knew everything possible about the failed mission.

"Well," Lorenz said, "it's a good thing we weren't depending solely on *your* efforts to deliver a message to those who would try to run us down." He picked up a remote-control device and silenced all of the equipment except for a thin and wide television screen with a black onyx frame that made it look like a window on the world.

"Our Czechoslovakian friends were able to carry out their mission without losing a soul—a soul that counted, that is," Lorenz added.

Then he pressed the Play button, and a black-and-white video appeared on the screen. The camera angle was distant and jerky, obviously taken from a moving vehicle.

Flickering images of a fenced-in area were followed by a shot of a station wagon leaving the gates of a military compound. The camera zoomed in from behind the station wagon, showing that the vehicle contained four men and some bulky equipment in the rear of the wagon.

"Do you recognize the area?" Lorenz asked.

"It's familiar," Erhard replied. "But I can't place it from this angle."

"It's Hangelar."

"Hangelar! But you can't—"

"Oh, but we can," Lorenz said. "And we did. Watch."

THE STATION WAGON MOVED at a moderate speed as it traveled a narrow road flanked by flat swaths of grassland.

Wherever the vehicle was headed, the driver was in no hurry. After the intense training that went on inside the Hangelar base north of Bonn, just leaving the compound was a threat.

The wagon continued on a straight path for several miles before the brake lights came on and it slowed to take a sharp right-hand turn.

The men inside the vehicle were all highly trained members of GSG-9, the very outfit that was tasked with rooting out the Vampyr network of outlaw Intelligence agents flooding Germany and the rest of Europe.

They didn't notice the surveillance car.

Or if they did, they didn't recognize it as a threat. They had no reason to.

There was an aura of invincibility about the GSG-9 team, fostered by their years of training and their incredible rate of success in the antiterrorist wars. Especially on their own territory.

As the wagon came out of the turn and neared a jagged edge of forest, four men in black hoods stepped out from the trees.

The lead man held a top-loaded magazine-fed Stoner 63-A machine gun. Aiming from the hip like a black-clad nightmare, the assassin triggered a burst straight at the oncoming station wagon.

The clatter and blast of the Stoner was just the first barrage.

As soon as the first stream of machine-gun fire riddled the windshield, pocking away at the bullet-resistant glass, a second gunner opened up with a Stoner, pouring a concentrated fire at the same time.

The lead stream scorched through the air and ripped into the splintering glass.

With his vision suddenly blocked by the imploding windshield, the GSG-9 driver lost control of the car. In an attempt to take evasive action, he steered it toward the right of the road—and into the path of a machine-gun burst that cut through his neck like a guillotine. As his head jerked backward on sinewy threads, the nose of the station wagon plummeted into a culvert.

The car doors opened.

From the front passenger door a boot came out, covered with a river of blood that streaked down over the leather. In a feeble attempt to touch the ground one last time, the man's toes rocked from side to side, like a red-drenched scythe slicing the air just above the grass.

A high-explosive round touched down in the culvert, launching a lethal spray of shrapnel that disintegrated the man's foot.

The third man on the hit team fired another explosive shell from the 5-round revolver-action Arwen 37 that was pressed against his shoulder.

The fourth man triggered several short burst from a Beretta 12 submachine gun, the weapon favored by many of the operatives of the Czech Intelligence services.

The simultaneous barrage blew the wagon into the air like a tin can, its gas tank exploding in white-hot sheets of flame that incinerated everyone inside the vehicle and turned it into a burned-out metal husk.

While one of the tires from the trashed wagon rolled crazily down the road, the four men in black double-timed it down the short slope, circled the flame-racked wreckage and waved down the surveillance car that had been trailing the vehicle since it left the compound.

Konrad Lorenz pressed the Stop button, fading away the image on the screen just as easily as the lives of the men in the station wagon had faded away.

"That operation was carried out by a group of monks," Lorenz said. "You know of whom I speak."

"Of course. I've dealt with them many times myself." The Czech STB agents had picked up their nickname of "monks" from the monastery outside of Prague that they'd taken over and used as headquarters for their international operations. The STB had a reputation for brutal finesse, as demonstrated once again by the exiled agents who'd carried out the Hangelar hit for the Vampyr network.

"That operation—as well as a few others—was part of a simultaneous attack to demonstrate our power once and for all. To show our hunters the error of their ways. But now I'm afraid any gains we might have made were neutralized by your bungled assault."

Erhard started to protest, but Lorenz raised a hand. "That is all forgotten now. I am bringing in a specialist of my own to counter the Executioner. I'd hoped to have him here to join you and Cusa, but this one still likes to believe he is a free man. He is taking his time about coming under my protection—although he is the target of an international manhunt and risks his life with every step he takes."

"Who is he?" Erhard asked.

"His name is Strashmir," Lorenz said. "Cass Strashmir. He is one of my countrymen who is much like this Executioner. A champion. A marksman. And more important . . . a fugitive. He will do whatever has to be done."

"Why are you telling me this?" Erhard asked. "You usually keep the names and numbers of your specialists secret from me."

"This time is different," Lorenz said. "You are the one who will work closely with him, since I want to keep this identity secret from him for the time being."

"You don't trust him?"

"I don't like to be in a position where I have to trust anyone," Lorenz replied, glaring at the fair-haired German. "I prefer to *own* them."

In the background Erhard could hear the soft footsteps of Simona Lascue, who timidly looked his way as she momentarily appeared in the hallway before disappearing from sight again like a frightened child. "I've noticed."

"Our monk friends will meet Strashmir in Vienna," Lorenz continued, "where they are particularly strong."

"No argument. Their covert operations in Vienna are second to none." With Vienna so close to Austria's northern border with the Czech Republic, the

STB renegades had had years to prepare for the day when they had to flee their own country. Vienna had long been the playing and preying grounds of the Czech operatives. In the days before the Berlin Wall had fallen, the grand old city had been like an international clearinghouse for the East and West Bloc operations. Much of that covert apparatus was still intact.

"From Vienna the monks will escort Strashmir safely to one of *our* safehouses, where you will meet him. From that point on you will assist Strashmir in locating the Executioner and putting him to rest once and for all. Then you and I can get back to our main concerns."

Survival was their main concern, Erhard thought. But it was always so much nicer when you could survive in style. Once the Executioner was out of the way, they could get on with the business of creating their underground empire.

But it still bothered him that Konrad Lorenz assumed an aura of command. After all, Erhard thought, they were in *his* country. It was his network that had helped Lorenz survive in the early days.

"If your man is as good as you say," Erhard said, "then I agree to task myself to him until the operation is ended. But when it's over, you and I have a few matters to negotiate."

"Such as?"

"Such as an equal share in the spoils of war. And make no mistake, now that you've attacked Hangelar, we are in for one hell of a war."

"It can be won," Lorenz said. "If we use the right weapons, they'll have to come to terms with us. And at the moment, Cass Strashmir is the right weapon."

CHAPTER SEVEN

Cass Strashmir clutched the Baby Browning automatic pistol concealed in the side pocket of his coat, nodding easily as the police officer questioned him about his destination.

The Austrian policeman had been following him since Strashmir had wandered through the Hauptplatz and lingered by the Trinity Statue, perhaps subconsciously looking for help from above. But the white stone cherubs had proved to be of no help to the Romanian exile.

When Strashmir had left the statue in a measured stroll, the officer kept pace behind him.

At first the broad-chested officer maintained a discreet distance. But he was drawn like a magnet to the Romanian, gradually closing in on Strashmir and striking up what seemed to be an idle conversation.

But the officer controlled the conversation every step of the way, just as he controlled the direction they moved in. He steered Strashmir out of the bright spring sun and into the shade of a green awning in front of a staid old jewelry shop.

Strashmir's back was against the glass while he dueled with the officer in conversation, trying to project the image of a tourist who was hopelessly lost. Just another tourist seeing the sights of Linz, Strashmir told him, a German tourist who'd come over into Austria for a much needed vacation.

He hoped his Romanian accent had been submerged deep within his new persona.

"You looked a bit out of sorts," the policeman said. "Lost and confused. I thought I would talk to you."

Strashmir nodded again. "That's it entirely. I've been walking around for too long looking for a bookshop. I'm a collector, you see." He hunched his shoulders and shook his head in wonder. "This was supposed to be a holiday, but now I feel like I've run a ten-mile marathon."

The laughing policeman studied him with narrowed eyes. The eyes behind the curtain. Strashmir knew the routine. The man was about to make up his mind whether to send him on his way or question him further.

Something had tipped him off, Strashmir thought. What it was, he couldn't be sure.

Strashmir had been trying to look the part of a man without a care in the world, which was difficult for a fugitive to carry off. Maybe he'd achieved that look too easily and seemed like an aimless wanderer.

This was his last chance to play the lost tourist, Strashmir thought. He had to throw out another piece of information to win the policeman over. A dozen lies came to mind, none of them convincing. Then his eyes were drawn to the policeman's left hand. A wedding ring.

"My wife will have my head if I'm not back at the hotel for brunch in an hour," Strashmir said. "She'll think I'm out chasing the girls."

The policeman nodded. "They do like to keep track of us," he said. "What hotel are you staying at?"

Strashmir rattled off the name of a hotel he'd picked up when he came into the Linz railway station and stopped at the Hotel-Zimmer & Gieldwechsel office for information. The boat dock. Soon he would be on his final leg of the journey, the steamboat trip down the Danube to Vienna. And thence to freedom.

If the policeman let him go.

One shot to the chest would do it, Strashmir thought. Or perhaps a knife hand to the throat—core his Adam's apple with the slighty bent rock-hard claw of his fingertips.

Strashmir didn't want to kill him. But he would if it came down to a choice between him and the police officer. He would pull the trigger, then try to vanish into the streets of Linz.

Perhaps he would shoot.

He really wasn't sure of anything anymore.

He had blood on his hands several times over, but none of it from innocent men.

Strashmir inhaled slowly, testing his legs, ready to strike. There was really no other way out for him. If he was taken in by the authorities now, he might never walk out. No one would believe his side of things.

While all these thoughts swam through his mind, the policeman leaned forward in a conspiratorial crouch and dropped his hand on Strashmir's left shoulder.

"Between you and me, my friend," he said, "I suggest you go back to your hotel and keep the wife happy. Forget your search. Come back another time."

"The best idea I've heard all day," Strashmir said. He took his right hand out of his pocket and shook the policeman's hand, then vanished back into the flow of tourists.

Halfway to the hotel he took a side street, then moved on down toward the Schiffplatz where the steamboats were docked.

The last thing he needed was for the policeman to have second thoughts and look for him near the hotel. He thanked the imaginary wife he'd conjured up—the best kind a twice-divorced man like himself could have, he thought.

One more close encounter, he thought. There'd been many since he'd begun his journey from Bucharest so long ago.

Like the thousands of other Securitate chameleons caught in the capital after the shooting stopped, he had soon shed his uniform and mingled with the crowds filling the great square.

He'd recognized the faces of many other Securitate officers, the secret of their profession etched in their hard eyes. And like many others in the suddenly lost league of operatives, he'd joined the exodus out of the capital.

He'd gone underground, staying with those rare souls he could trust not to turn him in. Their numbers had dwindled quickly as more and more scapegoats were manufactured by the new people in power, making him a wanted man.

It hadn't mattered that he was innocent, or as innocent as a man in his position could be.

All that had mattered was that his picture had circulated on an unofficial watch list that accused him of murder and embezzlement, rape and brutality. Crimes that many of his fellow officers had committed as a matter of course.

Crimes that were now laid upon his shoulders.

In order to continue living as a free man, he'd had to flee his own country, following in the footsteps of Konrad Lorenz, who now offered him shelter.

It was known to his colleagues as the Underground Express. Many of them also called it the Last Exit, because those who took the route were never seen again.

Konrad Lorenz offered them escape from the law and a new identity.

For a price.

There lay his problem. Because he wasn't a thief, he had no riches to trade for his new identity. But he had something else.

His skills were high currency in the underworld. He'd been a champion gymnast and sharpshooter. He'd also been a member of the antiterrorist squad, although by strict definition that meant he should have gone after some of his colleagues who were now offering him a safe harbor if only he would turn criminal.

It was a crazy world.

Strashmir stopped at a small street-side café and took a table at the back where he could watch the city flow by him. He ordered a cup of coffee from a young waitress who took his mind away from things for a short while.

He smiled, fancying that he attracted her. Perhaps even in disguise his good looks came through to her. No, on second thought, maybe all she saw in him was a potentially good tipper.

He had tried to look like a prosperous businessman with a somewhat larger than usual overcoat to hide his weapon.

The weapon, he thought.

That was what had given him away. Not the sight of it. Just the knowledge of it. The policeman had seen something in Strashmir that marked him as a threat.

He sighed, leaned back in his seat and absently dropped his hand in his pocket.

The Browning was a compact automatic pistol, deadly enough in the right hands. But maybe it was time to get rid of the weapon he'd kept with him throughout his roundabout exodus from Romania.

He'd carried the Browning on him or near him at all times as he'd skirted the eastern border of Hungary, then on to Prague and finally down to Linz.

He was tired of trains.

Tired of flight.

As he looked around at the people in the café, he wished that he could trade places with any of them, take someone's identity for a while and escape the silent footsteps he could always hear pursuing him in his imagination.

He finished his coffee, glancing at the waitress as he left her a generous tip.

Then he headed down to the docks to find a watery grave for the pistol.

His soul would feel much lighter going into Vienna without the gun.

CHAPTER EIGHT

A thick cloud of cigar smoke plumed across the long wooden conference table in the darkened room, drifting like war clouds across the silent battlefield gleaming from the television screen.

Mack Bolan sat at the middle of the table in an olive-drab sleeveless fatigue T-shirt, his shoulder wrapped and his ribs bandaged, his hand curled around a white ceramic cup of scalding black coffee.

Gina Salvie sat next to him in a pair of jeans, and a faded blue work shirt that was rolled to the elbows, looking in a lot better shape than the Executioner. But she'd been good to look at to begin with, so Bolan didn't feel so bad.

Gus Sinclair, a stogie jutting from a corner of his mouth, looked as if he was ready to go on camera any second and bring joy to the world.

Only Brognola looked the same way as Bolan. Like hell. He'd arrived at the farmhouse at the break of day in the company of a couple of blue suits and sunglasses who'd been detailed to him as around-the-clock bodyguards. Ever since his arrival, Brognola had been either dishing out information or gathering it in.

But fueled by several cups of coffee, he continued with his briefing, determined that the farmhouse crew shared in all of the Intelligence at hand.

"That was supposed to be my transport out of the base," Brognola said, gesturing at the television unit against the wall. On-screen was a freeze-frame of one of a series of photographs that had been put on videotape. This black-and-white blowup showed a twisted metal coffin on a roadside a few miles away from Hangelar. "But at the last minute I was called in for a conference with some of the GSG-9 brass."

"You think it was aimed at you?" Bolan asked.

"The hell of it is, Striker," Brognola said, "we don't know for sure. It could have been a blanket attack on the GSG-9, or it could have been meant to take me out. All we know for sure is that four good men are dead, and the Vampyr network has some awful good Intelligence connections."

"Yeah," Bolan said, "we found out firsthand."

The head Fed nodded. "I almost had both of you on my conscience." He looked first at Bolan, then at Salvie. "I'm sorry I sent you into that firefight. We fell lock, stock and barrel for some gray information that was floated our way by previously solid sources."

"That's a scary thought," Sinclair said. "It means either they kept some agents in place all these years just to feed us this information, or else they've reached into the heart of the Intelligence network. We won't know who to trust."

Brognola looked the man straight in the eyes. "Scary is right. It's a regular horror story any way you look at it. We're up against something a lot bigger than we thought going into this operation. And even then we figured it was a heavy-duty group."

The big Fed unfroze the tape for a moment until another black-and-white blowup appeared on-screen. This one showed the aftermath of an attack at a small pastoral village outside of Cheltenham, England.

In the background of the photo was a cluster of well-kept garden-ringed cottages. But in the foreground were the charred sticks-and-stones remains of what had been similar homes. All that was left of the walls were the jagged ruins above the foundations. Broken glass from the window frames was scattered on the ground.

"This was a relay station near our Cheltenham, England, base, where we had a small group of NSA and CIA techno-spooks vacuuming up and analyzing electronic communications Intelligence from all across Europe. Seven of our military people were killed in this rocket attack, as were two British liaisons. Ten more people suffered serious wounds."

"Why England?" Bolan asked.

Brognola shrugged. "This unit was recently tasked with tracking and tracing all communication references dealing with the Vampyr network. Their computers focused on key words that might tie in to Konrad Lorenz or anything to do with Romanian, Czechoslovakian or former East Bloc operatives. They were trying to put together an electronic mosiac that would have shown us the flow of Vampyr assets.''

Like a man who was showcasing a spook version of Dante's *Inferno,* Brognola raced through several more photographs on the videotape, all of them looking like gruesome postcards from Konrad Lorenz's Vampyr network.

From Rome came a photograph of a Fiat with a bloodstained driver's seat with the back cushion ripped apart by bullets. The deceased driver had been an American Special Forces officer recently attached to the embassy. He had been working on the Romania-Italy pipline of the Underground Express when his Fiat was blockaded in a traffic jam—and he was assassinated by a man in a policeman's uniform who appeared to be directing traffic. He was shot at point-blank range.

Another photograph showed the bloated corpse of a deep-cover Agency man who'd gone swimming in Lake Geneva with his hands tied behind his back. His cover as an international businessman had been in place for more than a decade. Recently he'd been investigating a maze of Swiss-Liechtenstein shell companies believed to be connected to Konrad Lorenz.

Brognola switched off the television set, then walked over to the long rectangular window. He raised the shade and levered the window open to let some air into the room.

"That tape was a compilation of some of the things we can see the Vampyr network throwing against us. Now, for some of the things we might not necessarily see until too late."

Brognola briefed them on the weapons caches that both the East Bloc and West Bloc countries had stockpiled across Europe during the days of the cold war. Arms, food and communications equipment were secreted away in several locations to outfit resistance groups who would be able to carry on the fight in case their country was invaded and occupied.

Some of the West Bloc sites had almost been forgotten during the upheaval following the fall of the Iron Curtain. But not by Konrad Lorenz. Several former West Bloc caches had been broken into in simultaneous attacks that liberated the weaponry and supplies. It had all the earmarks of a Vampyr operation.

Other troubling information had reached Brognola about black-market uranium suddenly coming from East Europe for sale to the highest bidder. According to the Intelligence passed on from the International Atomic Energy Agency in Vienna, much of the uranium had come from Romanian plants that processed it for use in nuclear-power programs.

Some of it was partially enriched, some was low-grade. Most of it had been recovered from the black marketers, but there was good reason to believe that higher quality uranium—almost weapons quality—was en route through the same pipeline. All indications pointed toward the Vampyr network as the supplier.

"In effect, what we have is a hostile Intelligence agency—hell, an entire underground military service—moving against us. They have access to critical information on our soft targets, on our industries and on a lot of skeletons in a lot of closets. They can put pressure on a lot of highly placed people to get them to collaborate with them. Unfortunately this network grows continuously as more and more rogue spooks turn to Lorenz for help. And Lorenz is targeting these seasoned operatives to neutralize anything we can send against them."

"They're also trying to scare us off from initiating further operations," Bolan said.

Salvie nodded. "Logically we have to wonder if *our* network has been penetrated or compromised. Our next step, supposedly, would be to think twice before going into action again. It's psychologically designed to keep us off balance."

"And?" Brognola prompted.

"It's not working, Chief," Salvie replied. "Not after what those bastards did."

"Same here, Hal," Bolan added. "As far as I'm concerned, Konrad Lorenz has signed his own death warrant. And we're going to deliver it."

The newsman pushed his long arms back from the table and sat straight up, meeting Brognola's gaze. "I've been working undercover for years now," he said. "Enjoyed the hell out of it, too. You want me to play it that way, fine. You want me to put on a uniform, I'll do that, too. Just aim me in the right direction."

Brognola smiled. "All right. Enough of what they've been doing to us. Let's start figuring out what we can do to them. Here's the situation. We're coordinating with GSG-9, the Austrians, the Belgians and the British. We've had a strong relationship with the Germans for years now. It won't end because they're absorbing the East German services, but it will complicate matters.

"Until we can get those sources who used to belong to the Stasi," Brognola continued, "we're going to concentrate on strictly an old-boy network. People we know and can trust. Any Stasi files that come our way we'll look at, but we don't regard as the bible. A lot of our initial leads will originate from recently recovered Stasi files, but we'll verify everything ten ways from Sunday before we act on it."

"What's our position here?" Bolan asked. "Officially."

"Officially we don't exist. Officially I wasn't even at Hangelar when the hit came down. But unofficially we've got unlimited manpower. Once we get a target, if we need any help we get whatever we ask for. Aside from the manpower, we're bringing in some heavy-duty mind-power to help find Lorenz.''

"Oh, no," Salvie groaned. "Not psychics again."

"Relax," Brognola said. "I'm not talking about psychics. Though they have their place."

"Yes," the woman replied. "In a storefront shop reading palms and telling fortunes."

Brognola shrugged. "They've had some successes. We used them to good effect when the Red Brigades grabbed Dozier. They helped in the search. They've also come in handy for locating subs on underwater maneuvers."

"Lorenz is big," Salvie conceded, "but I doubt he's got a submarine yet."

"Whatever assets he's got, we'll find sooner or later. But I'm also interested in what he's got up here," Brognola said, tapping his forehead. "That's why we're bringing in a psychiatrist to work with our team."

Gus Sinclair shook his head. "What's he going to do? Analyze them to death?"

Brognola shook his head. "This guy's got top clearance. He's experienced with the mindset of these types. We can use him to anticipate Lorenz's moves."

"Whatever works," Bolan said.

"Oh, he'll work, all right," Brognola said. "Once he gets here he'll do a full-bore briefing on Ion Cusa that might turn up things we miss. In the meantime, let's see what we can find out for ourselves. What's Cusa's condition?''

"He's groggy, hungry and scared," the Executioner replied. "He has some superficial wounds, but he's doing much better than he lets on. He told us enough to keep us interested in him, but he's held back a lot that we already know. I thought it best to wait until you were here before we start the next round."

"Let's do it," Brognola said.

THE EXECUTIONER WAS the first one into the room where Ion Cusa had been moved for interrogation. Bolan nodded to the guard, who left without saying a word, certain that the group of four well-trained operatives had nothing to fear from the Romanian.

Especially in his present condition.

He was weak and tired, looking a decade older than in the last session. His condition was obviously weighing heavily on him, although he tried not to show it.

Cusa's hands were bound behind the back of a wooden chair with a black nylon cord, not severely enough to cause pain, but enough to make sure he was immobile.

Even so, conditions were better here than in the cellar room where he was kept between interrogations. Cusa looked almost glad for the diversion.

"We've got some more questions," Bolan said. He switched on a bright light aimed at Cusa's face, which kept him from looking at Hal Brognola and Gus Sinclair as they entered the room and dropped into seats near the wall.

They hung back like inquisitors in the shadows while Bolan and Salvie pulled a couple of chairs close to Cusa, their grim faces staring hard at him.

Cusa's gray head shook from side to side in exaggerated despair. Once again the actor had taken his stage. "I've already told you everything I can," he said.

"Not quite," Bolan replied. "You've just started."

The Romanian shrugged. "What do you want me to say?"

"For starters, say something that will convince my friends we should keep you alive."

Cusa laughed. "It's too late for you to exercise that option," he said. "I know how the democracies work. Since I'm already in your custody, you'll play some games, but you won't kill me. Too many of your people have seen me."

"I got some bad news for you, Cusa. Officially no one has seen you. You're not in anyone's custody. This place isn't on the map. It doesn't exist. Neither do we. And if we don't like your answers, pretty soon *you* won't exist."

Cusa tried to gauge the expression in Bolan's eyes, but the light kept him from seeing. He shook his head. "I know what you are trying to do. You moved me here and now you are just using, eh, psychological pressure to make me think—"

"No," Bolan interrupted. "Don't think. Just talk. Tell us everything you can about Konrad Lorenz and his network. His front companies. His sphere of operations. The Intelligence agencies he worked with before and the ones he deals with now. I want to know every step he's taken since he fled Romania. Understand me? You talk or else the next place we move you is a cemetery."

"Of course I will talk," Cusa said. "But all I can tell you is what I've already told you the first time—"

Bolan stood slowly and started to drag his chair across the floor. Turning toward the shadowed faces of Brognola and Sinclair, the Executioner growled out a command. "Kill him," he said. "He's had his chance."

Once again Cusa saw the warrior who'd done so much damage to his men at the château. As Bolan reached the door, Cusa called him back. "Wait! Wait! There *are* some things I can tell you."

Bolan spun around. "So tell," he said, grabbing the chair and sitting down.

The story came out once again, this time with more details, more names. And, as if the threat of death had penetrated Cusa's masks, his English improved dramatically.

More important, Bolan thought, the things he said made sense, judging from the Intelligence they already had on Lorenz, who was notorious for compartmentalizing his operations on a strict need-to-know basis. Everything Cusa said reinforced that pattern of behavior.

Cusa had been kept isolated from the corporate arm of Lorenz's empire, concentrating mainly on the military arm. But he knew some of the safehouses and some of the shell corporations that had sprung up and dissolved, living only long enough to transfer funds for the Underground Express.

But the names, or at least the locations of the dummy corporations, might be useful in reconstructing the connections Lorenz had used and the path he'd taken. And perhaps the path he would take.

Cusa also knew the type of plunder that Lorenz was moving out of Romania and the Czech Republic with the riders on the Underground Express—crown jewels stolen from the treasury, gold bullion, currency, paintings, sacred books. It was just like World War II all over again, when the thieves of the night had descended on countries in chaos, determined to steal their art and their soul while war raged on.

Though Cusa didn't know the specific destinations for much of the plundered fortunes, he knew the kind of facilities Lorenz set up to handle them: private institutes and asylums in England; resorts and spas in Germany and Austria; private-detective agencies in all of those countries to absorb the steady flow of ousted Intelligence agents and provide them with cover.

It was a crook's tour of the underworld, led by one of Lorenz's greatest pupils.

Cusa also had some names, including that of Axel Erhard, the former Stasi operative. But Erhard had kept his distance, joining with Cusa only on military operations. Other than that, the Romanian had no idea what identity he traveled under or where his base was.

But the name that piqued Bolan's interest was Cass Strashmir, the man who would soon join Konrad Lorenz.

Interpol was looking for him and had put him on the watch lists distributed to police and customs agencies around the world. And Romania had labeled him as a figutive and enemy of the people, wanted for genocide.

According to the information circulating on Cass Strashmir, the man was the devil incarnate. Or at least his right-hand man. Atrocity after atrocity had been attached to his name.

"He sounds as bad as Konrad Lorenz," Bolan observed.

Cusa laughed bitterly. "Before long he'll sound even worse. His crimes are increasing daily. Whenever the police run into an unsolvable case, they attribute it to him. He makes a perfect scapegoat."

"Is any of it true?" Bolan asked.

Cusa shrugged. "He was one of us. A difficult man, however, always going his own way. But he was good at what he did. A cold and hard professional—much like you—who didn't give a damn about the rules. This stubbornness of his was tolerated as long as he produced. But when word of his excesses reached the ears of the public, nothing could protect him anymore. He had to go underground. And when one of us goes underground, sooner or later he has to go to Konrad Lorenz."

"All roads lead to the Romanian," Bolan said. "Which road is he taking?"

"His own road," Cusa answered. "All I know is that he was supposed to show up in Vienna. The monks are taking care of it."

"The holy men of Prague?"

Cusa nodded. He continued unraveling the threads of the empire that he knew about. But at one point he suddenly stopped, almost as if the sense of betrayal had overwhelmed him.

A case of conscience.

"Keep talking, Cusa. Or the next interrogator we bring in won't be so nice. We're relatively straightforard, but this man is a monster. A mindbender. He's a psychiatrist who won't care how deep he has to dig to get at your secrets, or what damage it causes. He'll make sure you tell him everything there is to know about the life and times—and maybe the death—of Ion Cusa."

Cusa resumed talking.

And as he listened to the Romanian spill his guts with a newfound respect for life, Bolan couldn't help thinking that using a psychiatrist might help them after all. Or maybe just the threat of using one.

CHAPTER NINE

The white-hulled steamship plowed through the
sunstruck Danube as the current wound its way
through the Wachau region, now and then passing
the ruins of riverside castles that had long crumbled
back into the rock from which they'd been hewn.

Sitting in the glass-paneled passenger lounge on
the front deck, Cass Strashmir felt perfectly at ease
for the first time since he'd left Romania.

A lot of it had to do with the fact that he'd dis-
carded the pistol back in Linz, giving him something in common with the rest of the passengers who
sat on the comfortable chairs sipping their drinks in
the cool spring air. Without the heavy feel of the gun,
a weight that pressed equally on the mind and the
body, he didn't feel as if he was in a combat situation anymore, that he was going to have to fight
someone to the death at any moment.

Without the gun he felt like an innocent, instead
of a man on the run. The sense of belonging to the
rest of humanity, if only for a short time, had re-
vived the persona that had long lain hidden beneath
the outward armor of his Securitate identity.

Perhaps at the end of this final leg of the journey from Linz to Vienna he could pass more easily as a tourist. He had several hours to wile away cocooned in the comfortable roar and throbbing of the steamboat's engines.

It was scheduled to dock at Reich Bridge early in the evening, which gave him plenty of time to lose himself in the simple pleasure of being.

It was no random choice that led him to the steamboat. When he was a younger man, a freer man, Strashmir had loved the feel of riding on a river, totally cut off from the rest of the world until the journey's end. Man and machine were in sync in the flow of mist, oil and steam.

On the river there were no petty tyrants to listen to, no Machiavellian gambits to unravel. There was just peace and quiet, the weightless sensation of a human soul adrift in a current.

He closed his eyes and sank deep into the comfortable cushion of the armchair, and as he fell into a half sleep he also fell deep into the current of memory.

Once again a chillness of spirit swept through his mind, haunting him with the cold December nights when Nicolae Ceausescu and his government were toppled.

ON THE NIGHT the dictator fell, Cass Strashmir was with a Securitate rifle team in one of the tall gray and drafty buildings that ringed the palace square.

Army tanks filled the square, carrying wildly shouting soldiers, as well as the Romanian protesters they had refused to fire upon, the protesters whose ranks were now swollen with soldiers who'd gone over to the side of the people.

The government was falling, and men like Cass Strashmir were in their glory.

Soon the madness would end.

The revolution had spread from Timisoara, near Romania's western border with Hungary. Then, in rampant contagion, it spread across the country and finally erupted in Bucharest itself.

In many of the cities the police, the militia and the army refused to move against the revolutionaries.

Part of it was a matter of patriotism. The police and the military welcomed the revolt against Ceausescu. But part of it was a matter of mathematics— *the entire country was in revolt.*

Twenty-three million Romanians couldn't be silenced any longer.

Even the security forces recognized that.

Already many of the Securitate units had broken away from Ceausescu, staying away from their posts. They had tasted the freedom that was blowing in the cold winter wind, freedom heralded by the burnt bound books containing the dictator's speeches, freedom heralded by the hated Communist government's flags whipping in the wind with their centers cut out.

Other Securitate units hadn't decided yet.

And still others were biding their time.

Freedom hadn't come yet to the people.

No one knew who was in control.

It was impossible to predict what course the revolution would take from moment to moment. So many forces were at work that no one group had risen to the top.

The streets leading to the palace square were packed with protesters who moved head-to-head, chanting and crying after years of repression, cheering at their brethren who had stormed the hated headquarters of Ceauşescu and now stood on his balcony pronouncing victory for the revolution.

It was an ocean of humanity, a tidal wave that surged and rushed endlessly through the square.

All Strashmir and the other agents could do was to wait it out and do what they thought best to help maintain order.

They'd poured like ants from one of the underground tunnels that connected the Securitate base in the central-committee building to several other government buildings that faced the square.

The entire city was riddled with subterranean tunnels where the secret police could crawl from one listening post to another, from safehouses to arms cache to escape hatch.

The miles of tunnels had several underground levels. All of it was designed so that Ceauşescu and his inner circle could creep and crawl in secret, far away from the eyes of the people, who loathed and feared the monstrous dictator and the monstrosity of a government he'd created.

The dictator and his apparatus leeched everything it could from them, coloring the once bountiful Romanian landscape a bleak shade of gray.

Cass Strashmir knew the crimes well. He had witnessed the systematic, organized plundering of the country's resources. And because he was human, he'd done nothing to stop them. Despite the revulsion that he felt, he played his part in the Securitate.

It wasn't just the corruption and the murderous nature of the Ceauşescu regime that bothered him. It was the bureaucratic ineptitude that bankrupted the country. The agricultural industry in Romania could feed its people and bring in needed currency. But instead, the divine rulers of Romania had diverted sorely needed funds to create ill-run factories that produced little income but created a lot of waste.

The ruling class didn't worry about the poverty of the people. While common citizens often went without food or heat and light for their homes—as if they'd been cast back into a fuedal darkness—Ceauşescu's inner circle lived like kings. Whatever whims or needs they felt were instantly met.

While his people scraped whatever they could to survive, Ceauşescu had a billion-dollar palace built to his order—as if a great building could make the one who lived there a great man.

But now, their voices raised in thunderous chants, the only building the people wanted for Ceauşescu was a tomb—"Romanians join us!" and "Death to Ceauşescu!"

The cries roared in ragged cadence across the square and echoed down the side streets of Bucharest, floating in the air like a thunderous flag.

It was a majestic feeling.

Strashmir was a part of history. Unfortunately, he thought as he gazed down into the square from his high window, all these years he'd been the wrong part of history.

He'd been a trusted member of Directorate 5, the special unit of the Securitate that handled presidential security and protection for foreign dignitaries.

The unit also handled antiterrorist operations, spearheading paramilitary operations against the armed bandit bands that controlled many of the rugged, secluded areas in the mountains. They were the smugglers, thieves and murderers who supposedly didn't exist in the paradise of Nicolae Ceauşescu.

The tyrant had made conditions so bad that many of the criminal gangs and terrorists felt they had little to lose. And men like Strashmir were sent to do battle with these men who preferred death to living under Ceauşescu's thumb.

It was crazy. In a way Strashmir almost admired many of the desperate men he'd hunted down. They stood their ground for what they believed in. Strashmir had spent a lifetime standing his ground for something he couldn't ever believe in. He knew it too well. He knew the rot at the heart of it.

The world inside the presidential palace, where Ceauşescu had always been surrounded by Securitate soldiers, was a world that not even George Orwell could have dreamed up. Orwell's visions of *1984* and *Animal Farm* were pale shadows of the paranoid and powerful apparatus that the dictator had set up inside the central-committee building in the heart of Bucharest.

But tonight the building was surrounded by thousands upon thousands of demonstrators and protesters and army units that had gone over to their side.

Tonight, Cass Strashmir thought, perhaps there was a god after all.

At least that's what it seemed at first.

But then another Securitate unit made contact with the radioman in Strashmir's group. His voice was excited, full of hope. Loyal Securitate forces had managed to spread out throughout the city in strategic sites just like this one.

They had sniper teams all over Bucharest and they had troops ready to move in large numbers.

The Securitate was preparing to launch a massive attack on the airport.

They were planning to take back the television and radio stations that had been occupied by the protesters.

And they were planning on taking back the streets.

The Securitate was preparing for war.

Inwardly Strashmir was stunned. But he didn't show it. Instead, he studied the faces of the other Securitate men with him, faces that suddenly shone with hope as the heavy whir of helicopter blades sounded above.

Securitate helicopters were sweeping down the wide boulevards of Bucharest, dropping leaflets warning the people to get off the streets and go back home before it was too late.

More instructions came across the radio.

Securitate snipers were supposed to stampede the people off the streets.

If possible, they were to avoid killing anyone. The initial attack would be psychological. If the crowds dispersed, matters could be brought back under Securitate control.

And one order had to be followed at all costs. Under no circumstances was any fire to be directed at the central-committee building. Securitate "defectors" had managed to infiltrate the leadership of the group trying to set up an interim government.

He shook his head.

True to form, Securitate chameleons had suddenly become neoreformists, wolves in sheeps' clothing, who no doubt were helping maintain a state of chaos among the revolutionary councils.

They were working side by side with the army and the civilians, listening in on all of the planning sessions to find out the direction the coup was taking.

And then they were transmitting this same information to the Securitate units spread across the city.

Strashmir shook his head. A sinking feeling came over him as first one man then another started moving around the darkened room with a fanatic spirit he had seen in so many of their faces. It was the look of men who wanted to rule others. The look of men who would do anything to keep their hold on them.

Each man took up a position by a separate window, his sniper rifle easing out of the sill and nosing down toward the milling crowds.

No, Strashmir thought. Not now. Not when it had been so close. But the other men didn't even consider thinking for themselves. They were hard core. They were ready to shoot.

Puffs of smoke billowed from the windows of another building to their right.

It was like a dam breaking. Volleys of sniper fire poured out from many of the other towers that surrounded the square and the central-committee building.

Tracer bullets seared the night, crisscrossing one another in an amazing pyrotechnic light show.

At first the bullets whined overhead, but then they started chipping into the square itself, digging up the stones.

The crowd suddenly began screaming, the chants of revolution quickly forgotten and the shrieks of survival uppermost in their minds.

Strashmir stood by his window with his rifle by his side and looked down into the square.

T-72 tanks began to roll, their lids clanging shut, their turrets swinging around toward the sniper buildings.

Army soldiers swarmed ahead and behind the tanks, many of them grabbing hold of the screaming civilians and shepherding them from the fire.

A band of army scouts clutched the foregrips of their Romanian modified versions of the AKM and headed across the square at full speed, instinctively racing for the buildings where the enemy sniper fire was coming from.

And Cass Strashmir realized *he* was one of the enemy.

He snapped.

The psychological straitjacket that had been strapped on him since he was a youth ripped at the seams. He was no longer going to take part in the insanity that swarmed around him.

Almost as if their rifles were magnetically drawn toward the people in the square, the rooftop snipers started picking out their soft targets, hitting the civilians as they scattered in every direction.

The snipers dropped them with blood-spattering precision.

They weren't trying to keep the protesters away. They were trying to put them away.

The people who'd been crammed into the square moments earlier stampeded like a herd of cattle as death rained down on them from above.

Huge gaps opened up in the midst of the crowd as it instinctively tried to move away from the center.

Just as instinctively, like huntsmen who'd beat the bushes to flush their prey, the snipers fired at the outer rims of the circle, knowing they would have plenty of time to pick off those who were still in the middle of the circle.

The invisible army of Securitate snipers shot at anyone in the square, regardless of whether they were uniformed. It didn't matter if the target carried a weapon. All that mattered was that it lived and breathed—until a Securitate bullet singed the air and took it down.

Streams of lead poured from every direction.

At the height of the barrage Strashmir saw a thirtyish woman spinning around in the middle of the street, struck by a high-powered round that hit her in the back and finally sent her sprawling face first onto the concrete.

Her hands spread out in front of her on the concrete as if she were trying to swim away to safety. But all she could do was swim in her own blood.

The eight-year-old child she'd been dragging along suddenly tumbled head over heels onto the ground beside her, trying to lift her dying mother.

A second round whined into the concrete next to the child.

The shot came from the window next to Strashmir's.

"No!" he shouted. "You can't—*we* can't!" Then words failed him. Something more primitive, more powerful than words came out of his mouth in a thunderous scream.

The deafening roar sounded as if it had been ripped from his conscience in earsplitting rage when he realized the men beside him were firing into their own people, men he assumed would be as horrified as he was by the slaughter below.

Like a man hypnotized, Strashmir charged the kneeling sniper at the next window, grabbing his forearm and prying it free from his weapon.

Strashmir kept on pulling until the leverage forced the man to spin crazily on his feet. The man tried to gain his balance but crashed headfirst into the wall, splintering through the plaster that dropped on his head in a powdery avalanche.

The two other riflemen in the room looked at Strashmir, their eyes wide with shock that one of their own had turned on them, going amok in the heat of battle.

"Stop!" Strashmir shouted. "Hold your fire!"

The sniper farthest from Strashmir shook his head in disbelief. "We're following orders!" he snapped. "Interfere with us and *you* will be shot." Without giving Strashmir any more thought, he turned away and resumed firing into the square as if he was some murderous automaton unable to break his programming.

"I'm interfering," Strashmir said, reaching for his side arm, a 9 mm parabellum Borsig automatic.

The sniper closest to Strashmir wore a look of pleasant surprise on his face, like a man who had eagerly accepted a duel to the death. In his mind this was treason.

That meant Cass Strashmir was fair game.

He swung his rifle toward his comrade.

But there had been a split-second delay caused by the backward motion required to pull the rifle barrel from the window and aim it at the new target.

It was a split second too long.

Strashmir squeezed the trigger and shot the man point-blank in the middle of his forehead, scattering pieces of bone and brain into the window frame behind him.

Like a puppet without his strings, the sniper crumpled to the floor, his rifle spinning end over end out the window.

The other sniper made his move, whipping the barrel of his rifle toward Strashmir.

But Strashmir was already on the move. He stepped to his right, moving just ahead of the rifle barrel that was tracking him as he aimed the Borsig automatic at the man's midsection, firing until the other sniper was flat on his back with blood running from his mouth onto the floor.

And Cass Strashmir was Securitate no more.

He left his past behind him in that room on the top floor.

But he also left one man alive, who made it his mission in life to implicate Strashmir in the murders of the civilians in the street.

When a band of army scouts and armed civilians cleaned out the buildings around the square in a room-to-room search for snipers, the man that Strashmir had thrown into the wall reversed their roles. He claimed it was Strashmir who had fired on the people in the square and when the others tried to stop him, Strashmir executed them in cold blood.

It was the first of many false claims that dogged Strashmir's steps as he vanished into the underground. Each month more lies and more crimes were added to his legend until soon he was a monstrous criminal in the eyes of the people he had tried to save.

A sudden blast of the steamship's horn yanked Strashmir from his reverie. Sitting straight up, he saw the rapidly approaching Reich Bridge quay.

The war that haunted his dreams was over.

Another war was about to begin.

CHAPTER TEN

Hooded figures ran softly across the rooftop of the modern gray stone-and-glass apartment complex on the outskirts of the Ringstrasse that circled the old-town section of Vienna.

Some of the men wore respirators and antiflash goggles, and carried a lethal array of weaponry. The strange-looking protective devices gave them the appearance of creatures who had just dropped from the sky.

Others carried black ropes and lightweight eaves-dropping equipment that looked like fishing gear. The miniature microphones and cameras were weighted just enough to keep them balanced when they were lowered on well-oiled pulleys down the chimneys that studded the rooftop like redbrick stalagmites.

Standing close to the edge of the rooftop, his camo-streaked face turned away from the crisp night wind racing over the skyline, Mack Bolan leaned back and tested the rope harness he'd rigged to the chimney nearest the corner of the rooftop.

He was part of the drop team that would go over the side as soon as they got the word.

If they got the word.

Now that the teams were in place, there was always the chance that second thoughts would kick in from the higher-ups who ran the operation from their command post across the street. Hal Brognola and his covert counterparts in GSG-9 were working closely with the commander of the Austrian antiterrorist unit who'd committed his Cobra unit to the Vienna strike.

The gray-haired chiefs were physically where they belonged, Bolan thought, safely ensconced in one of the apartments they'd commandeered from the occupants so they could observe the strike teams, as well as the streets below.

But Bolan wasn't so sure the spook chiefs were mentally in the right place. It was a sensitive operation, and it could be aborted at any moment if any of them felt it was out of control.

Their fears were understandable. If something went wrong, the ex-STB men holed up in the fourth floor of the apartment building could do a lot of damage. They had to be taken out instantly and simultaneously to keep them from launching a dangerous counterattack against the team or any civilians in the area.

The problem was that Cass Strashmir hadn't shown up for his rendezvous with the Czechs yet.

And now the Czech "monks" were getting restless, suspecting that somewhere down the line Strashmir had been compromised. That led the monks to think that they themselves might be in jeopardy.

The window of opportunity was closing.

If the strike team didn't get the green light soon, the heavily armed and wary Czechs were going to move out. And they wouldn't think twice about causing civilian casualties if they came under attack.

There was also the chance that Strashmir would hook up with the Czech arm of the Vampyr network somewhere else and do even worse damage further down the road.

A road with Mack Bolan standing right in the middle.

As he crouched near the edge of the rooftop, one more black-clad shape in waiting, the warrior forced himself to breathe out the tension that had built up inside of him ever since they'd arrived in Vienna with a GSG-9 unit and liaised with the Cobra team.

The German and Austrian antiterrorist units had worked well together in the past, often with U.S. and British counterparts attached as observers—or more often than not, participants.

Most of the countries that had been neutral or allied to the West during the cold war had welcomed the assistance of any Special Forces crisis unit that could help them take down the enemy. That was one of the reasons the members of the joint task force wore hoods. Aside from the intimidating psychological effect it had on their opponents, the hoods kept their faces hidden. It was impossible to tell their identities, let alone their nationalities.

Multinational task forces were the rule these days, rather than the exception. They had to be, Bolan thought. Otherwise, it would be a new world disorder rather than the new world order all the democracies were talking about.

For this operation Bolan had come into Austria as a specialist attached to the German unit. If anything happened to him, there would be no mention of an American presence.

Just one more unknown soldier gone to rest.

Bolan glanced over at the neighboring rooftop where another backup unit was approaching the rubber-sheathed plank that had been thrown down to connect one building to the next.

The chasm between the gray stone-and-glass apartment buildings fell seven stories to the dark strip of alley below. It wasn't the place to be if you didn't like heights.

Nor was this the business to be in.

Any second now half the men on the roof had to be prepared to rappel down the side of the roof like spiders on a web, easy targets if the Czechs heard them coming.

In the street below, a team of electronic techs worked out of unmarked Cobra surveillance vans parked at the curbside.

The vans were equipped with laser mikes and sophisticated cameras with night-vision lenses. The mikes beamed lasers onto the windows of the corner apartments, picking up the sound vibrations of voices against the glass, then bouncing the lasers up to the command post where Gina Salvie monitored the voices through audio decoders.

The laser mikes kept the strike team informed of the state of mind of the Czechs while the cameras scanned the streets for any sign of Cass Strashmir.

Other cameras were trained on the apartments from observation posts on surrounding rooftops, as well as cameras that silently snaked down the chimneys, transmitting clear pictures of the Czechs and their weapons.

By now the assault team knew the number and position of most of the armed monks.

The surveillance units had swept all the nearby rooms with the laser mikes to make sure none of the occupants in the adjoining apartments were part of the Czech team. Then the Austrian Cobra unit had filtered out through the hallways, quietly evacuating the apartment dwellers out the back entrance after alerting them by phone.

An incredible amount of work had been done by the special units to get to this point.

Acting on Intelligence that Brognola and the GSG-9 provided on the Czechs and their probable locations—courtesy of Ion Cusa's confessions—the Austrian Cobra unit conducted a massive surveillance operation throughout the city, finally narrowing the focus of the search to this cadre of known Czech nationals outside the Ringstrasse.

Most of the credit for zeroing in on the monks so fast belonged to one of the gray-haired Austrian chiefs who'd been brought out of semiretirement just for the case. Theodoric Ingram, an aristocratic type who still kept his hand in the covert trade, had weeded through thousands of files and photos he'd gathered during his cold-war days as a specialist on Soviet penetration of Austria. Their main target had been Vienna because of the international delegations that routinely met there. And the main East Bloc Intelligence service sophisticated enough to carry out that infiltration belonged to the Czechs.

Ingram was a walking encyclopedia on the monks. His presence had cut hours off the search. And once his groundwork led to this apartment complex, the high-tech snoop gear confirmed that they had the right spot.

Now all that was needed was for Cass Strashmir to make an appearance to complete the package.

The Executioner exhaled quietly and raised his black-gloved hand overhead to pull himself up from the wall he'd been leaning against. Then he studied the street below through a hand-held thermal imager, sweeping over the surveillance vans, the Mercedes communication cars and the agents who were walking in apparently random patterns.

Bolan also studied the regular traffic that continued to flow through the streets, taxi and sports cars picking and dropping off men and women sampling the nightlife. It was still relatively early in the evening, still a busy street.

It all looked so normal below, the warrior thought, right down to the horse-drawn black-laquered *Fiakers* making their regular rounds. The horses clip-clopped through the streets while the homburg-hatted drivers looked straight ahead, with lovers and other couples sitting in the backs of the carriages, oblivious to the silent war brewing above them.

"Go."
  "Go."
  "Go."

The team leaders spoke the words softly but cleary, accompanying each command with a hand gesture so there would be no mistake.

The Czechs were getting ready to close up shop, spooked by Strashmir's absence.

It was time to close them down.

Mack Bolan rappeled down the east corner of the building while several feet to his left and just out of sight, a Cobra team member descended the west corner.

Working the black nylon ropes, they dropped like spiders, kicking out into the air several stories above the street and touching down with their soft-soled shoes against the concrete before pushing off again.

From the windows Bolan passed on the way down came the sounds of television sets and radios. They'd been kept turned on even though the occupants had been cleared out, lending an air of normalcy to the night.

The warrior's feet scuffed softly on the concrete as he came to a stop one floor above the STB apartments. To the right he saw several other spiderlike forms coming to a standstill parallel with him just above their targets.

They steadied themselves, then looked around to see if their fellow rappelers were in place.

Then the men looked up at the roof, where they could see the silhouette of their spotters etched against the sky. They were using a combination of tugs on the rope and hand signals to make sure there was no mistake.

Bolan braced himself, ready to push off from the building in a wide airborne arc that would swing him like a pendulum down to the target window.

It was all a matter of timing and precision—and a solid belief you were going to come out of the operation alive.

To keep from getting entangled in the rope and hanging out there like a sitting target, Bolan needed enough momentum to carry him through the bottom half of the window. If his timing was right, he'd sail into the room like a man coming off a playground slide, then land on his feet in the middle of a minor Armageddon.

The rubber-soled shoes would take most of the impact, while his body armor, goggles and Frankenstein respirator would protect him from the shards of glass.

All that would protect him from the panicked terrorists inside was his own quick reactions.

Flash-bang grenades and gunfire would be sounding from all directions. The doors to the apartments would be blown off their hinges by shaped charges that would also knock out any booby traps the Czechs had planted to prevent intruders from coming through the door.

The plan also called for neutralizing the monk who now waited on guard in the front-entrance lobby of the apartment building. At the first sign of anything unusual on the street, the monk was ready to hit the buzzer-intercom system connected to each apartment.

A plainclothes Cobra unit was slated to take out the guard. Thanks to the cooperation of the newly installed Czech government, which was more eager than most when it came to exposing the corrupt activities of many of their former Intelligence operatives, the Austrian Kommando unit had been able to identify the monk with absolute certainty. He was a former military Intelligence man who'd been implicated in murder, black-marketing and arms smuggling to underground groups in Austria and Germany.

Bolan craned his neck back and looked up into the sky. Time to do it. The numbers were running down.

Almost as if the men on the rooftop had heard his thoughts, the spotters gave the rappelers the ready sign, a wide chopping gesture that set them on their mark.

Ten seconds to go in.

With a calmness that came from years of conditioning, Bolan began the countdown in a state of mind that was almost in slow motion. At this stage of the operation, ten seconds could seem like an eternity.

One thousand and one.

And if someone mistimed the move, they might have all of eternity to regret that mistake.

One thousand and two.

Suspended high above the street from a black nylon lifeline, Bolan felt exposed and vulnerable. If the monks had accomplices in the street, the men on the side of the building were easy targets.

Hanging by a thread.

One thousand and three.

The Executioner could feel the tension starting to spread through the rest of the team. It was like a psychic band encompassing them, a second sense that spread out from each man as he approached the point of no return.

They were synchronized weapons about to be thrown into battle.

One thousand and four.

Bolan mentally rehearsed the move, picturing himself swinging through the air and successfully landing inside the apartment. Subconsciously his mind would program his body to carry out that same maneuver.

As long as he trusted his instincts, he would be okay.

One thousand and five.

Just five more seconds to go, Bolan thought, tightening his grip on the taut rope in his gloved hands.

And then the world as he knew it shook to its very foundations as a tremendous blast boomed inside the corner apartment.

The echo bounced off the walls in concussive force as the directional charges lowered down the chimney went off ahead of time. Either the explosives were faulty or someone had jumped the gun. Whatever happened, it was time to go in.

Time to crash the party.

Bolan bent his knees and tensed his calf muscles. Then with a rapid push he sailed out and away from the building, a six-foot-three-inch, two-hundred-pound pendulum swinging out into space.

As his hands guided the movement of the rope, the warrior held his legs straight out in front of him like an iron-muscled battering ram that would rocket through the glass when gravity pulled him toward the window.

In midswing his plans suddenly changed.

A wild-eyed monk was looking out from inside the glass window, his hands furiously tugging up at the bottom of the window frame.

It all happened in a split second. As Bolan reached the end of his outward arc, the window rolled upward.

Both warriors got a close-up look at each other at the exact same time.

The man from the Czech terror team had a short, ax-shaped crew cut and a pointy little beard that made him look almost like a bewildered bohemian.

But the way his hand instinctively reached for the Czech-made Brigant automatic in his hip holser dispelled that split-second image. The man had military training.

In the next instant Bolan was going to find out just how good that training was. Even as the man freed the Brigant he was shouting something in his native language, a harsh bark alerting his comrades.

The Executioner had two choices.

He could divert his downward arc and try to push off from the building again—hopefully avoiding the 7.62 mm slugs from the 8-round single-action pistol.

Or he could maintain his attack.

Instinct took over.

When it came time to hit or run, the warrior in him went for the hit. Everything was so clear to him, every choice, every risk, the well-oiled gleam of the Brigant as the barrel cleared the holster and was turning toward Bolan, the rush of the wind as the Executioner sliced through the air almost in free-fall...

Mack Bolan's left foot cocked straight back, then pedaled forward in the first part of a pinwheel kick that gave his right foot enough leverage and power to snap forward just as his momentum carried him into the room.

The warrior's heel caught the Brigant-waving gunman in the bridge of the nose, breaking free the bone and pushing it deep into his brain. While the monk went down a dead man, one shot from the Brigant went off from the impact and studded the floor with a 7.62 mm bolt. Then the weapon skidded on the bare wood.

Bolan came down hard on his back, spreading both hands to break his fall. As he rolled to his right and scrambled to his feet, he tugged the Heckler & Koch MP-5 free from its harness and aimed at a trio of Czech gunmen who stood in the middle of the room, dazed.

The monks were still stunned by the afterblast of white-hot novalike stun grenades tossed by the dark shapes who filled the room from three sides.

There was no hesitation from any of the attackers. This was war, and you didn't wait for the other side to get off the first shot.

Bolan fired a 3-round burst into the Czech who was standing straight ahead of him. The man had a two-handed grip on his submachine gun, ready to go to work as soon as his mind recovered from the shock of the flash-bangs.

But the 9 mm stream of lead from the Executioner's SMG made sure the shock was permanent.

Bolan's man went down.

The second and third Czech hardmen dropped to the floor in a heap, kicked off their feet by bursts from the other men on the assault team. Sharp bursts of gunfire sounded from the adjoining rooms that were raided by the other team members.

Bolan joined the others in a room-to-room search through the apartments, past shattered doors, grenade-blasted fireplace windows and the battered, bleeding bodies of the monks.

There was no pity in Bolan's heart.

The rogue monks were part of the Vampyr network, and they deserved to go down. Images of the innocent civilians slaughtered at the château south of Koblenz were still fresh in the warrior's mind. So were the black-and-white photos of the GSG-9 unit that had been trashed at Hangelar—perhaps by the same gunmen who were now clutched in the cold invisible embrace of Morpheus.

For the next few minutes Bolan and the other commandos scoured the apartments for any hidden Czech hardmen. There were suitcases full of guns and ammo, as well as scattered papers: Eurail passes, airplane tickets. Czech and Austrian documents, identification cards, car keys.

It was a miniature Intelligence network, a well-staffed and equipped outpost for Konrad Lorenz's Vampyr network.

There were closets full of clothes, as well as cash—stacks of money in all denominations and currencies. Enough to live well anywhere in Europe.

Whatever their beliefs, Bolan thought, *these* monks obviously never got around to taking their vows of poverty.

But the money couldn't buy them out of this one. Their bill was paid in full.

All that was left of the outpost was a cordite haze of battlefield smoke that lingered over the invaded rooms.

Now that the situation was all clear, Bolan joined the exodus of black-clad men as they filed from the apartments one by one, making room for the next set of teams filtering into the monk's nest.

The new teams would turn the rooms upside down until they'd gathered up every last bit of evidence, every clue that could lead to the next stop on the Undergroud Express.

DOWN IN THE LOBBY one clue was still alive.

Barely.

The former Czech officer had been taken out by a middle-aged man in a tweed jacket and a black-brimmed hat with a bright orange feather stuck in the hatband.

Seconds before the assault began, the plain-clothes Cobra commando had scurried up the steps into the lobby, carrying his umbrella in his right hand and a bouquet of flowers in his left.

As the door swung closed behind him, the Cobra had moved over to the intercom unit built into the wall and begun to scan the nameplates while murmuring the name of his imaginary sweetheart.

Under the watchful eye of the Czech lookout, the conservative-looking commando moved closer to him, making it almost impossible for the Czech to do any damage even if he managed to draw the pistol from his bulky underarm holster.

Something spurred the Czech into action at the last possible moment. Maybe it was the look in the commando's eye. Maybe it was just the suspicious timing. Whatever it was, the Czech started to reach for his weapon.

His hand froze in midair as his head banged against the intercom panel.

Moving so fast that the Czech couldn't follow the direction of his attack, the Austrian commando had spun and speared the monk's throat with the blunt end of the umbrella.

Following through with a short push that snapped the monk's head against the wall, the commando kneed him in the groin with a smash that lifted him off his feet.

The commando flipped the umbrella around and clubbed down hard the Czech's collarbone. As the man crumpled from the blow, the commando used a supple but rapid twist that hooked the curved end of the umbrella around the man's neck.

Using the leverage of the hook, the Austrian flung the man face first against the wall and caved in the side of his ribs with a front snap kick.

The monk was unconscious by the time he reached the floor, his hand never even having a chance to reach his weapon.

It had taken a little more than five seconds to put down the assassin and change his mind forever about the wisdom of working with the Vampyr network.

He was damaged, but at least he was alive.

THE HORSE-DRAWN CARRIAGE clopped to a graceful halt in front of the old-city coffeehouse in the spired and gabled core of Vienna.

With a surprisingly athletic step, the man with the snow-white hair and mustache skipped down from the carriage onto the cobblestone.

He turned with an exaggerated bow and helped the raven-haired woman in the black velvet dress down to the sidewalk. After generously tipping the driver, he guided the woman down the street. Pausing at a street corner, he discreetly tipped her, too.

The woman from the escort service laughed and clung to his arm. "You sure you want it to end so soon?" she asked. "This could be an evening to remember."

"It already is," the man replied.

"But all we did was take a ride." The gleam in her eye took a few years off her age. Too bad all of her "dates" couldn't be like this one.

"A fine ride it was," he said. "With the finest company imaginable. But I have to be off."

"You sure? We haven't really done anything."

The man shook his head. "On the contrary. You saved my life tonight. I really needed your company." He leaned forward, kissed her on the cheek, then walked away.

Cass Strashmir looked behind him once. It was habit. Just as his exhaustive security measures were habit. Such caution had kept him alive these past few years.

Just as it had kept him alive this night.

He'd been uneasy about the rendezvous with the Czechs. The carriage ride was the perfect way to conduct surveillance of the monks' safehouse. He'd made several circuits of the apartment building, gradually recognizing the patterns of a covert operation in progress—unmarked vans; the apparently random but strategic paths the strollers were taking—well-conditioned, hard-eyed strollers who always seemed to be in the vicinity of the apartment house.

Shortly after he'd decided to pass up the rendezvous and meet up with the network at a later time. Strashmir's suspicions were proved true by the sudden barrage and subsequent sirens that echoed through the streets of Vienna while he casually slipped away.

Soon he would leave Vienna behind him—along with the white hair and mustache he'd adopted for the night.

CHAPTER ELEVEN

"Long-haired men in long coats and long-haired women in short skirts," Gina Salvie reported, sweeping her binoculars over the small band of people filing back and forth from the brightly painted tour bus to the recording studio.

"And a dog with no coat," Bolan said, watching the short-haired wiry boxer running in circles around the group, getting underfoot as they finished unloading the bus.

"Somehow I don't think we're looking at a hit team here," Salvie said.

"Unless they're carrying machine guns in those violin cases. As far as I know, that went out back in the forties."

The two of them were watching the musicians from inside their Volkswagen surveillance vehicle parked on the roadside fifty yards past the complex of houses and studios that bordered the Vienna Woods on the outskirts of Neuwaldegg.

Their surveillance wasn't obvious, since several other cars were parked on the roadside, with many of the occupants long gone on the sight-seeing paths that splintered into the dense woods.

Many of those sightseers were also part of the massive surveillance team that had descended on the area to follow up on leads discovered in the Czech safehouse.

But now they were there, it was difficult to see what VolksHaus Studios could possibly have to do with a group of hard-core terrorists. "These people look too legit to be involved," Bolan said. "They're more concerned with mandolins and madrigals than murder-for-hire."

The Executioner swept the complex once more to match the layout with the specs Austrian security had provided them. Branching out from the main building were several stone-walled houses used as living quarters for engineers and musicians who stayed there while recording for the small label. There were also former granaries that were now full of electronic equipment and casette-duplicating machines.

The main building was a glass-walled studio with a covered walkway that led to a former stable converted to a garage. On the edge of the property nearest the woods was a pair of underground grain storehouses that had fallen into disrepair and now looked like subterranean dugouts for cave dwellers.

The phone number of the studio complex had turned up in a search of the apartment in Vienna. A slip of paper had been found on the body of one of the slain monks who'd carried it in his wallet along with several changes of identity. The dead man had been identified as the leader of the action arm of the Czech group who'd planned all their operations.

But the find had turned out to be a mixed blessing.

The slip of paper had several other phone numbers scrawled on it in a nearly illegible script, making it easy to misread the numbers.

No names, just numbers, which meant they could be chasing after a wrong lead. Or they could be zeroing in on another outpost.

At the moment it looked perfectly innocent, like the headquarters of a small independent folk-music label would be expected to look. But then covert command posts were supposed to look innocent.

"Hold on," Salvie said, listening through a pair of slim headphones. "Sinclair's on the air now. Here we go." She turned up the volume on the audio monitor as the voice of the wired deep-cover broadcaster sounded from inside the studio.

Instead of his usual high demographics, today Sinclair was broadcasting only to a cadre of twenty or so special operatives scattered throughout the Vienna Woods.

But they were a highly attentive audience. One word from Sinclair and they would storm the studio.

But at the moment that didn't seem likely at all.

The receptionist in the studio had recognized Sinclair after a bit of gentle prodding from the well-known broadcaster.

He told her he was putting together a documentary series on the voices of Europe and wanted to include a feature on folk music called "Beyond the Borders," a sampling of music from around the continent.

"What do you want from us?"

"I'd like to interview people involved in keeping this music alive," he replied. "And I'd like to start with you."

"That's a good beginning."

CHAPTER TWELVE

The paneled gallery of Schloss Ingram was a veritable museum, displaying full suits of armor from every age of Austria, each gleaming suit standing in procession down the gallery as if the ghosts of their ancient owners were lined up for inspection by the present master of the venerable old castle, Theodoric Ingram.

Gobelin tapestries hung from the walls like shields of wealth commissioned by succeeding generations of Ingrams to grace the walls of one of the oldest existing castles in the province of Carinthia. As Ingram was proud of saying, Schloss Ingram was just twenty miles—and two thousand years—away from the town of Klagenfurt.

It was a medieval treasure house.

But the real treasures were kept in a much safer place—the private suites of Theodoric Ingram. In a gabled wing of the schloss overlooking the well-stocked stream-fed pond, Ingram kept those rare objects that only he, his wife and a few collectors and dealers knew existed.

There by the wall-length oriel windows jutting out over the water, he kept the priceless acquisitions made possible by the Ingram wealth.

The suites were laid out like interconnecting gallery rooms, small showrooms for golden crosses sheathed in velvet, glass-cased medieval clocks that kept perfect time. And then there were the longer glass-covered display cases of swords, halberds, daggers and battle axs, all refinished and restored, resting on bloodred cloth.

Muzzle-loading long-arms and pistols were displayed in cases and racks on the walls, complete with accessories and ammo, enough to outfit a small army.

The weapons gave Ingram a particular pleasure on those rare occasions when he took them from their cases and handled them, affecting the poses of the long-departed warriors who'd used them.

The Ingram collection was more than an expensive gathering of objects. They were the object of his life. Seeking out, acquiring and then displaying these treasures was one of the few self-appointed tasks he could master these days.

Aside from the occasional call from his former colleagues in Austrian Intelligence—like the recent request for help in netting the Czech terrorist nest— his greatest challenge in life was sitting back and watching the family fortune grow.

Another challenge, pleasing but psychologically threatening, was trying to create an heir for all of the

Ingram glory. His first two wives had proved to be barren. The latest was a gorgeous woman in her thirties who'd come from the proper family and would one day bring on the next generation of Ingrams.

And if *she* proved barren—it couldn't be his fault, despite what those foolish doctors said—then he would acquire yet another gorgeous young wife. That was what fortunes were for.

The thought of the need for another scion of Ingram, plus the thought of Karen herself, made him decide that it was time to try again. At ten o'clock in the evening he left his brightly lit collection and headed down the hallway leading to the master bedroom.

SHORTLY AFTER MIDNIGHT Theodoric Ingram sat straight up in bed. Karen was beside him, lost in a wine-drenched sleep among swirls of satin sheets and pillows.

His mouth was dry, parched. Perhaps he too had drunk too much wine. Sometimes it was hard to keep track of these things. Or maybe the dryness was caused by the fire, he thought, as flickering shadows from the bedside hearth washed over them and enveloped the room with a warm, dry aura.

Ingram looked around the room with slightly watered eyes, trying to see what had pulled him from sleep.

Trying to listen to the sounds of night.

The wind rushing against the windows was a bit unsettling, eerie almost, but Ingram never wasted time on fear. The Ingram family was well insulated from the rest of the world by centuries of wealth and breeding that provided for the highly trained security staff manning the schloss twenty-four hours a day.

Here in the high castle it was heaven. Nothing on earth could touch them.

But then he heard the sound that had wakened him, an echo sounding from a dark dream. It was coming from outside the narrow antechamber that led to the master bedroom.

The outer door shook again—and something shook deep inside Theodoric Ingram.

The steady pounding increased, the rumbling through the corridor, growing louder and louder as if a great fist were hammering away at it.

Karen stirred beside him, murmuring something softly. Her lips curved in a smile. She was laughing, lost inside a dream far removed from the waking nightmare he found himself in.

The pounding changed to a methodical rhythm over and over in the same violent cadence.

"What in God's name..." Ingram whispered as he swung out of bed and silently stepped onto the cold stone floor. He shrugged into his robe and slung the belt around him, quickly tying a loop in it as he headed toward the door.

It wouldn't do for the lord of the manor to be seen in disarray—even when he was this angry.

Someone was going to pay for this, he thought. Perhaps it was one of the new security men who didn't understand the royal Ingram need for privacy. Or perhaps one of the old security men who no longer cared.

Ingram slipped softly into the antechamber and closed the bedroom door behind him.

The outer door shook again.

He stepped back instinctively, then regained his courage and demanded to know what was going on. "Stefan!" he hissed. "Is that you? What is the meaning of this?"

The pounding stopped suddenly, but there was no answer.

"Who's out there? What are you doing? This kind of disturbance will not be taken lightly."

Silence.

At first.

Then he thought he heard footsteps rapidly shuffling away as if whoever was out there had finally come to his senses.

That was better, Ingram thought, pausing for several moments until the pounding of his heart subsided. Then he lifted the small iron bar that latched the door shut. It was more of a decorative piece than an actual barrier. A good push on the outside door would crumble the eroding stonework and rip the hinges from the wall.

He stepped back and pulled the door inward.

Darkness.

The outer hallway was dark, and so was his private gallery at the end of the hall. *Disgraceful!* Someone had turned out the lights when they left.

Ingram always kept some lights shining on his collections. But now the only light that came into the room was the dim moonlight pouring through the gallery windows.

A break-in? he thought. But then he dismissed it immediately. Not here. Not in Schloss Ingram.

He called out the names of all the guards, but there was still no response.

Ingram shook his head as he walked down the darkened hall to the gallery rooms. Heads would roll for this, he thought.

As soon as he stepped into the first room he felt eyes upon him. It was just a feeling, a remnant from the days when he was an active officer and such things were second nature.

''Who's there?'' He meant it to be a bold challenge, but his voice was weak and tentative, like that of a stranger exploring a new realm. It was the voice of a man who suddenly knew what it was like to feel vulnerable again.

As Ingram's eyes adjusted to the darkness, he could make out several bulky shapes scattered around the glass cases. One was directly in front of him about fifteen feet away, and the others were scattered to his left and right.

Oh, dear God! he thought, moving like a hypnotized man down the narrow aisle between the long rows of glass cases.

Part of him wanted to find out what the shapes were, and another part didn't want to know at all. But the strange combination of fear and fascination propelled him forward.

At the end of the aisle he found Stefan Grieg.

The ex-army officer and private security man who'd been chief of staff for five years lay flat on his back, his open eyes locked forever onto the ceiling.

There was a wide canal of blood running from his stomach to his groin. His hands were neatly folded across his breastbone as if he were part of an exhibition that was now showing in the private gallery of Theodoric Ingram.

A dark red trail stained the carpet, showing the direction that his body had been dragged.

Stefan Grieg wasn't the only casualty.

Off to Ingram's left was another part of the exhibition, Warren Steiger, the next in command. His head was twisted around at an awkward and painful angle, certainly not the position any living person would assume. Steiger's normally placid face was twisted into a grotesque death mask.

Turning to his right, he saw two more of his uniformed security men sprawled dead on the floor.

The tableau was too much for his shocked mind to absorb, freezing him where he stood. He'd spent only a few seconds looking at the obsessive, deliberate and demented carnage visited upon his gallery, but it seemed like forever to the old-guard Intelligence man.

His security staff had been slaughtered.

Even worse was the way they'd been brought here to mock Ingram in the heart of his private kingdom. The grisly masque had been put on for his benefit.

But the cases were still intact. What did the intruder want? And why had he left?

And then, as a footstep deliberately scuffled on the gallery floor, Ingram realized the intruder hadn't left.

Ingram spun and looked left and right, but he saw nothing but the glass-cased reflections of moonlight spilling through the windows.

Moonlight and shadows.

The Austrian aristocrat slowly backed away, a cold stream of fear running up his spine from the awful knowledge that someone was watching him from somewhere in the dark.

Someone capable of killing highly trained officers at the peak of their skills.

For a moment Ingram thought of calling out to his wife. But no, that might force the intruder into action. At least now he had a few more seconds to possibly get away.

Flick.

The lights came on from the far end of the room where a blond-haired man in brown clothes and black boots stood looking perfectly at ease. He was almost baby faced, but his hard eyes held a cruelty that took years to acquire.

A pistol was holstered on his hip.

The man glanced down at the bodies scattered about, like a superior studying the work of his underlings. And then his deep laughter filled the air.

"Were they really the best you could find," the intruder asked, "especially now when there's so much wicked talent roaming about?"

"Who are you?" Ingram demanded.

"You want my name?" The man stepped forward in precise military steps. His confidence totally overwhelmed Ingram. Maybe a few decades ago he would have been capable of facing down such a man. But not now.

The stranger stopped a few feet from him. "Please allow me to introduce myself," he said, bowing curtly. "My name is Axel Erhard. Perhaps you've heard of me."

"The files," Ingram said. "Your name turned up in the files on the monks."

"Yes, the files. I must congratulate you on your work in identifying our poor friends in Vienna—our poor dead friends, thanks to your execution squad."

"I was asked to help—"

"And help you did," Erhard said. "You must have some very fine sources in the Intelligence community."

Ingram found himself nodding dumbly as he instinctively stepped back from the menacing ex-Stasi man.

Erhard instinctively moved forward to close the gap. "I regret to inform you that we also have our sources in the community. They identified you as the architect of our destruction."

"I didn't mean—"

"No. Of course not."

"It was just information. I had a lot of experience in that area, and when I was asked—"

"Oh, I understand," Erhard said in a calm and conversational tone. "It's quite simple. You gave us up without a second thought. Planned the attack, the murders. It was all done very well."

Ingram stopped moving. There was no sense in going any farther. He knew he couldn't get away from this man. And the look in the man's face made it clear that he was enjoying every minute of this.

"But I think you are a much better organizer than a killer. What do they call you these days? Graybeards? Old boys? Old soldiers? The kind of man who still has what it takes to plan an operation and pull the trigger from afar, but unable to do it up close. But a killer nonetheless."

Ingram felt some of his nerve coming back. He heard an inner voice talking to him once again. It was a faint echo of the man he once was, talking to the man he'd become and telling him not to back down any more.

"Killer?" Ingram repeated, glancing at the bodies of the slain security men. "You murdered these innocent men in cold blood and you dare to call me a killer."

Erhard shrugged. "Actually I didn't kill them. My associates did that. They'd tell you themselves, but they're busy elsewhere—going through your files to see what they can find. But I promise you they'll be back soon enough."

The German stepped back and gestured at the treasure-filled cases. "They'll be returning here to gather up these priceless objects you've collected for us."

"Impossible," Ingram snapped. "My collection is too well-known around the world. If you try to sell them anywhere, there will be such an outcry—"

Erhard's laughter drowned him out.

"It's true," Ingram insisted.

"Some of your pieces may be well-known," Erhard agreed. "But the rest are part of your private hoard, little-known objects that will bring a great price."

"No reputable dealer will touch them."

"Who needs reputable men?" Erhard queried. "They are of no use in our profession. Believe me, Ingram, we already have a place for your ancient books. Your sacred artworks. And for all of your weapons and relics. One of our subsidiaries in England will have the honor of matching your pieces with deserving collectors."

Ingram steeled himself for what was coming. The man wouldn't be telling him all of this unless he was sure the information would do Ingram no good.

He was as good as dead. A gun, Ingram thought, if only he kept a gun in his bedroom. If only he had a gun in the pocket of his robe right now he could erase that grim smile from Axel Erhard's arrogant face.

But he'd grown too complacent, too confident in the skill of the armed men he'd entrusted to guard Schloss Ingram. And now he knew the castle was about to be taken.

"What goes through your mind, Ingram?"

The older man shook his head.

"I really want to know."

"Why?"

Erhard shrugged. "Who knows? For comparison's sake, I suppose. I'd like to know what men in your position think. What final words they have to say. That way perhaps I'll know what to say when my time comes and who to say it to."

"You're insane."

"No, no, no," Erhard scolded him. "Homicidal, yes. Insane, no. But please. Answer my question. Go ahead and answer. You'll live longer that way. What are you thinking?"

The Austrian sighed and looked straight into the hard blue eyes of his interrogator. "All right. I'll tell you. I'm thinking that you're going to kill me in cold blood and there's nothing I can do about it."

"You'd be surprised at the number of people who say such a thing," Erhard replied. "But let me correct a slight mistake you made in your last words. You see, you said 'in cold blood.'"

Ingram heard voices coming from one of the stairwells leading up to the private chambers.

Guttural laughter.

Boasts.

The voices of men who knew they had just inherited a fortune. The voices of predators.

"Blood isn't cold," Erhard continued as if he were engaged in a rational debate. "Blood is hot when you first shed it. Scalding, in fact. You tend to get used to it—but even so, there are many of us who try to recapture the sensations of that first time."

Lecture finished, Erhard suddenly spun away from Ingram and smashed a hammer-fist onto the nearest glass case. The shattered glass fell in sections onto the carpeted weaponry.

"Excellent taste," he said, reaching through the opening and grabbing a silver inlaid sword with a long and broad-curved blade. His hand clenched loosely around the hilt, sliding down toward the disk-shaped pommel as he slashed downward through the air to test the balance.

"You can't just kill me," Ingram said. "I'm unarmed."

Erhard cocked his head and considered Ingram's desperate remark. "Arm yourself," he suggested.

Ingram glanced around the room, regarding the encased weapons with a different eye now.

Daggers.

Swords.

Maces.

Before, they had been collector's items. Now they represented his only chance to escape with his life. Finally he settled on a Spanish sword with double finger guards. Its edge was sharp, and the guards were sturdy enough to trap his adversary's blade.

He took it from the case and turned to face the German, feeling as if he were reliving some duel from ancient days, confronting an opponent who stalked him for all eternity, lifetime after lifetime, always leading to this spot.

He thought of his wife in her bed, still sleeping peacefully. But how much longer would there be peace?

"Now," Erhard said.

Ingram raised the Spanish sword—then he saw blood in the air, saw the sword falling to the ground with his hand still attached to it.

Erhard completed spinning around, following the upward momentum of the first stroke, the blur of the blood-slicked sword too fast for the dazed and armless Ingram to follow.

Now the sword was moving level—it chunked once through Ingram's neck, toppling his tendril-trailing head into the air like the broken bust of a bloody statue.

Ingram's head rolled onto the floor with a dull thunking sound before it came to a stop at the base of one of the display cases.

The rest of Erhard's team filtered into the room, looking at the headless corpse.

The German strode over to Ingram's severed head and picked it up as if he'd been doing it all his life. Then, with the pommel of his sword, he smashed an opening in one of the delicately painted windows.

Shards of glass dropped into the pond like glittering rain.

Holding the head by the hair, Erhard swung it through the opening, out over the water. "Make a wish," he said.

It dropped with a loud splash, like a coin in a wishing well.

He turned and casually placed the curved sword on a glass counter. Gesturing at the fortunes under glass, he turned to the black-clad crew who'd helped him carry out the revenge hit and said, "Help yourselves."

Then he went to pay his respects to the woman of the schloss.

CHAPTER THIRTEEN

The yellow sail flapped loudly in the wind that swept across Lake Constance, carrying a trio of female sailors close to the shore in a small but fast sailboat. Their shocking pink-and-green wet suits seemed designed more for attracting attention than for protecting them from the elements.

Two men on land *were* watching them closely while they walked along the lakeshore path from Uberlingen, the small German town just across the border from Austria where Cass Strashmir had rendezvoused with Axel Erhard.

As the sailboat raced past the shoreline, one of the women leaned over almost parallel with the water, her adventurous eyes sweeping briefly but daringly at Strashmir.

The Romanian bowed toward the brightly plumaged brunette and flashed a perfect smile in return. Though he was in his late forties there were still traces of the handsome leading-man quality that many a young woman had fallen for.

Even as he was drifting into the stage where his looks were more the craggy and weathered face of a character actor, he still attracted women. He just didn't know how to keep them, a fact reinforced by the dwindling form of the brunette as the sailboat picked up a fresh wind and took her away from him as suddenly as if she were a mirage.

Once the woman was out of sight, Strashmir resumed his role of an actor, a role played by every fugitive, as well as by the men who hunted them down.

Beneath the fast-moving clouds, along the wind-driven water, Strashmir was on stage once again. This time he was performing in front of a dangerous and unseen audience.

The director, of course, was the blond-haired martinet walking alongside him—Axel Erhard, hatchet man, hard-core killer, the brand-new guardian angel who welcomed him into the fold.

Lake Constance was the perfect site for the two operatives to hook up with each other. The internationally known resort lake had borders on three countries: Austria, Germany and Switzerland. It was a good point of arrival—or departure—for those nameless riders who traveled on the Underground Express.

And at the moment there was no shortage of conductors for the underground passengers.

Discreetly shepherding the two men as they walked along the shore was a scattered cadre of Erhard's men, former secret police who knew how to maintain their anonymity under any conditions. And if that anonymity was broken, they had enough firepower on them to decimate anyone foolish enough to identify them.

Strashmir and Erhard slowly led the covert parade along the shore. The two of them were smiling, apparently chatting amiably in German like a couple of time-killing tourists on holiday.

Despite their seeming camaraderie, Strashmir and the German were actually coming to terms.

And almost to blows.

The fair-haired German knew Strashmir was a headstrong sort, but he'd at least expected some kind of gratitude from the Romanian exile.

But it wasn't forthcoming. Instead, the agile and aging Romanian acted as if *he* were the one offering a way out for Axel Erhard.

"How fortunate for us that you chose Constance as the site of your second coming," Erhard said, tiring of the quarrelsome and wary Romanian.

Strashmir nodded pleasantly, as if he were accepting a familiar compliment.

"But you mustn't overestimate your worth as a savior," Erhard continued. "We are capable of surviving without you."

"Yes," Strashmir said. "I've seen the results of your work splashed all over the media. You managed to kill an old man in an old castle. And you also managed to kill his young wife in a most gruesome way. Most impressive."

"They were targets," Erhard said matter-of-factly. "So they were hit. Simple as that."

Strashmir nodded. "And then there were those ferocious tourists in Koblenz. I believe that massacre, as the newspapers term it, also had your signature."

Erhard's face reddened. Normally he wouldn't have reacted so quickly. But it was hard to deal with the fact that, in effect, this man was his replacement.

"They, too, were targets," Erhard protested. "Not of my choosing, but certainly my doing. The blame—or credit—lies with Konrad Lorenz. There will be other such targets. If you have any reservations about this kind of work, say it up front."

"Very well," the Romanian said. "I have reservations about this kind of work."

Erhard loudly exhaled, indicating his frustration. "There's been much talk about how troublesome you are to work with. More trouble than you are worth... if you ask me."

"I didn't ask," Strashmir replied. "Nor do I think it is your station to question such matters. I've come here to offer my services to Konrad Lorenz."

The German abruptly stopped walking. He looked out at the shimmering blue line that was Lake Constance beneath a strong wind. "Your credentials are impeccable," Erhard said, reverting to a false and friendly tone.

"Kind of you to say so," Strashmir replied.

"So impeccable that half of the security services on the continent are after you, Strashmir. I think you'd do well to remember there's a price on your head, and unless you cooperate fully with us, someone just might try to take it."

"I'll cooperate as much as necessary. Enough to learn about the targets I choose to take. Enough to study any Intelligence you've gathered and to share mine with you. But when I go out into the field, I work alone."

"Not this time," Erhard said. "We will be with you every step of the way."

"I see. You will point out the women and children you want me to shoot?"

"We will provide security."

"As you did in Vienna," Strashmir said.

Erhard looked hard into the eyes of the Romanian, eyes that other men might turn away from. But Strashmir met the German's threatening gaze indifferently, making it clear that Erhard's wrath was of no concern to him.

"Listen well. You are here because there is no other place for you to go. You can either spend a lifetime—a very short lifetime—on the run, or you can come in from the cold into the warm embrace of Konrad Lorenz."

"That is why I'm here, as we so laboriously arranged," Strashmir said. "But where is Konrad? I'd prefer to discuss any further details with him."

"He's right up there," Erhard replied, gesturing toward an arrow-shaped car park that was perched on a leveled-off plateau with a broad vista of the lake. Several vehicles were parked on the roadside lookout, their windshields and chrome trim gleaming in the late-afternoon sun.

Strashmir followed Erhard's gesture, then casually noted the position of the backup team spreading out over the bright green grass.

"Let's go."

"Not yet," Erhard replied.

"Why not?"

"Konrad is waiting for my signal," he said. "If I give him the all clear, then you will meet him. But if I signal otherwise, you will be blasted to pieces, hit with enough lead to sink your sorry carcass to the bottom of the lake and take you straight down to hell itself."

"I see." Strashmir stepped closer to Erhard, hands in the pockets of his windbreaker, steel in his eyes. "In that case, I insist you come along with me."

Erhard laughed curtly. "Perhaps you are what we need," he said. "Perhaps Konrad was right all along."

The German turned toward his men who were scattered on the hillside. Then he looked toward the car park and gave a short wave.

"Come along," Erhard said, his voice full of sarcasm. "Come on and meet the master of us all."

"We already know each other."

"Of course," Erhard said. "The two of you are old and dear friends."

"No. I said we know each other. That is all. Friendship has no place in Konrad's life."

Erhard laughed again. "You *do* know him."

TEN MINUTES LATER Cass Strashmir sat beside Konrad Lorenz in the back seat of a sky blue Volvo that toured the eastern shore of Lake Constance on the German side.

It was part of a leisurely moving fleet of cars that were providing a security escort for the chief of the Vampyr network.

Lorenz's small entourage had even included a platinum-tressed woman whom Strashmir vaguely recognized. She was very familiar, but he couldn't completely place her, especially since he'd been permitted only a brief glimpse of her when Lorenz had ushered her out of the car and welcomed Strashmir in.

Now the woman was traveling in the vehicle behind them.

The car ahead of them contained Axel Erhard and some of the hard-eyed bodyguards who'd shadowed him back in Uberlingen.

After preliminary pleasantries that neither man really felt, Konrad Lorenz got down to business.

"We can talk freely here," Lorenz said, lightly tapping the glass shield that separated the back seat from the indifferent driver up front. "First I think we should establish the matter of trust. To be honest, I am somewhat disappointed in the lack of faith you've shown me."

"It wasn't directed toward you," Strashmir replied. "Nor toward anyone. It was simply a matter of survival. As part of my routine I considered every meeting, every communication to be compromised. And then I would prove to myself it wasn't compromised before going any further."

"That created a lot of complications for my people. Sometimes you were where you were supposed to be, sometimes you weren't. At times you dropped out of sight for so long I wasn't even sure you were still part of the network."

Strashmir shrugged and leaned back in the soft cushion, watching the forest flying by on both sides of the road, here and there a gap of blue water showing between the trees. "As I said, it was routine. Fortunately so, judging from what happened in Vienna."

"Yes," Lorenz said. "That was bad for us. They hit us hard there. But we made up for it, believe me."

Strashmir nodded. "I'm sure you repay them in kind at every opportunity."

Lorenz fell silent, studying Strashmir as if he could look into the depths of his soul.

Strashmir was familiar with the technique—always keep the other man off balance, always make him think you know more than he does. Make him think you are in control.

He returned the gaze. But it didn't take much to figure out what kind of mind lay behind those tombstone eyes. True, Lorenz had changed somewhat on the outside.

The leader of the Underground Express looked much lighter than before and, amazingly, much younger, as if he'd undertaken a comprehensive program to change his physical appearance. But there was still that unavoidable quality about him. The quality of a murderer. Even though Lorenz sat at the top of an invisible empire, he was a murderer just the same.

"We haven't come this far to play games," Strashmir finally said. "Show your hand, Konrad. Tell me what you want."

"Very well. We have worked together in the past. Me in the headquarters, you in the field. You performed well on some very sensitive operations. Heroically, in fact."

"I did what I could and I did what was needed," Strashmir replied. "No more than that."

"But it was always enough," Lorenz said. "And that is why I have tolerated your eccentric approach. You're the best I know of in this delicate line of work. I propose that you and I work together again in much the same capacity."

"You want me to kill people."

The Vampyr chief raised his eyebrows, then exploded in laughter. "You always go straight for the throat. No euphemisms for Cass Strashmir."

"I guess I am not that sophisticated. I like to know where I stand at all times and what we are talking about. That way there can never be any misunderstandings."

"Then understand this," Lorenz said. "There's a man I want you to kill."

"That's all?"

Lorenz shook his head. "No. That's for a start. There's actually a list we must take care of. It is a short list, but it contains some crucial names."

"Name them."

"The first one is not actually a name," Lorenz said. "It is more of a title."

"Yes?"

"I want you to kill the man known as the Executioner."

Now it was Strashmir's turn to laugh. "You're not the first to want such a thing. You won't be the last."

Lorenz looked taken aback. "Are you saying you can't do it? Or you won't do it?"

"I'm saying I might never get the opportunity. He's been in the field for years. Sometimes even his own people were hunting him. No one came close."

"Maybe no one of your skill ever went after him," Lorenz suggested. "Believe me, we can make sure you have the opportunity. Even as we speak we have men tracking him down. Men on both sides of the law who work for me whether they know it or not."

"Tell me where and when," Strashmir said, "and I'll tell how I'll do it. That is, if I agree to come in with you."

"Good. What does it take to convince you to join us? To get you to leave your present position? Maybe you enjoy the challenge of looking over your shoulder every minute and wondering who or what is coming after you. But I think we can make your position in life a much happier one. And in its own way, a fairly stable one."

"To begin with," Strashmir said, "I want to know everything about your operation that will concern me and my assignments. I want no secrets. I want cooperation from men like Axel Erhard, and I want total command of any military action I undertake."

"You have it."

"I also want to know what your plans are for me after I kill the Executioner."

Lorenz smiled. "I'm glad you're so confident. If you manage to kill the Executioner, there will be more work for you—but none so difficult as him. And there will be great rewards for you between assignments. You can name your price."

As he spoke of the great benefits of working with his network, Lorenz began to sound like an aboveground CEO bragging of the power and reach of his multinational corporation. "Anywhere you want to go in Europe, we can send you. We have a presence there. And a power."

Flicking his fingers as if they were pointers on a map of the world according to Konrad Lorenz, the Vampyr chieftain began reciting a litany of European spots where his network had influence.

"Marseilles, Nice, Cannes, the Côte d'Azur, Zurich and London," Lorenz enthused. "We mustn't forget London. We are growing quite strong there. In fact, we're setting in motion a plan that may lure the Executioner to England. Some priceless objects he and his people may attempt to locate are currently on their way to one of our British outposts. We may let the Executioner find them—or he may find them through his own resources. Either way, if he goes there, we'll make sure you're waiting for him."

"It is like the old country," Strashmir said. "Hunts, lures and endless schemes. Now all you need is a hunter."

"I've told you my terms. Now tell me if you are joining us."

"I have terms of my own," Strashmir stated.

"Go on."

"I want to return to Romania. I want my name cleared. I want the truth to come out. I think you can help in that regard."

"I understand your plight," Lorenz said. "Similar to mine. Believe me, when the madness ends and the confusion stops, you and I will go back to clear our good names."

"That is my price."

"Done," Lorenz agreed, a look of satisfaction on his face. He had just bought the services of the man most likely to rid him of the Executioner, and he'd gotten off cheaply. All he really had to give to the man was hope.

As the Volvo once more rode past a clear stretch of beach looking out toward the lake, Konrad Lorenz told his newest recruit some of his other tasks.

There were certain members in the organization who appeared to be increasingly untrustworthy, maintaining too many contacts with the Intelligence services. They might have to be dealt with in a final method. But there was one other name on Lorenz's list that was given a high priority.

"Harold Brognola?" Strashmir repeated when he heard the name. "But that's insane. He's very well-known in Intelligence circles. Too well-known. Too powerful."

"He's on the list," Lorenz said. "And he's more reachable than the Executioner. We almost had him ourselves, but somehow he got away from us at the last minute."

"Go after him and you go after the United States government and every Intelligence service cooperating with him."

"Exactly," Lorenz agreed. "If we neutralize Brognola, we might not even have to take out the Executioner. Remember, it is Brognola's connection with the Oval Office itself that allows the Executioner to team with international agencies. Otherwise, he would just be one man on his own. Get rid of Brognola and we get rid of the Executioner's protection.''

''If we go after these people,'' Strashmir said, ''there will be no end to the struggle.''

''That's one way of looking at it. But I prefer to see it another way. If we don't go after them, then sooner or later they'll be at *our* throats.''

Strashmir leaned against the window and pressed his hand against his forehead, momentarily closing his eyes.

But it wasn't a dream. Konrad Lorenz was still with him when he opened his eyes.

He'd chosen sides in the covert war that was breaking out all over Europe, he thought. Actually he'd been *chosen* by the wrong side.

''Tell me one thing,'' Strashmir said. ''Are you prepared for an all-out war?''

''On any front you wish. Financial or military. We have weapons for sale, and we have weapons for use.''

As the Volvo drove deeper into the heart of Konrad Lorenz's empire, Strashmir knew that before too long one of those weapons would be in his hands. But where would it be pointed? he thought.

CHAPTER FOURTEEN

The man in black stood on the narrow stone bridge across the stream that rippled alongside the farmhouse near Germany's western border with Luxembourg.

It was past midnight, and the Executioner couldn't sleep.

Nor could he do much thinking. His mind was too full with the corpses on his conscience.

He thought back to the Austrian Intelligence man he'd encountered briefly back in Vienna just before the operation went down. Ingram had been huddled with Hal Brognola helping to map out the outpost of the ex-Czech security ops when Bolan had conferred with the head Fed on some details.

He'd seen Ingram up close, a pleasant if somewhat pretentious Old World sort. Bolan had met the type before, men who couldn't quite let go the reins of power they'd held in the covert services and did what they could for the cause.

Ingram did what he could, and now he was dead.

So was his wife. By all reports, she had been a stunningly beautiful woman. Of course, that was impossible to tell from the photographs taken after the Vampyr crew had hit Schloss Ingram.

Bolan shook his head, forcing the image out of his mind. If he hadn't pushed so hard in his attempt to nail Strashmir, then maybe none of this would have happened. Maybe Ingram and his wife would still be sleeping a gentle sleep in their luxury-laden schloss. But the warrior knew that "maybes" had no place in war.

Dark gray clouds rolled overhead, but now and then a clear patch of sky showed above, dropping a reflected carpet of stars in the fast-moving stream rippling below him.

The stars shimmered in dizzying glory for a few hypnotic moments that took his mind away from the body counts credited to the Underground Express. But then the reflected stars vanished as the thick clouds rolled overhead once more.

Now the stream looked black, as black as the Executioner's chances of finding Konrad Lorenz before he struck again.

The thirst for action parched his soul, but for now there was little he could do.

Since they'd come back into Germany on the special flight to Saarbrucken International Airport that Brognola had arranged for them, Bolan was left with little to do but think about what had gone wrong.

He and Gina Salvie were on hold for the moment, taking a much needed break to patch up body and soul before another target was located and they were sent out into the field again.

Doing time on the farm, he thought.

Downtime.

Most of the other teams were out there actively following leads, and their absence at the safehouse made the long spell of inaction weigh heavier than usual on the Executioner.

He felt as if he was in a state of limbo waiting for a sign from one of the gods above, the god of war who had controlled his life since his family was murdered so long ago.

Motion on the periphery of his vision drew the Executioner's gaze toward the gate house, where a couple of tall, dark shadows were moving.

The guards patrolling the area were changing shifts. Bolan knew their routine well, though they didn't know his.

The farmhouse was still a protected site, but it wasn't as heavily guarded as it had been the last time the Executioner was there. Ion Cusa had been moved to another house on the covert circuit, where he would continue to be debriefed until he'd provided every last shred of evidence.

A detachment of the special-ops men who usually manned the farm had gone off with Gus Sinclair in a small caravan of sports cars and news vans.

Sinclair was playing up his role as an independent news producer working on a story about the changing political, social and cultural boundaries of Europe, showing how lives had changed now that people were free to move around the continent.

In reality Gus Sinclair and his crews were chasing down the leads that turned up in the recording studio in the Vienna Woods. Though most of the people working there really were involved in the music industry, quite a few silent partners used the small studio as a clearinghouse for many of their financial transactions.

The problem was that most of the companies who had business dealings with the studio were legitimate. And the shell corporations that did business with the studio hid their trails beneath a blizzard of paperwork and secret bank accounts.

Hal Brognola was also zeroing in on Lorenz's network with a special team of computer experts assembled in Frankfurt.

A computer search of the names of emerging East European businesses had flagged thousands of companies, some long established, some brand-new. What they had in common was that they either branched out into marketplaces formerly dominated by Western European outfits, or else they'd bought the Western European companies outright and were now staffing those enterprises with many of the people who used to live behind the Iron Curtain.

Brognola's team was tracking the influx of people, as well as tracing where the money came from, in the hopes of turning up black-market and secret police links to the emerging businesses. If they were successful, they could start unraveling the secret threads of the network and find a new target for Bolan to concentrate on.

Until then the warrior was on standby.

He hated the waiting, but it was a good chance for him to recover fully from his wounds. His shoulder was almost back to normal again. It had been aggravated by the assault on the Vienna safehouse, but hadn't been enough to keep him down.

Bolan used his enforced free time to use counter-exercises on the shoulder to lessen the pain. He'd also built up his wind by running hard across the grounds of the farm, getting to learn every bit of the terrain in the process.

Footsteps sounded in the tall grass, drawing his attention away from the water for a few moments.

Gina Salvie was approaching from the path that led from the farmhouse, her statuesque figure silhouetted in the moonlight. It was funny, he thought. In the dark he could see her clearer than ever before.

It was all in the way she moved.

Soft-spoken body language.

She, too, was restless, trapped in the lull between the storms. Sometimes the downtime was hard to weather. When you were in the field, no matter how bad your situation was, everything was black and white. It was pure and simple. You did what you had to in order to make sure that you survived and the other guy didn't.

But in the off moments there was more than enough time to summon up the feelings that had to be submerged in battle.

Salvie paused at the edge of the high grass, her hands deep in the pockets of her unbuttoned white cardigan as she looked toward the bridge.

A few moments later her footsteps lightly tapped on the wooden slats of the small bridge as she joined him on the railing, her red hair shining.

"You can't sleep, either," she said.

"Can't sleep," Bolan agreed, "can't think."

"Sometimes there's a lot to be said for that," she replied. "Sometimes thoughts get in the way." She turned and faced him directly, twisting her hands in the pockets of the sweater and pushing it taut over her figure.

The warrior had seen the woman in many guises, but tonight was the first time he saw this side of her. And it was definitely a nice view.

"We've been through a lot together," she said, her hand reaching up to his shoulder.

"A lot of pain," Bolan agreed. "So?"

Her hand reached for his other shoulder. "So maybe it's time we go for something a bit more pleasurable."

Bolan laughed. The attraction between the two of them had been there since the beginning, but they'd had to push it aside, masking their feelings.

Until now.

His hand slid around her waist just as she tossed her head to the right, her long red hair fanning the air with a pleasant scent.

He leaned over, pulling her up as he pressed his lips against hers. And then he felt her firm body and soft curves working against him.

"This might not be the best idea we ever had," he said. "Working as partners like we are."

"Right," she said. "But it'll be nice finding out."

AT FIVE O'CLOCK the following morning Bolan was returning from a morning jog around the perimeter of the farm, a collar of sweat seeping through his sweatshirt despite the chill in the air, when he saw the black Mercedes rolling up the narrow drive.

He picked up his pace, catching the driver just as he stepped out near the wraparound porch.

It was one of Brognola's black-suited bodyguards and couriers.

"Got a package for you, Striker," the man said, handing him a small satchel.

"What is it?"

"Some late-breaking news from Hal," the man replied. "Plus a pair of tickets and a list of names, addresses and phone numbers to learn and burn."

"Any news is good news at this point," Bolan said, glad that something was breaking. Brognola wouldn't have sent a courier unless something was in the works.

He glanced inside the satchel and saw several videotapes, airline tickets and a slim leather-wrapped notepad.

"Thanks." Bolan clapped the man on the shoulder, then hurried inside the farmhouse to the communications room and started watching the series of videos.

The first one was a series of news clips about the large-scale theft of sacred relics from Czech churches and Romanian monasteries. Now that the governments no longer exerted direct control—and protection—over them, the irreplaceable altar pieces, goblets and paintings had become fair game for organized bands of looters who often conducted their raids at gunpoint.

The next tape contained interviews with Interpol officers and art-recovery squad members from several countries who outlined the likely fate of the priceless objects.

The first stage on the road to the underground art market brought them to dealers and collectors in Germany and Austria. They would often attach phony provenances to the stolen goods, then ship them to their contacts in France and England.

Sometimes the objects would be sold immediately to private collectors who didn't care if they were stolen, or in some cases relished the thought that they were stolen.

Other times the objects would be kept off the market for years until the heat wore off. And then suddenly a "find" would be made, and the objects would go into the legitimate market.

Brognola had put his people to work assembling a crash course in the black-market art trade, including a partial inventory of some of the pieces stolen from Theodoric Ingram's schloss that were the talk of the underground.

The big Fed had ended the presentation with some reliable Intelligence that a group of Lorenz's men were en route to England with the pieces at that very moment.

That was where the address book came in. Included in the book were the names of dealers who deserved watching, known criminals who could be squeezed for information and some authentic contacts in the field who'd cooperated with authorities in the past.

There were also several "magic" names and phone numbers of Intelligence and police contacts the Executioner could call upon—the usual get-out-of-jail-free cards that free-lancers might have to play in order to stay in the game.

The Intelligence was solid but not definitive. It might play out or it might not. But if nothing else, Bolan thought, at least it would put him in the same stomping grounds as the Vampyr network.

Bolan viewed the tapes once more, learning as much as he could about the world he was about to invade. Then he thumbed through the address book, imprinting the names and numbers on his memory.

Midway through the warrior's last viewing of the videotaped Intelligence, Gina Salvie came downstairs in jeans and a T-shirt.

"Watching cartoons?" she asked.

"More like a travelogue."

"Oh, really?" she said. "I hope it's someplace warm."

"Pack an umbrella," he replied. "We're off to England."

CHAPTER FIFTEEN

The main headquarters of the Brutus Foundation was located in a gray building on Bond Street amid London's more successful barristers, bankers and art dealers.

It towered over its limestone neighbors, a fairy-tale castle with Gothic columns, turrets and leering gargoyles that silently prowled the upper storys.

The foundation had been in existence for only ten years but already had acquired a sterling reputation. It fit in well with the upscale businesses that flourished on Bond Street since the 1700s, when royalty had first started building their mansions in the district. Shops patronized by the nobility quickly followed, establishing a dynasty of hotels, couturiers and rare-art dealers that still reigned.

In the more recent section known as New Bond Street, Southeby's had expanded from specializing in rare books to treasures of all types. Now more than a score of art dealers had followed suit, setting up shop to see to the needs of collectors and prominent organizations like the Brutus Foundation.

Along with works of the old masters, the dealers offered a steady stream of gold and silver treasures, ranging from Thracian drinking cups unearthed in Bulgaria to Dark Age miters spirited from digs in Britain and Denmark.

The art experts on Bond Street could quickly establish a provenance for the treasures and in some cases, with just the slightest clues, trace their heritage back thousands of years.

Quite conveniently many of those same experts were totally at a loss when police investigators came to them in attempts to trace rare objects to the looters who had acquired them in the first place.

It was all part and parcel of the magic offered by wizards of the establishment.

In one form or another the Brutus Foundation was a major benefactor of that wizardry. It had so many subsidiary companies and splinter organizations that nearly every respected group on Bond Street had connections with the foundation without being aware of it.

One banking syndicate that had the audacity to conduct an investigation found so many foundation links to official bureaus, church officials and universities that it was almost like a secret government. When the bank suddenly lost several of its larger clients, the investigation stopped. Almost miraculously the bank's former clients returned.

The Bond Street headquarters of the foundation lived on without bother, investing in and trading lost art treasures, funding digs throughout Britain, funding historical research proposals and carrying on respected, if unknown, activities.

Rumors on the street had it that the Brutus Foundation was making a major bid to acquire several rare artifacts that were coming in from Austria.

It was common knowledge that the artifacts were en route. But it was uncommon knowledge who was bringing them in. Nearly every dealer on the street was putting out feelers and getting ready to pay the high price for first crack at such a collection.

No one really knew how extensive the Austrian collection was, but the word going around Bond Street was that there were enough artifacts to fill a castle.

SEVERAL MILES SOUTH of Bond Street in a reconstructed fourteenth-century monastery in Richmond by the Thames, a man who was known these days as Aldric Whitelaw sat working in the real headquarters of the Brutus Foundation.

It was through Whitelaw that the tainted treasures had come to the foundation.

He was tired. It was early morning, and he'd been working all through the night cataloging many of the recent additions to his underground inventory.

At the moment he was poring over an archaic and faded twelfth-century manuscript that dealt with the holdings and doings of an Austrian knight named Theodoric Ingram.

The knight had been killed shortly after he'd returned from the Crusades, barely having the time to install his plunder in the castle before a band of freebooting mercenaries cut his throat and took the plunder for themselves.

Funny how history had a way of repeating itself, Whitelaw thought. Ever since medieval days, the Ingram family had embarked on a personal crusade to gather up the history and the heraldry of their noble military clan. Many of the weapons that had recently arrived at Whitelaw's monastery were once held in the hands of an Ingram. And the Theodoric Ingram who most recently departed the world had died in a vain attempt to hold on to some of the same treasures as his ancient namesake.

Whitelaw pushed aside the manuscript to stretch his legs for a few minutes.

He had an endless task in front of him—appraising and inventorying the shipments of plunder that were constantly arriving at his headquarters from drop sites all around London, courtesy of Konrad Lorenz.

Whitelaw could barely keep up with the ones that were already delivered, let alone the additional shipments Lorenz told him were coming.

He would have to price the items in the collection, provide provenances for many of them, then distribute them to the Brutus Foundation and other outlets they controlled in England, their first stage on the underground market.

It was hard work, but he was well paid for it. Plus he no longer had to take part in the covert part of Lorenz's operations. As long as he handled this end of the affair, he didn't have to participate in some of the more gruesome activities of the Vampyr clan.

He and Lorenz had planned well for times such as this back when they were in the Securitate.

It took a man of vision like Konrad Lorenz to see that Ceauşescu would fall. It took a man of even greater vision to set up an apparatus that would take care of all the Securitate chieftains on the run—like Aldric Whitelaw.

Whitelaw's respectable cover was years in the making, and hopefully would last for years to come. He enjoyed the role he was playing and spoke well enough to convince almost anyone he met that he was a born Englishman. He had almost convinced himself that the images of Romania that now and then swam through his mind were nothing but dreams.

He paced the relic-strewn gallery to work out his stiffened muscles. The gallery was an uncharted sea of medieval manuscripts, paintings and tapestries everywhere he looked, a sea he traveled endlessly, day and night.

To the Bond Street chairman of the foundation, such a mess would seem sacrilege, especially since many of the manuscripts were of an irreplaceable nature.

But to Aldric Whitelaw, sitting in the maelstrom of manuscripts and artworks was like having a private audience with the masters of old. It was a privilege that few could ever enjoy. Only the rich. Only the protected.

Despite his appreciation for the ancient times, unlike the scholars and salesmen with gilt-edged tongues who worked at the foundation, he wasn't one of those thin, white-faced, bespectacled wraiths who haunted libraries.

Whitelaw was a very physical man who religiously balanced his painstaking appraisals of rare treasures with strenuous workouts in the basement armory. It was a trait he'd picked up from Lorenz years ago. The fact that they were both still alive spoke well for it.

And Whitelaw reveled in the respect such a body won from the fairer sex, his other main pursuit when he wasn't making himself and Lorenz wealthy men.

At first glance Aldric had a deacon's look about him. But the glint in his eyes quickly dispelled any saintly illusions about him, illusions that were quickly shattered by anyone who followed him in his twice-weekly ritual walks in the heart of London, which always led him into the arms of streetwalking priestesses he found beneath the Eros statue in Piccadilly Circus.

Strangely enough recently he'd felt that he *was* being followed, as if someone were trying to look beyond the illusions he'd set up. But with so much activity in the streets, so many bright lights and promises drowning his senses, it was impossible to tell.

THE PHONE RANG an hour later. Aldric Whitelaw was once again pacing the treasure-lined gallery. He glared at the instrument as if his look alone could stop it from ringing. He wanted to complete his work before dealing with the outside world—one of the reasons he often toiled through the night until a specific amount of work was completed.

Sitting back down at his desk, Whitelaw picked up the sixteenth-century rondel dagger he used as a letter opener and idly tapped the narrow blade into the aged desktop while the phone rang.

That was the main drawback in his present line of work. He *couldn't* refuse the requests that came his way from Konrad Lorenz at all times of night or day.

"Yes?" he said, finally answering the phone with an irritated hiss in his voice.

"Aldric Whitelaw?"

He felt cold suddenly, as if someone had dropped an ice-cold shroud around him. The voice was hard and abrupt, the voice of a man who knew his own power.

"Do I know you?"

"That's not important," the caller said. "What's important is that I know you."

"What do you want?"

"The truth."

The Romanian held the phone away from him as if it were a weapon aimed at his head, a weapon that had already done its damage.

There was no explanation for the shiver that suddenly raced through his body. It was a cool spring morning, but the elbow-patched, leather-lined cardigan sweater he wore usually kept the chill at bay.

This was something different, something that came from the voice. This was the call that he'd been dreading since he'd set up shop. The call or the knock on the door. The nightmare had finally caught up with him.

"Whitelaw? Are you there?"

The voice drew him back to the phone. "Yes, I'm here. I want to know how you got this number."

"A friend of a friend," the voice said. "Or maybe it was an enemy. It doesn't really matter how I got your number, does it? What matters is that I have it and now I'm using it to give you one chance to come out of this alive."

"Who are you? What are you talking about?"

"I'm talking about the Ingram collection. Just one of many that have come your way."

Whitelaw looked down at the manuscript. He looked over at the medieval-era swords that he'd lovingly unwrapped. They were still lying on top of their rectangular red cloths, looking almost like a three-dimensional tarot card.

The Death card.

Leaning against the dark wooden wall were shields bearing the millenium-old crest of the Ingram family, a crest that was now extinct. Seeing the shield made him think of a joust or a duel. And that *he* was involved in a duel right now, with some errant champion who was out to avenge the death of Theodoric Ingram.

Whitelaw's occult turn of mind made him flash back to the twelfth-century Theodoric Ingram for a moment. Maybe this was a champion summoned by the long-departed knight who sought vengeance against the thief who just a few moments before was poring through *his* ancient manuscript.

"Your silence speaks loud, Whitelaw," the voice said. "I take that as an admission of guilt."

"Of what?"

"I'm sure you're guilty of many things. But right now my main concern is the Ingram collection."

"That has nothing to do with me."

A hollow laugh sounded on the other end of the phone. "It has everything to do with you and why I'm making this call."

"And why is that?" Whitelaw asked. "How do I know this isn't just a crank call?"

"Because you would have hung up long ago if you'd thought so. This is real, guy. Dead real."

"I'm listening."

"I want Konrad Lorenz."

"Never heard of—"

"I want you to lead me to him. That's all. Cooperate, and you can walk away from this. Don't cooperate, and you won't have any more worries. Period."

"I don't respond to threats."

"How about bullets?"

Again Aldric Whitelaw felt as if an electric current were passing through him, searing his insides.

"Okay, guy. Time for an answer. Are you in or out?"

"Here's my answer," Whitelaw said. "One, I don't know who or what you're talking about. Two, you sound like a dangerous lunatic the police might be interested in."

"I work well with the police. By all means, bring them in. If you've got nothing to hide."

Whitelaw ignored him. "Three, if you knew a little more about what you're playing with, then you'd know enough to quit while you're still alive."

"Now who's threatening?" the voice said.

There was a click and a whir on the line, and in the background Whitelaw thought he heard another voice, another conversation.

It reminded him of a spook-shop monitoring center, the kind dating back to his former life as a Securitate agent where *he* spent a lot of time on the other end of these calls, testing and terrorizing suspects. Maybe that was it, Whitelaw thought. Maybe this was all just a bluff, someone fishing for whatever he could find.

"I'm going to terminate this call," Whitelaw said, his voice sounding more confident now. "But first I'll repeat that I don't know what you're talking about, and I don't want to know any more."

"Okay," the voice said. "But before I hang up, I'll tell you who this is."

"Go on."

"I'm known in some circles as the Executioner."

"That's not a name."

"You're right. Some say it's a trade—one you might get to witness up close. I'll be in touch."

The line went dead, giving Whitelaw the first chance to breathe deeply since the conversation had started. He hadn't realized the effect the call had on him.

He was in shape physically, but mentally he was flabby when it came to handling this kind of thing. It had been years since he was an active member in Konrad Lorenz's network, and now it looked as if it was coming back to haunt him.

This "Executioner" obviously had some knowledge of the foundation and Lorenz.

He had to alert Konrad to the possible penetration of the network.

Or at least he should.

He knew from past experience what happened to members of a covert apparatus when its cover was blown. The operation was rolled up from top to bottom.

And sometimes the operators were rolled up with it.

End of story.

Aldric Whitelaw closed the ancient manuscript and pushed it gently across the desktop.

It was time to put away the mask of respectability he'd worn for so long. And pick up the sword.

CHAPTER SIXTEEN

In the small hotel room near Covent Garden's open-air marketplace in the center of London, Mack Bolan put down the phone and circled the name of Aldric Whitelaw on a list of names he'd written on a sheet of hotel stationery.

"I think he's our man," Bolan said.

"Both of us have been saying that all last night and this morning," Gina Salvie replied, "with just about every call we made. And then we move on to the next one and *he* sounds like the one we're looking for."

"Yeah. I know. But this Whitelaw has a certain quality about him that you can recognize after a while."

"What quality is that?"

"Fear," Bolan told her.

Salvie shook her head. "That's no proof. All the people on that list have something to hide."

"This one was different. I could sense that he was ready to break. He wanted to run."

"My God," she said. "You sound like you're a predator."

"I am. Just play the tape back and you'll hear it yourself."

"And if I don't agree he's our man?"

"Then maybe I'll take him myself."

"We're in this together," she said. "In every way possible, we're a team."

"No argument. When I get a strong feeling, you listen to it. When you get a hunch, I'll listen. Hey, I'm not pulling rank. I'm just saying he's worth a hard look."

"We still have other names to check out."

"A hell of a lot of names," Bolan agreed. "It's likely that more than one of these guys are connected to Lorenz. But for now I'll put Whitelaw on the top of the list."

Salvie shrugged, then leaned casually on the hotel bed. The two of them had been calling numbers ever since they'd flown in through Heathrow the previous night and checked into the hotel.

Now the cycle was starting all over again. They had a day full of suspects to cover, then logistics to take care of, a possible liaison with the British.

And a possible showdown with the Vampyr network.

"Go ahead," Bolan suggested. "Play back the tape. And when you're convinced he's our man, we'll figure out how to play him."

The woman nodded and played back the tape, now and then rewinding it to check out Whitelaw's responses. "He's scared all right, but who wouldn't be if he got a call like that? You don't come across as the angel of mercy here."

"Damn right. I want this guy to be running scared. So scared he'll run right to Lorenz. And we'll be right behind him."

"If he's the right man, we will," she said. "Let's go check him out."

SHEETS OF COLD RAIN pelted London, momentarily sweeping the streets clean as the late-morning crowd fled for shelter.

Wearing a rain-slicked windbreaker, Mack Bolan ducked under the awning of a curio shop just off of Brompton Road along with a few Londoners caught in the sudden downpour.

It seemed too seedy a place to handle pieces from the Ingram collection, he thought, but he scanned the display windows out of habit. He and Salvie were doing a quick recon of some of the locations Brognola had identified for them.

They had nothing better to do at the moment. Whitelaw had temporarily left his Richmond manse, giving them plenty of time to check out the other suspects on the hit list.

Maybe they'd spooked him too soon, Bolan thought. But that was a risk they had to take with crashing into the London scene so suddenly.

Whitelaw was just one of many names they had on their suspect list, and they had to try a scattergun approach to see who ran.

Whitelaw had run. That was a good sign.

Unfortunately he'd run fast. They had no idea where the "reputable collector" had gone.

He would turn up. A man like that wasn't going to let a fortune slip through his fingers. Aldric Whitelaw would die first, and the Executioner would do his best to oblige him.

With a feigned lack of interest, Bolan glanced into the shop windows. It held no real treasures, just the usual tarnished but splendid junk that loosened the purse strings of those anxious to burn money and buy a piece of history.

When the rain lightened into a gentle mist, swarms of shoppers moved onto the pavement once more, hurrying to their next stop before the storm could catch them again.

The warrior strolled down Beauchamp Place, moving with the crowds spilling in and out of the sidewalk shops and cafés. He'd joined them by reflex, and fell into the same pace.

He was tired of the endless and sometimes aimless walking, but that was always part of any recon. They had to know who was the enemy, as well as who wasn't.

He and Salvie had split up so they could cover as many shops as possible as fast as possible. Initially they'd worked together, sometimes engaging the owners in conversation to test the rhythms of their speech to see if they were nervous or preoccupied about something.

On those occasions Salvie had the advantage. People found her a bit easier to talk to than Bolan. The Executioner made people nervous. Perhaps it was the cool, searching blue eyes that studied them with a well-learned wariness, aware that at any moment they could turn into moving targets or attackers.

The streets that had initially seemed so foreign now seemed familiar. On previous trips to London, Bolan had pretty much covered the town. But it had been a while since he'd toured the country. Now, after walking around for a while, the layout was coming back to him.

It would have been pleasant walking through London again, if not for the reason that brought him there. Konrad Lorenz's tentacles had reached far. Unless he was stopped soon, he might be impossible to stop at all.

Money had a way of erasing the past, and from what Bolan knew, Lorenz had enough to erase several lifetimes.

The rain hissed softly on the pavement in a hesitant and teasing prelude to another downpour that suddenly whipped down the street and drenched those caught in the open.

Bolan sought refuge in a secondhand bookshop, sandwiched between a pub and a deli, midway down Beauchamp Place.

He felt as if he were in a church the moment he stepped inside. Thick curtains were draped over the backdrop behind the books in the display window, isolating the interior of the store from the frantic passersby.

It was quiet except for the muted classical music that streamed from small speakers hidden like bookends on the crowded bookshelves.

The bookseller behind the counter looked up as Bolan passed. The man's faded blue denim shirt was rolled up to his elbows, and he was penciling something into a spiral-bound notebook.

On a rack of dusty and worn volumes near the counter, the warrior scanned the hard-to-read titles, thumbing the old cloth-bound spines to see what they were about.

The books on this rack were mostly old volumes of poetry. All of them were priced cheaply.

"Welcome," the bookseller said, tugging at his graying goatee as he looked up from his work. "Anything you're looking for, don't hesitate to ask."

Bolan nodded his thanks and drifted down an aisle with shaky bookshelves on each side looming over him like a sleepy forest, the pine and oak scents replaced by the musty smell of ripening books—like incense for the intellect.

With the Beretta 93-R rig weighing heavy under his shoulder, Bolan felt somewhat like an intruder in the peaceful shop. The weapons had been waiting for them in the hotel room Brognola had booked for them. So were the keys to a few cars scattered in parking lots and garages around London.

The cars were part of the free-lance fleet that the covert agencies kept around in case their people had to move fast.

Following a whim, Bolan headed toward the back of the shop toward a section full of horror and science-fiction books. He crouched down to one of the lower shelves and picked up an early edition of Bram Stoker's *Dracula*.

It was an annotated version of the classic horror tale, full of all sorts of uncanny lore dealing with the lives and death of the Romanian king of the undead. It not only provided the factual basis of the vampire legend, but offered a veritable atlas of Transylvanian geography.

As he thumbed through the volume, Bolan found that the life and crimes of Vlad Dracul ran neck and neck with the lives and crimes of Konrad Lorenz.

Both Romanian warlords had carved a bloody path to the top, both had fallen, and both fought to regain their positions of power.

There was something else they had in common, Bolan thought. Both men were hated and feared, and, strangely enough, respected by their countrymen.

In the end Vlad Dracul had been beheaded.

His fictional counterpart was snuffed out once and for all via a blade to the heart and a neck-severing knife thrust.

Bolan closed the book with a dusty snapping sound and put it back in the rack.

Too bad Konrad Lorenz wasn't as easy to kill, the warrior thought. Actually, killing him probably wasn't the hard part.

Finding him was.

PLAINCLOTHES OFFICER Bruce Campbell of New Scotland Yard walked down Beauchamp Place with a practiced casual gait, moving in and out of the shops as if he had nothing more on his mind than making a few choice purchases.

To add legitimate cover to his surveillance of the man whose passport proclaimed him to be Michael Belasko, Officer Campbell window-shopped a few stores behind him.

To add even more cover, at one curio shop he bought a white beer stein emblazoned with a Welsh dragon. After all, he had to look authentic.

The rain was coming down hard as he followed the American, but it didn't really bother him. As part of his plainclothes garb he wore a Burberry trench coat and a felt hat. It not only kept him dry but helped him blend in with the crowd.

Campbell liked to think he looked like a rising young businessman, perhaps a junior banker or an advertising man. The only thing connecting him to the Yard was the badge and ID in his wallet.

When Belasko stepped into the bookshop, Campbell ducked into an upscale pub across the street to wait him out. He didn't worry too much about his subject getting away from him. Not this time.

This wasn't a criminal investigation.

If anything, it was more of a bodyguard assignment. Although Campbell didn't know all the details, he knew that Michael Belasko, or whoever he really was, was considered to be on the side of the angels.

Or at least on the side of British Intelligence.

No one wanted him to get hurt on British soil. And everyone wanted to know what he was doing here.

Records showed that the Belasko name had turned up quite frequently over the years in England. Usually his presence occurred at the same time as some undercover operation that turned out favorably for the Yard or for their colleagues in the security services.

Officially the man who traveled under the name of Michael Belasko was hardly noticed.

Unofficially his presence was welcome—but deserved watching.

Campbell had been catching more of these assignments lately because he had the right temperament for it. To work on Chief Inspector Newhall's squad, covering everything from counterfeit artwork to kidnappings and bombings, you needed the heart and soul and now and then the growl of a bulldog.

The job entailed equal parts of paperwork and legwork and now and then a sudden encounter with violence.

The little cakewalk he was on right now had something to do with the recent influx of plundered artworks from Austria. But there was something else in the works.

Officer Campbell could feel it.

Michael Belasko was going to lead him to some very interesting places.

Otherwise, Chief Inspector Newhall wouldn't have taken such a special interest in the case. Newhall was working around the clock on this one, which meant that someone big was going to fall.

Not only was Newhall on the case, but the Intelligence types were also involved, the men who liked to keep their secrets, harboring them like the bloody treasures they were now trying to find. Campbell had no doubts that David Peake, the new man who'd just been attached to the monuments, fine arts and archives unit was from the spook brigade.

It was written all over him. He trusted no one, gave orders at every opportunity—but never any opinions—and treated Chief Inspector Newhall as if Newhall were the guest at the Yard.

Campbell sighed at the thought of Peake.

Whenever Intelligence was involved, something always crawled out from under a rock sooner or later. And sometimes it was the Intelligence people themselves.

He would find out more in time. But for now all he had to do was be patient and stay with his man.

Too bad he hadn't been assigned to the other subject under surveillance, Campbell thought. Gina Salvie was a lot easier on the eye than Michael Belasko.

No way he'd ever lose sight of *her*.

Campbell watched the bookshop from inside the pub, holding a frothy mug of lager close to his lips without drinking it. Except, of course, for a sip now and then.

It was past noon already, and so a drop of brew for lunch wasn't a capital crime.

All part of the job, he thought. And there was another reward in the pub. The brown-haired barmaid was a looker, and she had the kind of magic in her eyes a man rarely glimpsed these days.

Too bad he was on duty. She kept looking his way.

Another time, perhaps. But she kept on looking at him.

His aura must have hooked her. That had to be it. The scent of danger had handcuffed yet another poor wench.

She was coming over to him.

"Hey, mate, you going to nurse it to death or buy another?" she demanded.

Before he could reply, Campbell saw the door of the bookshop swing open and out came Belasko.

"Well?" the barmaid said. "What'll it be?"

"Nothing, love. I've got to sprint. Another time, though, count on it." He paid for the beer and slowly walked out of the pub.

Campbell followed his man at a distance, hoping he'd do something a bit more exciting than seek out another bookshop.

And then Campbell caught himself. He'd been starting to treat this as a lark. Soft duty.

But he knew that despite the man's apparently harmless stroll, Belasko had seen a lot of action under a lot of names.

He was a friend, true. But a dangerous friend.

AT THREE-FIFTEEN in the afternoon Chief Inspector Newhall dropped a folded copy of the *Times of London* on the corner of his desk and sipped black tea from a chipped white cup.

A crack to the left of the handle had crept slowly over the years, a stone spiderweb covering more and more of the cup each year. But the cup still held up. It didn't leak, and the loop in the handle accommodated his thick fingers just fine.

Newhall fortified himself with a deep draft of the strong tea, then regarded the mountain of paperwork that had been accumulating on his desk.

Several folders were crisscrossed on top of one another in order of priority. Unfortunately the priorities kept on changing, and the pile kept on getting bigger.

There was too much information for one man to sift through, analyze, then act upon. But he had no choice. Newhall commanded just one of several units working on the case—one of several who passed their information to the spook shop.

It was an impossible task, but the men of the Yard were all used to doing the impossible when asked.

Newhall picked up the top folders and quickly scanned through them to see which ones demanded a more in-depth study.

Surveillance reports of Michael Belasko.

Surveillance reports of Gina Salvie.

And then there were follow-up reports on the places that the two of them had visited. It was a never-ending spiral. Now the Yard would have to check out the same shopkeepers that Belasko and the woman had visited.

And these were just the most recent reports.

An epidemic of computer data and hard copy had been flooding his desk lately, most of the Intelligence having to do with artifacts from Romania, the Czech Republic and Austria suddenly appearing in art shops around London.

Many of the shops were run by dealers who didn't look too closely at their provenances or the backgrounds of the people who provided them.

With this latest Austrian collection supposedly tied in with an underground network staffed by rogue Intelligence officers, Newhall was prepared to go to any lengths to see that his end of the operation held up. Too many people would be looking over his shoulder.

It was an international case now, which meant that his international reputation was at stake. If things went well, no one would ever hear his name.

But if things went wrong, his name might end up on the front page of the very newspaper sitting unread on the corner of his desk. And his career might end right along with it.

They wouldn't go wrong, he thought.

But then the phone rang.

It was Officer Campbell calling in with news of the surveillance. Things had gone wrong. Out-bloody-rageously wrong.

Michael Belasko had dropped out of sight, and so had Gina Salvie.

Neither of them had displayed the slightest sign that they knew they were being watched, right up to the moment when they vanished. Both of them shook their watchmen in the subway at Piccadilly Circus.

Newhall shook his head. He had special teams he could call in to find them. But considering the kind of people in the underground network, he wondered if there would be anything left to find.

CHAPTER SEVENTEEN

Cass Strashmir jogged easily through the wild forest across from the curving road that fronted Aldric Whitelaw's monastic palace on the edge of Richmond.

He was traveling relatively light this night. His only real extra weight was twenty pounds of precision metal, the Heckler & Koch PSG-1 sniping rifle complete with tripod and 6×42 Hensold Etzler scope.

Strashmir had two 20-round magazines for the rifle, though that was certainly overkill—unless the man he was waiting for showed up with a small army. But according to Whitelaw, when the Executioner had called back to press him for a face-to-face, Whitelaw got him to agree to a private meet.

Perfect, Strashmir thought. He hated crowd scenes. People tended to get in the way and they also ruined the beauty of the moment, their panicked screams echoing long after the event was finished.

The Romanian assassin dropped to the ground and propped himself up on the crest of a slight grassy knoll that looked down on Whitelaw's residence.

He'd scouted out the woods several hours earlier to determine the best vantage point.

There was a twenty-foot-high ridge of jagged earth directly behind him, providing plenty of shadow to keep his silhouette unseen in the moonlight.

Strashmir fixed the tripod in the hard earth, then adjusted the buttstock until it fit just right against his shoulder. He scanned the facade of the former monastery that had been converted into a place where only money was now worshiped.

The Hensold Etzler scope's built-in low-light illumination made the west side of the house seem as plain as day.

He couldn't miss.

Strashmir swung the barrel slowly from left to right, tracking imaginary kill targets in his mind's eye.

Then he waited calmly in the woods as he'd waited so many times before in so many different places.

He was totally at peace.

This was his weapon of choice.

This was his territory.

And right now this was his world, a world viewed through the cross hairs of a high-precision semi-automatic sniper's rifle.

MACK BOLAN RESTED his left hand on the steering wheel of the dark green Ford station wagon parked just outside a stone wall on the edge of Richmond Park.

The station wagon he and Salvie had driven from London was hidden in the shadow of a huge oak tree with gnarled and curving branches cascading in all directions like a wooden waterfall.

After a few more minutes passed, the Executioner glanced at his watch and pressed the illumination button on the side.

"Almost time to go," he said.

"If you ask me, it's past time. This place gives me the creeps."

"I can't think of anything getting to you—not after what we've been through."

"Sometimes the nighttime does," she said. "Especially when you don't know how it's going to end."

Bolan nodded.

He understood that sense of unease.

Or maybe it was just the dark and ancient majesty of the nearby forest that gave Richmond Park its wild and medieval character. It felt like something primeval was on the loose.

Walking through the park during the daylight was like taking a trip back into the past to a time when it had been the hunting preserves of London royalty.

It was a peaceful escape for Londoners who took a bus or rode the subway to the station by the park. A perfect day trip.

But at night the park changed. It seemed almost like an otherworldly landscape that never quite stayed still because of the strong breeze that hissed and whipped through the overhead boughs.

Most of the time it was just a steady breeze, but now and then a shrieking wind raced through the woods, bending the corallike silhouettes of the tall and distant treetops.

For a superstitious man it wasn't a good place to kill time before attending a potentially dangerous rendezvous.

But Bolan wasn't superstitious.

And after his earlier recon of Aldric Whitelaw's estate, the warrior thought they could wait there undisturbed.

After a few more minutes Bolan switched on the ignition. The radio came to life once more, bringing in some slow British blues from a London FM station.

"Now's the time," Bolan said softly.

"I'm sure as hell ready. I've had enough. Any moment I expect Robin Hood to come swinging down from the trees."

The Executioner spun the wheel slightly and eased the Ford wagon over the rough terrain onto the main road heading toward Richmond.

He planned on arriving early enough for the rendezvous so he'd have enough time to scope out the area one more time.

He didn't expect a full house at Whitelaw's manor.

When he'd spoken to Whitelaw on the phone for the second time, the man seemed straightforward. Or as straightforward as a man with his background could be.

Whitelaw had made it plain that he was ready to deal some information in exchange for amnesty.

It was SOP in the covert world, the kind of bargain Bolan had made more times than he could count. He didn't like it, but there was really little other choice.

It was the same at all levels. From street crimes right up to the big boardroom rip-offs, the main reason most cases were solved was because of the informants.

You either bought them or badgered them until they were ready to give up the game.

Once you put the fear of God—or a gun—into them, then it was confession time.

Aldric Whitelaw had been around long enough to know the score.

If he talked, he walked.

"Do you know who I am?"

"Of course I do," Whitelaw replied, looking at the man with the chiseled weathered face. "You're the man who threatened to kill me."

"I don't want to," Bolan replied. Keeping his hands in his pockets, the warrior opened his windbreaker wide enough to show the Beretta holstered in his underarm rig.

Whitelaw looked long and hard at the Ford wagon that Bolan had parked under the carport.

When he was satisfied no one was concealed in the car, Whitelaw opened the door wide and gestured for the Executioner to step inside the mansion.

His senses fully alert, the warrior crossed the threshold and walked slowly down the marble hallway.

His gaze swept toward the end of the T-shaped corridor, where it split off in two directions. He looked and listened for any sign that Whitelaw had company.

"There's no one else here," the man said. "I like to do my selling out in private."

"Then do it."

Bolan continued to check the place out of habit. He and Salvie had made sure no one else was in the house before he pulled up to the carport. During their last recon of the grounds, the Executioner had studied every room of the building through the night-vision lens of a compact pocket scope.

But this was still enemy territory and no matter how safe it looked, Bolan wasn't going to take any chances.

"This way," Whitelaw said.

Bolan followed two steps behind the man and to his right, ready to take him out at any second.

Whitelaw had no visible weapon, but it would be easy enough to conceal a weapon somewhere in the house.

Walking with the dignified air of a statesman about to sign a peace treaty with a long-time enemy,

Whitelaw led the Executioner to a cathedral-windowed library on the west side of the house.

Several old wooden desks and tables were covered with manuscripts and ancient but expensive-looking goblets. The Old World wealth was casually on display.

A few easy chairs were randomly stationed along the floor-to-ceiling bookcases; glass doors led to a balcony overlooking the grounds of the former monastery. This was the room where Whitelaw conducted a lot of his business, Bolan thought. That was a good sign, making it *seem* as if Whitelaw really was intent on dealing honestly with him.

They sat across from each other at a long mahogany table by the glass doors.

Wearing the look of a man who knew the other player had better cards, Whitelaw raised his hands and said, "This is your affair. What do you want to know?"

"Everything."

"That's kind of broad, isn't it?" Whitelaw gestured around at the volume-filled library. "As you can see, I'm a man of many interests."

"Okay. So you're a well-read thief. How about we narrow it down to a book title—*Everything You Always Knew about Konrad Lorenz but Were Afraid to Tell.*"

Whitelaw offered a thin smile. "I see that you're familiar with the classics. But you've made your point."

Leaning forward, his clasped hands sliding smoothly across the polished surface of the table, Aldric Whitelaw spoke in carefully measured and cultured tones.

Almost as if he *were* lecturing about one of his classics, he began to outline his end of the operation and how it was tied in with Konrad Lorenz's network.

Whitelaw was one of the most cooperative informants the Executioner had ever encountered. And precise. In just a few minutes the man had given him several leads to the ring that brought stolen artifacts into England.

There were antique dealers in London, as well as several storehouses located on the outskirts of the capital. The ring also smuggled in East European fugitives. Those with fortunes were well hidden. Those without fortunes were treated almost like indentured servants, waiting at the beck and call of the Vampyr network.

And the calls came often. Lorenz had several operations in the works at all times.

Though Whitelaw had a solid knowledge of the art-smuggling operation and the crews who protected them, he claimed not to be as familiar with the routes taken by the fugitives on the Underground Express.

Other than guessing that the traffickers were connected to some legitimate company that provided authentic cover for them to move men and matériel across international borders, Whitelaw wasn't able to mention any of the specifics.

"The smuggling crew is also the enforcement arm for the network," Bolan suggested. "The action arm that does all the killing for him?"

"I try to stay away from that end," Whitelaw said. "I'm a businessman, not a criminal."

The distinction was lost on Bolan. Here was a man directly tied in with a murderous organization that trampled on innocent people all across the continent, and Whitelaw figured it was just business as usual.

"I understand that," the Executioner replied. "What I don't understand is your sudden change of heart."

Whitelaw shrugged. "I realized I had no choice when you came onto the scene. If I tried to fight you, another one of your kind would come along."

"What kind is that?"

"An army, I presume. And as I've said, I'm a businessman, not a henchman. When you threaten that business, I have to either retire...or cooperate with you."

"Right," Bolan said. "But this cooperation is all very sudden, isn't it?"

"Why act surprised?" Whitelaw asked. "I have the feeling you've made these kinds of bargains in the past."

"A time or two."

"Exactly. And you're quite good at it. Your first call to me was a bit melodramatic, but it was effective just the same. Today you sounded more reasonable. And I, too, am a reasonable man. I accept that I have no other choice."

"Just like that," Bolan said.

"Just like that," the man repeated, snapping his fingers and smiling.

"What about Konrad Lorenz?" Bolan asked. "This could lead to his downfall. But it might take a while. In the meantime things could get hot for you."

"I've looked the situation over. And you said the magic words—*his downfall,* not mine. I believe that I can hold out until that happens. That is, if I can trust you."

"Play by the rules, and you've got nothing to fear from me," Bolan told him.

"I thought as much. I figured you for a real bastard, but a bastard who keeps his word."

"As long as you keep yours. But I'm still curious about the reasons why you changed your mind so suddenly. Usually it takes a bit more."

"Disappointed you didn't get a chance to strongarm me any more?" Whitelaw asked. "You want to see why, I'll show you why." He pushed away from the table and headed to the glass doors.

With Bolan one step behind him, the man unlatched the doors and pushed them outward. Then he stepped out onto the balcony that looked out onto the forest surrounding his palace.

"This is why I'm informing on Lorenz. I want to keep this. All of it. If I have to cut off one of my associates to do so, that's a small enough price to pay."

People had been sold out for a lot less, Bolan knew, but there was something in Whitelaw's words that bothered him, an undercurrent of challenge that had been submerged until now.

Now that they were out on the balcony, Whitelaw seemed combative. But at the same time, he was trying to keep his distance from Bolan.

The Executioner looked out at the surrouding forest, its rolling treetops looking like a soft mountain of shadow. It was a terrific vantage point, but he was interested in more than just the view.

Instinctively he scanned the woods as if it were enemy terrain. When he looked back at Whitelaw, the other man was regarding him with a superior look—as if he were the victor. As though some battle had been fought and won in his head.

Bolan gauged the man's stance and saw no weapon in his hand. He saw no aggressive stance, as if the man were preparing for an attack. But in his eyes he saw death.

The Executioner looked back out over the woods one more time and saw a brief glint in the distance. Just for a moment.

It could have been the moonlight striking on rock, or just a trick of the eye.

But under the circumstances, it was long enough to make him act.

Bolan dived to his right.

In that split second he saw a red-hot flash searing through the blackness. The sheet of flame came from far in the woods, across the main road.

Aldric Whitelaw was also moving. Like a man moving in slow motion, the man hunched his shoulders and raised his hands with their palms outward as he backpedaled a few steps.

Blood erupted from his shirt, staining the area around his heart a deep red. He shook his head in disbelief as he crumpled to the floor of the balcony.

As he hit the floor, Whitelaw sought out Bolan, as if to accuse *him* for still being alive.

And then the man died with a soft exhalation of air, his last image the hard, cold eyes of the Executioner.

"Striker!"

Salvie's voice floated up from the woods below, where she'd been on lookout. "Striker! Are you okay?"

"I'm fine!" Bolan shouted. "Whitelaw's down. For good."

"It came from across the road," she shouted.

"Yeah. I saw it." He drew his Beretta 93-R from its rig and scrambled across the balcony on his hands and knees, staying out of the line of fire.

The woman's voice floated up to him again, sounding farther away this time. "I'm going after him."

"Wait for me," Bolan shouted back.

But there was no answer.

He cursed, but then he thought about what he would do if the position was reversed. He wouldn't wait around for someone to hold his hand while he crossed the road.

She was good and had a chance of getting to the sniper.

She also had a chance of ending up like Aldric Whitelaw, his eyes blank and staring, his arms spread out and his warm blood oozing onto the balcony he'd claimed to love so much.

Bolan made it to the edge of the balcony and looked out through the narrow vertical spaces between the thin stone columns.

He could go back inside, but with the light shining from inside the room, he'd be exposed to rifle fire for a crucial moment. And even if he made it inside, there would still be plenty of light from the windows for him to make a good target.

The warrior dismissed the idea. No matter how fast he could cross the kill zone, it would still be long enough to die.

His other alternative was to swing up and over the railing, then drop into the brush below.

The sniper might still have a chance to pick him off, but he'd need a lot of luck to hit a fast-moving target in the dark.

As he crouched there in the shadows, still another alternative came to Bolan.

He could play it safe and wait it out. The sniper wouldn't stay on his mark for too long. Not with the echo of the shot drawing curious neighbors.

Then he thought of Gina rushing into the woods.

The Executioner holstered his Beretta, grabbed the railing with one hand, then pulled himself up and over.

He sailed down to the ground below and crashed into the brush.

CHAPTER EIGHTEEN

As he stalked uphill through the forest toward the sniper's nest, Bolan flicked down the front handgrip on the Beretta 93-R.

His left hand curled around the grip, and his thumb hooked through the extended trigger guard, giving him more control as he held the 9 mm pistol like a submachine gun.

The selector was in the 3-round-burst mode, and the weapon was carrying a 20-round magazine.

Bolan was on the right flank, Salvie on the left. She was carrying a Heckler & Koch MP-5.

If the sniper was still there, he had some heavy-duty firepower to contend with.

But the Executioner doubted the gunman would still be around, not after he'd practically left a neon sign to give away his position.

They'd been able to see the light right after they crossed the road and rendezvoused at the base of the hill. It was an incandescent yellow, glowing brilliant in the dark green shadows.

The sniper had to have had powerful reasons for wanting them to find the kill site—exactly the opposite of most snipers, who wanted to hit-and-run and leave no trace of their presence behind him.

But the light burned brightly in the night, drawing them like moths to the shooting gallery.

Bolan could hear Salvie moving uphill, but just barely. Branches flapping back, twigs cracking under her feet and pebbles rolling downhill gave her away.

She was good and moved as silently as possible, but Bolan was attuned to this kind of hunt. His senses were alert for even the slightest sounds.

And right now he was almost expecting to hear another sound—the sharp report of another shot from the sniper's nest.

The light suddenly seemed to grow brighter as the warrior crested a small wooded ridge.

Now that the screen of forest was thinner, he could make out the strange foot-long device that was casting its eerie aura against an earthen backdrop.

The sniper had planted a light stick in the ground, one of the plastic-coated glow-in-the-dark tubes that covert forces had carried around for years as instant sources of light when they were trapped in dark situations.

Nowadays the sticks were popular with kids who used them as little more than toys or curiosities. But many a covert operator still carried them, especially those who'd been in the field for a long time.

Bolan realized that their sniper was of the old school. He took three steps around a cluster of closely grown trees at the edge of the clearing, giving him a clear view of the sniper's nest. Behind the light stick there was a small slanted dip in the ground and a cliff behind, a perfect hidden pocket of earth for the gunman.

The warrior emerged from the trees with the Beretta trained at the edge of the gully just in case the sniper was still there.

"Clear on the right flank," he shouted.

"Clear on the left," Salvie answered.

"You see what we're dealing with?" Bolan asked.

"Got it in my sights."

"Cover me."

As he jogged toward the light stick, the warrior spotted a small square box sitting next to the light.

A pack of cigarettes.

Or maybe a pack of explosives.

The possibilities flashed through Bolan's mind in a split second. Whoever had lain there had had plenty of time to rig a booby trap, although it was an unlikely move for a sniper who would favor a quick and clean kill. Why go to such lengths to kill a man? Bolan thought.

The warrior kept running until he was past the light stick, then instinctively dropped down into the position the sniper had assumed just a short time ago.

A quick search of the area revealed that the sniper had left some metallic fingerprints behind—indentations in the earth from the tripod that had supported the rifle.

From this vantage point he had a clear shot at the doors leading to Aldric Whitelaw's balcony—and Bolan.

It was a long shot, but a skilled marksman could hit his target from that range.

But who was the intended target? Bolan or Aldric Whitelaw?

Had the marksman made a mistake and misread the faces he'd obviously studied through a sniper scope?

Or was Whitelaw the target all along?

"You all right?" Gina called out, her voice floating from the edge of the woods.

"Yeah," Bolan replied. "So far, anyway."

The Executioner looked around him until he found a splintered tree limb with a long branch stripped of its bark. Holding it like a fishing pole, he eased it forward until the tip of the branch pressed against the cigarette box. Palming the bottom of the branch with his left hand, he pushed the box over, while at the same time scrambling off to his right and rolling downhill to safety.

The cigarette box flipped softly onto the ground.

"What happened?" Salvie asked, appearing at the edge of the woods.

"Nothing."

Getting back to his feet, he saw that the cigarette box had opened and a matchbook spilled out.

Bolan scooped up the matchbook and gave it a quick once-over. The cover showed a picture of a sprawling rustic-roofed inn with a medieval look about it.

"The Bell and Oak Inn." Bolan read the name off the matchbook. "Ever hear of it?"

"No."

"Me neither. But it looks like I've been invited to lunch there."

"What do you mean?"

"Here," Bolan said, handing her the matchbook. "Take a look inside."

Salvie flipped open the book and read the message scrawled inside in tall, flowing script:

> We have to talk.
> 3:00 tomorrow.

Beneath the message was the writer's initial—*S*.

"Any idea what *S* stands for?" she asked.

"Yeah. Looks like the guy we were looking for in Vienna has found *us*."

"Strashmir," Salvie said, handing back the matches.

"Right. Unless Konrad Lorenz has another sniper with the same initial running around on the loose."

"What do you figure he's up to?"

"Looks like we've got a sniper on our hands who wants to do some talking before he does any more shooting," Bolan replied.

"You going to show up?"

The Executioner glanced at the matches. "If he's paying, sure."

She laughed and said, "You're a hell of a cheap date." Then she got serious. "But what if it's a trap?"

"Then he still pays. With his life."

CHAPTER NINETEEN

The Bell and Oak was a thatched-roof inn sitting close to the road that led from London to Windsor. White picket fencing cordoned it off from the well-traveled highway. Several tall oaks were scattered about the grounds of the inn, shading a forlorn-looking wishing well.

The sign hanging out over the front entrance showed a silver bell dangling from a sturdy weathered oak.

With its stone walls and leaded-glass windows, the inn looked as if it had been plucked from the Middle Ages and dropped intact there in the Midlands, complete with costumed wenches who moved quickly from table to table to keep up with the steady afternoon crowd enjoying the sun on the terrace.

On his way from the crowded parking lot, Bolan scanned the outside tables, then walked through the open front door into the cool shadows of the inn.

It took his eyes a few moments to adjust to the darkness before he was able to scan the bar and the crowded but cozy tables inside.

A top-heavy hostess who could have stepped from a screen version of *The Adventures of Moll Flan-*

ders looked his way as she returned from one of the back rooms and headed straight for him.

"Mr. Belasko?" she said.

"Yes," Bolan said, somewhat taken aback. "How did you know?"

"Your friend gave me a most vivid description. But believe me, it doesn't really do you justice."

"Thanks."

"Your table's over here," the hostess said. "Right this way." She led him to one of the tables that looked out at the front of the inn. Each table was separated from the others by tall wooden booths to ensure privacy.

And there, sitting calmly by the window, eating a meal, was his "friend" and assassin, Cass Strashmir.

The Romanian was an athletic-looking man with neatly combed and slightly graying hair. He had the build of a tennis player without an ounce of fat on him. And at the moment he looked as if he didn't have a care in the world.

"Mike!" the man said, standing up to shake his hand while the hostess fluttered away. "So good to see you again!"

Bolan shook hands with him, registering his strong and easy grip. Then he swung into the seat across from the man and said, "Thanks for the welcome, but as far as I know, we've never seen each other before."

"Oh, I've had you in my sights for a while," Strashmir replied, a smile lighting his eyes.

"I figured as much," Bolan said. "If you are who I think you are—"

"Oh, we both know who we are. Otherwise, we wouldn't be here having this nice chat. I'm Cass Strashmir and you're Mike Belasko. At least for the moment."

Bolan glanced up as the waitress zeroed in on him. "Just a lager for me."

"Nothing to eat?" Strashmir asked, carefully playing out his role of generous host. "The roast lamb has a wonderful mint sauce. I heartily recommend it."

Bolan shook his head and waved off the waitress. "I didn't come here to eat, Cass."

Strashmir shrugged. "Life is so fleeting—for some—that I've long made it a practice to take what little pleasures come my way. Good food. Good company."

"I'm not good company," Bolan said, a hard edge to his voice. "Matter of fact, I'm probably the last person you want to let this close to you."

"Two days ago I might have said the same thing," Strashmir replied, carefully cutting a slice of lamb. "But I've done a lot of thinking since then."

"And?"

"And I think we might see eye to eye."

"What if I think different?"

"Yes," Strashmir admitted. "There's always that chance." He picked up his wineglass and took a small sip, savoring the taste before swallowing. Then he looked slowly around the room, not long enough to stare at anyone, but long enough to get a make on the other occupants in the inn. "But, my friend, I don't see the rest of your army."

"Meaning?"

"Meaning I don't see any of your compatriots zeroing in on me as we speak. That means that you and I might come to terms."

Bolan was about to speak, but then he saw his waitress weaving through the crowd as she balanced a tray of frosted mugs. She spun by him and dropped the lager gently in front of him before moving on to the next table.

Strashmir raised his glass. "A toast," he said, holding the glass out to Bolan.

"To what?" the warrior asked as he lifted his mug and stared hard at the good-natured assassin.

"To the future."

"To the future," Bolan agreed, clinking his beer mug against the wineglass. "However long or short it may be."

Strashmir laughed. "I was told you were a hard-headed sort, but not that you had a sense of humor. Of course, a lot of that has to do with the fact that most of the people who've met you weren't around to report on it later."

Bolan glanced around at the other tables. No one seemed to notice their conversation. Sometimes the best place to talk discreetly was right out in the open.

The clinking of glasses, the clattering of silverware and the low murmur of the crowd blended into one steady sound that masked their voices.

"You seem to know an awful lot about me," Bolan said.

"No doubt you know much about me. There are few secrets about my life. Many lies, but no secrets. For men like us, it's only natural to learn as much as you can about a target before you kill him—I'm speaking hypothetically, of course. I mean you no harm."

"How do I know that?"

"Because you're sitting here in casual dress in a nice cozy inn instead of lying flat out in a funeral parlor weighted down by all of your medals. A place I could have very easily sent you last night instead of leaving a message for you."

Bolan raised his eyebrows. "You've got some wrong information there. I'm not military."

"Maybe not now," Strashmir replied, "but you were. It shows. And it's my guess you've got a lot of medals for your mettle."

Bolan found himself if not liking the guy, at least admiring him. The Romanian showed no sign of subterfuge. He looked like a man who was ready to put all of his cards on the table and say "Take it or leave it."

But then again Strashmir apparently was a master at living out false personas. Here he was in a foreign country looking totally at ease. The man spoke English exceptionally well, but like many people who learned it as a second language, he was a bit too formal with its use, marking him as a foreigner.

Cass Strashmir was a man running for his life, and Bolan was the one supposed to take it. Could he do it now, he wondered, knowing that Strashmir had spared him?

"Getting back to last night," Bolan prompted.

"Yes?"

"What makes you so sure you could have got me?"

"Maybe you are correct," Strashmir said. "From what I recall, you never quite stayed still, and most of the time you managed to keep Whitelaw between you and the open spaces."

"Instinct."

"Justified. Add to that the fact that you *did* move at the last minute," Strashmir conceded. "And I don't know if I would have hit you—the first time."

Bolan looked out the front window where a group of kids was heading for the wishing well, running in wild loops around the tall oaks.

Such an innocent world. For some.

"All right," the Executioner said. "Granted that you weren't aiming at me. That was yesterday. Where do we stand today?"

"That's up to you."

"I guess it is." Bolan took a sip of the lager, then pushed it off to the side of the table. "So what's to keep me from taking you down here and now?"

"Simple. You want to know why I brought you here."

"I'm listening."

Strashmir slid his half-empty plate away, then leaned forward, elbows on the table, his clasped hands cradling his chin as he spoke in a somber voice.

"First let me tell you that though I am a hunted man, I am also an innocent man. As innocent as anyone can be in this business."

"I've heard that claim a hundred times before," Bolan commented.

"In my case it happens to be true. Most of the crimes I allegedly committed were actually carried out by people working for Lorenz, or else he had his people manufacture evidence implicating me."

"You have proof of that?"

"The proof lies in what happened to me," Strashmir said. "Lorenz was the only man in a position to do it. He had the connections inside Romania to incriminate me. Many of his associates still cling to their positions in Romania, but fortunately they are outnumbered by authorities who want to bring him to justice. They are the people I will bring my case to once this is all over."

"What would Lorenz hope to gain from doing this to you?"

"My services," Strashmir replied. "It also discredits any knowledge I have about his activities. Who would believe a man who seems as guilty as Lorenz? That left me no choice but to go underground, a path that ultimately led to him."

"And to me," Bolan added.

Strashmir studied his clasped hands for a moment, gathering his thoughts before answering. "I *could* have killed you last night, but there's a reason why I didn't."

"Why's that?"

"The killing wouldn't stop there," Strashmir said. "Lorenz has too many targets on his list."

"Who?"

"Harold Brognola, for one."

"Why him?" Bolan demanded, the hard edge returning to his voice.

Strashmir shrugged. "You know the old saying, cut off the head, the body will follow."

"Not in this case, guy. If any of Lorenz's people hit Brognola, I'll follow them until the day they die—and that'll be the day I find them. Guaranteed."

"I gathered as much," Strashmir said. "That's one of the reasons I want you as an ally instead of an enemy. Because sooner or later *I,* too, would end up as an enemy on that list and then both sides would be hunting me."

"Why would Lorenz turn on you?"

"Because he would think I was a danger to him and he would get rid of me—just as he wishes me to get rid of other people in his organization he no longer trusts.''

"Who else is on this wish list?"

"It grows longer all the time," Strashmir replied. "He's targeted Intelligence officers from many of the European services on his trail. He's also gunning for some influential people who wouldn't cooperate with him despite the pressure he put on them. He wants to make an example of them.''

"What kind of pressure?"

"Whatever works best on the individual," the assassin said. "The threat of exposure. Financial ruin. Remember, Lorenz spent his entire career gathering sensitive information on friends and enemies alike. And many of our current East European leaders and prominent businessmen—who so skillfully reinvent their pasts—were actually willing collaborators with the regimes in power.''

"And Lorenz has a long memory," Bolan suggested.

"In most cases a photographic memory. He has evidence to back up most of his threats. So when he sends one of his people to contact these leaders to remind them of their real past, most of them prove to be quite cooperative.''

"Does he send people like you?"

Strashmir pulled back, as if he were offended. "No, of course not. People like me—people like you—we are the final threat. And I refuse to kill innocent men.''

"As you suggested before," Bolan said, "innocence is a relative term."

"That is why I am here, to establish my innocence once and for all. I want to go back to Romania and clear my name, but to do that I have to remove certain obstacles in my way."

"The chief obstacle being Konrad Lorenz."

Strashmir nodded.

"Why don't you kill him yourself?"

"It's not that easy. Not yet. He travels with a small private army, and he keeps me separate from his other businesses. As far as I know, Axel Erhard is the only one of his associates who knows his other identities and his place of business. By shadowing Erhard, I've managed to narrow his headquarters down to somewhere in Munich. If I convince them I'm still after *your* head, sooner or later I'll be able to get Lorenz. Or, perhaps with your help—"

"We'll both get him."

"Then we understand each other," Strashmir concluded. "I help you get Konrad Lorenz. You help me get my good name back."

"We'll do whatever's possible to bring out the truth," Bolan told him. "No guarantees. If things don't work out the way you want, we can still provide you with new cover so you can start over."

"That's all I ask."

Bolan nodded. It was a done deal. In a way he felt as if he were dealing with a mirror image of himself. Like him, Strashmir was also a man on the run, a man of principle, someone who couldn't give up his private war.

"I've got a list of my own," Bolan said. "Maybe we should compare notes."

"Agreed. Let's take a walk and I'll tell you some things I think you should know."

Five minutes later Bolan and Strashmir stood by the wishing well outside the inn, talking as old friends might.

Or old soldiers.

Strashmir explained as much of the workings of the Underground Express as he understood, giving Bolan an assassin's eye view of the network—names, places, drop points and covers.

In return Bolan helped fill in pieces of the puzzle with some of the Intel he and Brognola had gathered. Together they created a murderous mosiac that featured Konrad Lorenz at the center.

From here on in, the plan was simple. And deadly.

With Strashmir's help, Bolan's people would hit the outposts of the Vampyr network, gradually working their way up the ranks until they could strike right at the very heart of the empire.

But it all depended on getting good information and being able to move fast. Lorenz wasn't going to be standing still while the walls came tumbling down around him.

CHAPTER TWENTY

Pools of rainwater from the recent storm covered the unevenly graveled yard of the East End warehouse. A quartet of empty semitrailers sat in the yard, propped up on steel support legs. Bright yellow light gleamed from the windows of the boxlike dispatcher's office that jutted out from the rest of the building.

Parked alongside the dock leading to the office was an empty flatbed trailer. Midway down the dock was a series of concrete ramps leading up to hinged wooden bay doors, tall enough for flatbeds to roll in and unload cargo.

Flanking the ramps were weathered lantern posts that stuck out like gallows poles from the warehouse wall.

To an average person who bothered to give the complex a second look, it seemed like one more struggling East End business by the docks, trying to stay alive.

But the two armed observers scoping the yard through the windshield of a "borrowed" truck cab knew better. They were parked a hundred yards away, just outside the tall metal fencing that surrounded the neglected-looking warehouse.

The Executioner sat behind the wheel in a black knit cap and a black leather jacket, looking like countless other drivers, sailors and dockworkers who plied their trade in the East End. Salvie was also in black, making the two of them look like a pair of mourners ahead of the fact.

They knew the crumbling exterior of the complex was just a facade for a thriving concern. In fact, the warehouse complex was one of the most profitable subsidiaries of Konrad Lorenz's Vampyr network.

In addition to serving as a storage facility for the stolen art objects plundered from across Europe, the complex also served as one of Lorenz's underground armories. Using his Intelligence connections to set up phoney end-user certificates indicating foreign destinations for the arms shipments, Lorenz was able to purchase high-quality armament that invariably ended up right in the warehouse.

In turn, Lorenz sold the weaponry to underworld contacts or armed his own troops with it, troops that were now quartered somewhere inside the warehouse and had been originally slated to join Cass Strashmir on his stakeout of the Executioner. Lorenz had sent some veterans of his European kill teams to help out with the London operation.

Strashmir had managed to put them off by telling them that if he failed to pick off the Executioner they would have the chance to go against the man one more time.

That time was now, Bolan thought.

The warrior had no doubt they had the right spot.

Shortly before his death, Whitelaw had hinted at the existence of such a place by the river where contraband came in by boat and truck. Whitelaw didn't know the exact location, only that it was near the East End docks.

Strashmir had provided the address, confirming Whitelaw's claim that such a place existed.

Mack Bolan and Gina Salvie made a visual confirmation through the night-vision scopes of the surveillance gear they'd brought with them.

For the past hour they'd been reconning the site, taking plenty of time to study the restless and heavily armed man on duty inside the dispatcher's office.

His face was familiar. The man was one of the Vampyr gunners they'd seen in Koblenz shortly before the battle at the château, a former East German "soldier" who'd been seconded to the London trafficking operation.

Midnight was approaching when Bolan scanned the grounds for the last time. If they waited much longer, they risked a changing of the guard and possible exposure of their position.

"You see any guard dogs yet?" Salvie asked, instinctively tapping the stainless-steel Navy Model 22 pistol she'd selected from the small arsenal that

Brognola's people had provided. Known as a Hush Puppy, the silenced weapon was designed to take care of attack dogs as quickly and quietly as modern technology allowed.

"Sorry to disappoint you," Bolan replied. "The only guard I see is the two-legged one in that office."

"There's probably a dog on the premises," she said. "All of these places have dogs."

"You really don't like dogs, do you?" Bolan said.

"Not all of them," Gina said. "Just the ones who bare their fangs at me like I'm their next dinner. I had more than my share of close calls. Anyway, even without dogs, there'll be plenty of fangs tonight. These Vampyrs have teeth."

"So do we."

Bolan switched on the ignition, shuddering the tractor cab into life. Flicking on the headlights as he shifted up through the gears, the Executioner cruised down the road and swung the cab wide through the open gates.

After their earlier recon of the site, they'd decided on a frontal assault. Sometimes the best cover was no cover at all.

The headlights staggered over the building as Bolan bounced the cab over the ruts toward the main office. With the brakes hissing against the huge tires on the rear axle, he rolled right up next to the office, rattling the windows with the high-idling engine.

The man inside swore at him and vaulted off his chair as if he'd been stung on the rear end, grabbing a denim work jacket as he rushed out of the office.

A few moments later the man ran across the rain-slicked gravel, his hastily donned jacket barely concealing the holstered automatic under his arm.

He pounded on the driver's side of the cab and shouted, "What the hell are you doing here?"

Bolan rolled the window down. "I'm here to make a pickup."

"The bloody hell you are. There's no freight moving tonight. In or out of this place."

"You're wrong there, mate," the warrior replied. "It's right here on this log." He tapped a finger on his clipboard, then shoved it out the window and dropped it into the startled man's hands. "See? Somebody called for a pickup. Where's the trailer?"

"Listen here," the man said, menace crackling in his voice as he struggled to maintain control. "I've been here all night, and I didn't make a call. You've come to the wrong place. Now haul outta here while you still can."

"Easy there, mate," Bolan said. "Okay, I made a mistake. Give me the clipboard and I'll be on my way."

"All right," the man replied, raising it toward the window.

Then a flying door hit him in the face as Bolan flung the driver's door open.

The guard tumbled backward, skidding on the loose gravel in a vain attempt to regain his balance. His left hand flapped wildly under him as he sank into one of the puddles.

Bolan landed a couple feet away, training his Beretta 93-R on the man's forehead.

The fallen guard came to life, arching both feet upward and out, kicking Bolan's left knee and collapsing it into his right with a bone-jarring knock.

"Watch out!" Salvie shouted, clinging on to the hold bar at the back of the cab body as she leaned out the open door, aiming the stainless-steel Hush Puppy at the man's chest. "He's going for his gun."

It wasn't news to Bolan.

Even as he moved with the momentum of the man's kick, spinning around to face the gunman, he saw the black metal sliding out its holster.

He'd wanted the man to talk.

But he wasn't going to die on the off chance he could reach him. Plus he didn't want the man's automatic to go off and alert the others inside the warehouse.

Bolan snapped off a silenced round and pushed off to the right. The 9 mm parabellum round drilled into the man's chest with a blood-letting splat that knocked him back down into the puddle.

The warrior grabbed the man by the jacket and lifted his deadweight out of the water, then searched him for keys.

"Nothing on him," he reported. "Let's check inside."

They hurried up a set of concrete stairs, then slipped quietly through a pair of cheap metal doors painted a drab utility green. The doors led to a long corridor with a small office complex on the right. Beyond that was a low-ceilinged garage full of forklifts, oil drums and stacks of pallets.

On the left of the corridor was a wide wooden door on rollers. It was barred, chained and padlocked.

"Pretty stiff security measures for a run-of-the-mill warehouse," Salvie commented.

"Yeah, but just about right for a *warehouse*."

They could force the door with a charge of plastique, but the blast would give the troops inside plenty of warning.

From the general layout of the place that Bolan had committed to memory from Strashmir's description, blowing the door off the hinges would be the quickest way in, but it might also guarantee they'd never come out. Too many gunmen were holed up inside, ready to go to war.

They had to get the keys to go in quietly or find another way inside the warehouse.

Bolan and Salvie hurried back down the corridor and carried out a quick search of the office, rummaging through the old and scarred metal desk drawers to no avail.

"He's either hidden the keys or he never had them," Bolan said, looking out the office window at the still-running cab. "I'd say we used up whatever grace period we have."

"We've got to get in there fast," she said.

"We go the hard way."

Half a minute later they were back outside, with Bolan lifting the guard's body up to the cab where Salvie sat, helping to haul him inside.

"I don't see what we need him for," the woman stated, grunting from the man's weight.

"He can help with the introductions," Bolan told her.

"What are you talking about?"

"If they see him behind the wheel, they might hold off firing for a few seconds until they figure out what's going on. That might be just the time we need."

She tugged once more until the corpse's legs were dangling in the air and he was sitting halfway on the seat. "Maybe you're right. It just seems kind of ghoulish."

"He's not complaining, is he? Besides, if it was up to him, *we'd* be dead by now."

"Uh-huh," she said, unconvinced and unhappy at the prospect of riding shotgun for a dead man.

"Got him?" Bolan asked.

"Yeah. He's being really cooperative."

Bolan slammed the driver's door, then hurried around to the passenger side. After they propped the slain guard against the driver's side window, the warrior squeezed behind the steering wheel and put the vehicle into gear.

He drove back out into the middle of the yard, dimming the lights as he zeroed in on one of the concrete ramps.

"Get out the gear."

Salvie nodded. She pushed through the curtain and reached back into the sleeper compartment to take out a Heckler & Koch MP-5 submachine gun and two combat vests with well-stuffed pockets.

Then she reached back again and pulled out the M-203 grenade launcher with armor-piercing loads.

"Hold on," he said.

The Executioner stepped on the gas pedal as he worked the clutch, shifting gears rapidly until the cab's engine was whining and roaring in high speed as it sailed up the concrete ramp.

The metal grille on the square blunt nose of the vehicle broke through the wooden door as if it were paper, sending the hinged sections pinwheeling into the air.

The chromed vertical exhaust on top of the cab broke in two pieces when it hit the top of the splintering doorway, billowing clouds of smoke into the air.

Other than that, the damage was minimal.

The sound was maximum. But before the kill crew could gather its wits and weapons, the cab was in the middle of the warehouse, breathing like a battered dragon as it filled the air with fumes and fury.

The vehicle came to a screeching halt at the base of a huge stack of palleted crates, spilling them onto the floor with a thunderous crash. The crates split open and the contents skated on the smooth concrete floor, long-barreled automatic rifles spinning end over end like black metal *I Ching* sticks cast on the floor.

Shouts echoed from all corners of the warehouse as the hardmen who were quartered inside quickly responded to the breach of their temporary stronghold.

Footsteps clattered on the catwalks and platforms that ringed the upper stories of the warehouse. Soft-soled shoes skidded and scuffed on the grime-and-soot-covered floor as several of them converged on the tractor cab.

Sitting in the dim light that spilled into the warehouse through the smashed doorway, the cab looked like a chrome-toothed behemoth, the dim parking lights staring like eyes into the darkness.

"Turn on the lights!" one of the men shouted.

"Not yet!" another man replied.

"We've got to see what we're dealing with. Turn the goddamn lights on—"

"Might as well paint a bull's-eye on your head while you're at it," a gruff, authoritative voice said, growing louder and closer with each passing second.

"Wait until I give the word. Until then we got lights of our own."

A babble of East European voices joined the clamor, many of them sounding Slavic or Romanian.

Suddenly a half-dozen flashlight beams seared through the darkness, crisscrossing in the mote-filled shadows around the cab and striking brilliant reflections onto the chrome work as the first teams converged on the scene.

In the ambient light that lit up the immediate area around the loudly idling cab, it was easy to see that many automatic weapons pointed at the driver's window.

Some of the flashlights were mounted on top of revolvers or automatic rifles, with the beams targeting the path the bullets would follow.

Magazine clips snicked into place. Safety switches came off. Full-auto came on.

The grim-faced men nearing the cab still showed the effects of shock, although the surprise was slowly wearing off. They'd been jolted out of sleep, pulled out of late-night card games or hauled away from bouts with whiskey and wine bottles, the usual activities pursued by mercs the world over while they were waiting to be thrown into action.

Tonight it had come to them.

Their training showed in the way they approached the cab in a rapidly closing circle that cut off any avenues of escape. They were ready to fight.

They just didn't know whom they were fighting.

Then one of the flashlights spotlighted the face of the driver in the glass.

"Hold your fire!" shouted the man in command. "That's Berlitz in the cab. What the hell's he doing?"

"Must be crazy—"

"Or drunk. Bastard's been drinking again."

"He'll get himself killed screwing around like that. Get his ass down from there."

One of the men grabbed the hold bar on the side of the cab and pulled himself up to look into the window. "He *did* get himself killed!" he shouted. "He's been shot!"

While the words echoed in the warehouse bay like a low-rent requiem, the Executioner stepped out of the shadows between two tall stacks of palleted crates and aimed the M-203 grenade launcher at the truck cab.

In a practiced and simple movement the Executioner judged the trajectory of the armor-piercing round, then pulled the trigger.

The 40 mm round blasted from the muzzle and impacted against its target.

An atomic blast ripped through the fuel tank below the cab door, just above the running bar where one of the unlucky mercs happened to be standing.

He went up like a rocket, flame sprouting up his body and consuming him in a hideous scorch and crackle as his burned body was blown in the air.

The tremendous flash and roar from the explosion wiped out the first ranks of the hardmen who'd circled in on the cab, scattering them like ashes.

Fiery sheets of flame licked and stabbed at the clothes of the men in the second ranks.

As their clothes caught fire, they ran back from the blast like flame-ridden scarecrows, screaming.

Their cries of agony were drowned out by a second blast as the cab came down on its side, cracking open the reserve fuel tank.

The concussive force of the explosion shook the warehouse bay and blew out the windows at rooftop level, one after the other crashing in shattering harmony.

Some of the panic-stricken men fired their automatic rifles in wild bursts that emptied their weapons in a few short seconds, just long enough to cut down some of their own people who were immobilized by shock.

A few of the men instinctively turned toward the source of the 40 mm grenade and chopped away at Bolan's kill zone with controlled bursts.

The bullets seared through the darkness like steel rivets and ate into the wooden crates right where the Executioner had been standing a few moments earlier.

But now the warrior was at floor level, hugging the concrete while bullets and splinters flew overhead.

Gina Salvie stepped out from another aisle of crates and fired broadside at the gunmen who'd opened up on Bolan.

Using the afterimages of the flashes from their weapons to zero in on the gunmen, she took them down with deadly precision.

The muffled chop of the Heckler & Koch submachine gun drilled three of the riflemen at waist level, kicking them off their feet and into an untidy heap on the floor. A fourth man shouted out that he was wounded, then scuffled away into the darkness.

Salvie's covering fire gave Bolan enough time to scramble to his feet, keeping low while he burned off a clip from the M-16 barrel above the grenade launcher. Then he ducked back out of sight and slapped a fresh magazine into the assault rifle.

In the midst of all the carnage one of the hardmen managed to flick on the light switches on the side wall of the warehouse. Overhead fluorescent lights blinked into ghastly yellow brilliance one by one, except for the strip of lighting above the exploded cab, which sizzled and crackled in electronic death throes.

Looking up, Bolan spotted a man on a catwalk to his left, bearing down on Gina with a shotgun. The Executioner fired from the hip and triggered a burst at the catwalk, spraying the metal grate with lead.

The shotgunner managed to pull the trigger, but by then he was deadweight in free-fall, tumbling headfirst toward the floor. Two barrels of buckshot smacked harmlessly into the warehouse wall.

Bolan triggered another burst at the overhead lights, casting a few of them back into darkness with a loud crash of glass shielding and tubing. Then he headed toward Salvie, who was facing him with the Heckler & Koch to cover his back.

"Get down!" she shouted.

A split second before she fired a burst over his head, Bolan dived forward, sailing parallel to the floor. He landed hard on the concrete, scraping his chin with a teeth-crunching, flesh-shredding jolt.

It hurt like hell, but the man who'd been sneaking up behind him was hurting a lot worse now that he was carrying a trio of 9 mm slugs in his body.

The numbers had reached zero.

More time spent in the warehouse was killing time.

The shocked troops would be recovering their wits and preparing to launch a counterattack any moment now. Reinforcements might be on the way and perhaps even a small army of riot police. No matter what kind of contraband and armament were found on the site, the authorities wouldn't take kindly to having covert wars fought on their territory.

They'd delivered a message to Konrad Lorenz loud and clear. He could be hit hard wherever he set up shop. And sooner or later he'd be hit right on the home front.

"Move, move, move," Bolan shouted as he scrambled to his feet and raced down the left side of the warehouse.

But Salvie was already in motion, leading the way down the left side of the warehouse until she came to a fire door that was barred and padlocked.

She blew off the lock with a burst from the Heckler & Koch. Then, as Bolan pushed back the wooden bar, she kicked out with her right foot and knocked the door wide open until it slammed onto the outside wall.

They sprinted across the outside dock, leaped into the air like long jumpers, then came down running on the gravel yard. They headed straight for the back fence, slinging their weapons over their shoulders on the run.

Once they hit the fence Bolan and Salvie scrambled up the chain links like hard-core rockers crashing a concert.

Their feet smacked down on a hard dirt road outside the complex. Running in the dark, their breath coming in loud gasps, feet pounding on the pavement, the pair reached the Ford station wagon parked alongside the road without being seen.

They drove off slowly, winding their way back into the East End like a couple of night crawlers looking for some hell to raise.

A half hour later they pulled into a gas station, just long enough for Bolan to place a call to Inspector Newhall's office at New Scotland Yard. His previous call had alerted the inspector to the treasure trove he'd find at Whitelaw's mansion.

This one alerted him to the kill site they'd find at the warehouse, along with enough explanation to link it to Whitelaw and the Underground Express.

Then they drove southeast of London, heading toward Folkestone, where they'd booked a room in a bed and breakfast.

Their London excursion was over.

In the morning they'd take the ferry to France.

And then they'd take the war to Konrad Lorenz.

CHAPTER TWENTY-ONE

As dusk fell on the southern tier of the Black Forest in the middle of German wine country, Gus Sinclair sat in the crook of a wide oak tree like an electronic owl, his eyesight boosted by the high-powered Spy-lux Night Scope. To avoid detection, he was careful to move the scope slowly as he scanned the wooded terrain surrounding Roadhouse International, one more stop on the Underground Express.

He felt cramped from holding the position for so long, but that was an occupational hazard in his line of work. He'd found himself in the same position more times than he could count in his career as a newsman out to get a story.

But the information Sinclair and his crew were gathering this day wasn't for broadcast on one of the television networks that usually picked up his features.

Like all of the other reports they'd filed, the latest bulletins were going to a small but exclusive audience in Frankfurt, where Hal Brognola was coordinating the Europe-wide operation.

The Intelligence they'd previously collected on the BolksHaus recording studio outside of Vienna led them to its corporate cousins scattered across Austria, Czechoslovakia and Germany.

Each piece of the puzzle led to another stakeout.

Sinclair's people constantly fed videotape and surveillance photos to Frankfurt to keep Brognola up-to-date with their targets and movements. In turn, Brognola's people processed the Intel and sent the analysis and identification back out into the field, along with reports that came in from Bolan's end of the operation.

Soon they would act on all that Intel.

Sinclair glanced left and right, studying the rest of his "documentary" crew, who were spread out through the woods. Even though he knew their positions and their woodland-style camouflage that blended in with Norway spruce and fir trees, it was still difficult to pick them out right away.

They were silent statues perfectly blending in with their surroundings, a skill required by both news crews and Intelligence teams. At the moment they were acting as both, carrying SMGs and small arms, as well as their lightweight camera and sound equipment.

More weaponry and gadgetry was packed inside the small caravan of surveillance vans and Jeeps parked in the crowded lot of a winery on the Badische Weinstrasse where Sinclair had stationed a skeleton crew. Positioned midway on the "wine road" from Baden-Baden to Offenburg, the winery gave guided tours to tourists several times a day—and now and then to one of Sinclair's operatives.

From the winery Sinclair's field team had moved through the Black Forest on foot so they could come up on their target from the shelter of the woods.

Black Forest pines formed a postcard backdrop to the cluster of cathedral-roofed homes set back into the woods. A flat-roofed garage off to the side sheltered an eccentric assortment of tour buses, customized vans and delivery trucks that all bore the logo of Roadhouse International.

Roadhouse International was a full-service operation that provided roadies, engineers, transportation and lodging for touring musical groups.

Positioned close to Germany's southern border with Switzerland and its western border with France, the company was in the ideal position to move people and equipment back and forth across the international boundaries.

Some of the tour buses were new and looked as if they carried every creature comfort known to man. Others were restored and wildly painted old school buses with psychedelic murals on every square inch that wasn't covered by windows.

One of the buses had been converted into a rolling home with cedar siding and a peaked roof with skylights. It looked like a high-tech commune.

But the men Sinclair's crew had sighted on those rare moments when they stepped out of the buildings were definitely not the peace-and-love sort.

Brognola's Frankfurt team had identified one of the drivers for Roadhouse International as a former internal-security officer with the East German frontier troops during the cold war era. His name was Dolphe Hunsruck, a tall man with an aquiline nose and a long, storklike visage. He'd supervised troop activity in the land-mined and barbwired security zones along the border between East and West Germany. He'd also served a stint with Axel Erhard in the Stasi and apparently had taken part in several Stasi-related swindles that made him a wanted man.

When the Iron Curtain had come down, Hunsruck was one of the first to flee to the West. Erhard had used his connections to find a new identity for the man, as well as a new life with Konrad Lorenz's organization.

It was a life that might soon come to an end.

Using directional and laser mikes to eavesdrop on the Roadhouse crew, Sinclair's people had learned that Hunsruck was a marked man. His colleagues thought he was too erratic, too close to the edge. Apparently Hunsruck didn't respond well to the midnight roll calls that often sent him across borders as a bodyguard or an enforcer. The same went for the more dangerous orders that had him deliver shipments in desolate destinations.

Hunsruck was cracking from the strain, despite his inglorious past with the secret police.

The German had achieved a ruthless reputation during his years with the frontier troops for his unyielding enforcement of the shoot-to-kill orders in the security zone. Hunsruck was directly responsible for the deaths of his own countrymen who'd risked everything to escape East Germany.

But something in Hunsruck had snapped when he went underground with Lorenz's people. In the old days he at least had official sanction for his murderous acts. Back then he could always shift the blame for his crimes to the state and claim he was only following orders. But now he had no one but himself to blame.

The others considered him a risk, someone who might go over to the other side at any time, revealing everything he knew about the Vampyr network in exchange for clemency.

Sinclair's surveillance crew had heard the others talking about "dealing with" or "removing" Hunsruck from the operation. But they hadn't heard how or when.

But if Hunsruck wanted an out, Sinclair would give it to him. The next time the German made one of his runs, the "documentary" crew would cut him from the herd.

Brognola had given the newsman the green light to move from surveillance mode to intervention. They'd already gathered as much Intel on the Roadhouse operation as they could. So far, there'd been no direct connection to Konrad Lorenz or Axel Erhard.

Movement from one of the cathedral-roofed houses drew Sinclair's attention. He swept the Spy-lux toward the front door in time to see Hunsruck and another man appear on the threshold. Both men headed toward the garage where the buses and delivery trucks were parked.

Hunsruck stopped in back of a delivery truck that resembled an armored car. It had reinforced metal siding and narrow security windows that covered all angles from inside the truck.

This was it, Sinclair thought.

But then the two men lit up cigarettes. They were just killing time.

The newsman watched for several more minutes until the men turned back to the house.

He heard someone moving behind him, softly calling his name at the edge of his perception. Turning, he saw three of his men heading his way. The changing of the guards.

Good, Sinclair thought. He'd been out there so long he felt as if he were taking root.

Sinclair silently dropped from his perch, slightly scraping his wrists on the rough bark. His feet stirred a clump of leaves at the base of the tree as he headed to the relief team.

HAUSACH, TRIBERG, Furtwangen—the Roadhouse International truck rolled through the small Black Forest towns that had kept the past alive in the Old

World architecture of cottages and cathedrals with lofty spires towering above the treetop horizons.

Hunsruck drove at a fast clip past the villas and vineyards, the scenery painfully familiar to him from his previous runs through the southern reaches of the Black Forest toward the Swiss border.

Just past Furtwangen he took the east road that would eventually bring him to Lake Constance. There he would hand off the latest cargo of contraband to one more shadowy group connected to the Vampyr network.

Whatever the cargo was, weapons or stolen art objects, it was well hidden inside crates of musical equipment and huge speakers. Hidden well enough to pass a cursory inspection, he hoped. His chances of getting off with a light sentence would be a lot greater if he came in voluntarily and not as a low-level smuggler caught by the authorities.

His mood darkened with the fall of night.

He felt trapped. His own people were turning against him, and the enemy was getting closer all the time.

Though Erhard tried to hide it, rumors of the network's losses in Vienna, London and elsewhere were on everyone's lips. The Intelligence services and their action arms were closing in on Lorenz's ring.

Sooner or later one side or the other would get Hunsruck. It was inevitable, he thought.

Most likely his own people would get him first. Lately the signs were obvious that they didn't trust him, almost as if they could read his mind. More and more they'd been doubling on him wherever he went. One rider would come along with him to supposedly help guard the cargo, but Hunsruck knew it was really to guard *him*.

He knew the routine. It was the same as when he had run frontier troops at the border. One member of the two-man patrol units was always a fanatic marksman, loyal to the end. The fanatic would always be paired with a less trustworthy partner in case the partner had to be shot for not following orders—or if the partner tried to make *his* escape across the border.

Lately Hunsruck had had a lot of partners.

Tonight was the first run in a long time that he'd been allowed to operate on his own. Maybe they were trusting him again, he thought. Maybe he should make a run for it....

Hunsruck spun the wheel easily as the winding road made a sharp turn to the right. He knew all the dangerous curves, having committed the familiar route to memory. He knew every farmhouse perched close to the road that slashed through the legendary forest, the setting for so many fairy tales.

Ogres were still haunting these woods, Hunsruck thought, roles well filled by him and the other Vampyr soldiers.

The road followed a serpentine course as it passed a small lake encircled by chalets and an old-style tavern with a stone-and-timber facade. Just past the tavern came a tough stretch, with a lot of sudden dips and steep climbs.

Hunsruck gunned the truck up a long and steep hill, feeling the engine buck and strain from the effort. Even without the extra weight of the armored plates, the engine would have had a tough time of it. All of the trucks had seen a lot of service since Hunsruck came aboard the Underground Express.

A sudden gust of wind chopped through the half-open window on the driver's side. Cold with moisture from the nearby lake, it matched the chilly bitterness of his heart.

He felt drowsy all of a sudden, as if the wind itself had worn him down. It was an odd sensation that he'd never felt before, like an illness coming on all at once with no warning.

He was tired.

Tired and trapped in a no-man's land.

As he wound down a dark stretch of road cut off from the lake by tall trees with curling boughs blocking out the moonlight, he felt even more isolated from the men he worked for—and the man he used to be. A man who used to give orders instead of taking them.

After another ten minutes of driving, Hunsruck felt tears rolling down his cheeks. It was from the wind, he told himself. Only the wind.

The smell of the cold spring air and forest filled the inside of the truck.

A storm was coming, he thought. The wild, bristling wind was stronger than usual this night, strong enough to blow open the gates of sadness he'd kept closed for so long.

Something was wrong.

He felt dizzy.

Sweat beaded his forehead.

His arms were full of kinetic spasms that caused him to clench and unclench his hands on the steering wheel.

The forest seemed to grow before his eyes, tall dark trees jumping out at him, then falling back with only the long branches lingering behind as shadows on the windshield.

Cold, he thought.

Too cold.

An inner cold was freezing him from the inside out.

He stomped on the accelerator, and the boost of speed jerked the truck wildly around a curve. The wind rushed in through the windows, carrying the sounds of branches hissing in the wind, passing secrets. Secrets about him. Everyone was talking about him, plotting his death.

This was crazy!

He couldn't keep track of his thoughts anymore. Too many of them came floating out of the recesses of his mind.

As if he'd been drugged . . .

Oh, God in heaven, he thought, drugs!

They'd used some kind of drug on him.

And now he knew why they'd let him drive alone on this run. It was a one-way ride. It made a sick kind of sense. The East Bloc services were masters at creating "accidental" deaths to get rid of their enemies. It was their preferred method of removing enemy agents, as well as suspected double agents of their own.

With the KGB's help, the Intelligence services had created a wizard's brew of chemicals that would do the job: poison-tipped umbrellas that gave the victim a slight scratch at the time of impact, a scratch that hours later would lead to excruciating pain as the poison worked its way through the system; powders sprinkled on clothes that would eventually work their way into the victim's system.

And then there were the drugs used on prisoners for interrogation purposes, drugs that opened up a prisoner's mind so far that it could never close again.

Drugs to wake them, drugs to put them to sleep, he thought. And drugs to make them go out of their mind.

As he drove along the darkening road, he felt his senses start to dim. It felt as if a shroud of nothingness was starting to wrap him up in a strange cocoon.

The Vampyr operative wondered what drug his "friends" had used on him and how they'd slipped it to him.

Food?

Drink?

Powder?

But then Hunsruck realized it didn't matter how they'd given it to him. Unless he managed to counter its effects, soon nothing would matter at all.

SINCLAIR'S DRIVER found himself tapping the accelerator to keep up with the wildly rocketing truck he was tailing. The surveillance caravan had discreetly hung back ever since they had picked up Hunsruck when he left the headquarters of Roadhouse International.

Traffic was light on the Black Forest road, and now and them, to avoid detection as they pulled closer to the armored delivery truck, they turned off the headlights.

So far, they'd had little trouble keeping up with the truck.

But now it was a killing pace.

"What should we do?" the driver asked.

"Keep up with him," Sinclair replied, studying the truck through the Spylux viewer.

"He's driving crazy," the man behind the wheel said. "Like he's drunk out of his mind."

"Or scared. Maybe he made us. Stick with him until he goes off the road. Or until we have to stop him."

Sinclair picked up the radio transceiver and passed the word to the rest of the cars to keep up.

Then he sat back for the ride.

It was out of his hands now. It was totally up to his driver. Marty Deacon, who'd been keeping him alive for the past ten years, taking him through war zones and resorts alike, was in command when it came to getting them to where they had to go.

A cloud of exhaust plumed in the road ahead, smoke signals from an engine pushed beyond its capacity.

"God, look at him go now," Deacon said. "He's practically flying. Hold on to your shorts, Gus."

AXEL ERHARD'S strike force gathered at the side of the road, bordering the edge of one of the tourist paths that led into the Black Forest. Their vehicles were covered with brush and shadows.

The force had come up from the Lake Constance retreat for a rendezvous at the Roadhouse International headquarters near Offenburg. From there the combined strike teams would move against a target to be determined by Konrad Lorenz.

As usual, Lorenz kept his plans to himself, willing to unveil them only at the last possible moment. Only when Erhard called in to Lorenz would he learn the purpose of assembling another underground army.

In a way Erhard didn't mind. That took the responsibility off him. If there were failures—and lately there'd been several—he could place the blame on the Vampyr chief himself.

Erhard would find out soon enough what the target was.

But before they completed the drive up to the rendezvous, there was a small matter of business to be taken care of.

They had to confirm the "accidental" death of Hunsruck. Not only was this going to be Hunsruck's last ride, but it was also going to be the last ride for Roadhouse International.

The company had been in operation too long. Lorenz had determined that several Intelligence agents were looking into the corporate structure that bankrolled Roadhouse International and some of the other front companies.

Sooner or later the company would come under intense scrutiny along with the people who worked for it.

The company had to die.

Soon the body of Dolphe Hunsruck himself would be all that remained.

Shortly after his death, anonymous sources would send documents to the authorities that would implicate Hunsruck as the mastermind behind the operation.

And Lorenz would start another operation elsewhere.

Perfect, Erhard thought.

Almost perfect.

Hunsruck hadn't made his appearance yet. Or actually, Erhard thought, his *disappearance*.

Five minutes later, a bit ahead of his usual schedule, Dolphe Hunsruck made his fateful appearance.

"Here he comes," Bauman whispered.

Erhard glanced over at his lieutenant, who was crouched on top of the front hood of his Fiat like a gargoyle. Bauman was facing west with a predatory look on his face that reminded Erhard of a dog pricking his ears toward the sound of some unexpected intruder.

A moment later Erhard heard the whining engine of the truck as it made its chaotic approach through the woods, headlights stabbing out of the darkness.

Erhard waited calmly.

He felt like an ambulance chaser waiting for the planned accident to happen.

The truck whipped by in a metallic blur.

And then a short time later a convoy appeared on the road. It was composed of fast-moving vans and cars that were obviously trailing Hunsruck.

"No one was supposed to follow him," Erhard said.

"They're not our people," Bauman replied. "I passed on your orders myself. No one was to leave until we got there."

"Then who the hell are they?"

Bauman shook his head.

Somebody already had Roadhouse International under surveillance, and that meant they were very close to Konrad Lorenz's other operations.

Erhard shook his head. Lately he'd felt that on some occasions he was being observed. He'd done everything he could to shake any possible tail, and never noticed anything amiss. Earlier he thought that meant it was all in his imagination.

But now he thought whoever had been following him was too good to be detected.

A man with long experience and a solid covert reputation.

There were few candidates Erhard could think of, but Cass Strashmir was on the top of the list.

It seemed that ever since the Romanian had come on board, things had been falling apart at an alarming rate.

Could Strashmir be a mole? he wondered. Was the wanted assassin actually working for the other side?

Probably. And even if he wasn't, this was a good chance to get rid of him. After all, Konrad Lorenz had been depending too much on the Romanian assassin lately.

A man like that could be dangerous.

As the last car passed by, Erhard called over the rest of his men and outlined his plans for the newcomers.

Hunsruck was still going to die as planned.

But now he would have unexpected company joining him at his next and final destination.

THE WIND HOWLED through the windows in a rising and descending shriek, blending with the whine of the tires.

The eerie sounds increased Hunsruck's panic, and finally it was too much for the man to bear.

"Stop!" Hunsruck shouted.

For a moment everything was still and quiet, and he was in control again.

But then the trees came to life once more, whispering and hissing as he passed.

He floored the gas pedal, as if the added speed could help him outrace the hallucinations.

The crates in the back of the truck slid back and forth, crashing into the walls in a discordant cadence as the vehicle skidded around the curves.

Something ran into the road, black, shadowy and primordial, conjured up from the splintering borders of his mind and plunked down right in the middle of the road.

Part of him realized that the shadow was the last-ditch effort of his instinct for self-preservation, summoning up any image that would make him stop.

Part of him listened.

He slammed on the brakes.

The screeching agony of the tires chased away the shadow. The truck stopped dead in the middle of the road, sitting in a cloud of burned rubber.

Dolphe Hunsruck didn't know who he was, nor where he was.

All he knew was that he had to get away. He hunched his tall frame over the steering wheel and held tight as he pressed the pedal down to the floor.

The truck groaned, its nose skidding and shaking like a wild animal springing from its cage.

He felt as if he were flying as the truck whipped around an S-shaped curve.

Hunsruck looked down at the speedometer, but he couldn't read the numbers. All he could focus on was the red arrow banging against the far end of the meter. It looked like a second hand on a clock that was stuck in place, but still kept ticking.

Time was stopping for him, he thought. Time was stopping forever.

As the heavily armored truck reached the end of the sharply curving loop, it continued straight ahead, off the road and over a slight ravine.

Everything seemed to slow down as Hunsruck sat in the driver's seat watching the trees grow larger.

Then all of a sudden the sharp treetops of the Black Forest were sprouting up before him.

Hunsruck had a fleeting grasp of sanity again, a brief moment where the inner workings of the world suddenly seemed so clear to him. It was very simple. He was hurtling through the air in the front of tons of metal, and his world was about to come to an end.

The trees blurred by him, branches slapping at the truck like outstretched hands.

His senses were shattered, but his body was still moving on automatic pilot.

Hunsruck clutched at the handle and flung open the door as the momentum carried the truck forward. He jumped, then felt himself spinning in the air like a kite with no string.

A jagged spruce tip speared through his groin. He opened his mouth to scream, but the impact levered him forward until his face splattered against the bark.

CHAPTER TWENTY-TWO

Gus Sinclair was jerked back into the leather cushion of the Volvo's passenger seat as Deacon accelerated uphill.

The truck they'd been tailing had vanished.

"Where could it go?" Sinclair said.

"Could've turned off."

"Not at this speed."

"Right," Deacon said, more intent on closing the gap to the spot where the truck had vanished than guessing what had happened to it.

The high beams of the Volvo lanced into the sky as it crested the hill, then illuminated the first loop of an S-shaped curve.

Behind the lead car came the vans and vehicles of the rest of the surveillance team.

And now all of them were chasing shadows.

One moment the truck had been there, the next it was gone. It could mean anything. Maybe the driver had spotted them, or maybe it was a trap.

Whatever it was, Sinclair planned on being ready for it. He unholstered his 9 mm Colt Commander and sat back calmly in the passenger seat like a man getting ready to go to work.

The Volvo hurtled out of the loop, then started to race down a long straightaway splashed with patches of moonlight that streamed through the trees.

"Stop!" Sinclair said. "There it is."

"Where?" Deacon asked, slowing and pulling over to the side of the road.

"Back there." The newsman pointed behind him at the wall of forest that stood a short distance from the last curve. "The truck didn't make the turn."

As Deacon came to a full stop on the shoulder, Sinclair radioed the location of the crashed truck to the other cars. Then the driver slowly backed toward the curve where the rest of the convoy was converging.

"Right down there." Sinclair indicated a spot in the woods where moonlight shone on the metal panels of the Roadhouse International truck.

It was flat on its side, wedged in the midst of the broken and splintered cluster of oak and spruce it had smashed through. The path of ruin was easy to see from the edge of the road.

Sinclair grabbed a flashlight from the glove compartment and went to take a look.

Behind him the other cars came to a stop one by one. Car doors slammed, and several of the men ran out to join Sinclair on his downhill trek.

Stepping carefully in the wake of the mowed-down trees, the newsman approached the truck and peered inside the smashed glass at the driver's seat. Then he scanned the nearby woods.

There was no sign of the driver.

Deacon's footsteps sounded loudly through the brush as he moved off to the side of the truck and began shining his flashlight in the wall of trees.

"Oh God!" he shouted. "Up there." Deacon's voice cracked with pity as he spoke, a sound that Sinclair had heard only rarely during the time he knew the hardheaded driver.

Sinclair stepped through the brush, pausing for a moment when a sharp oak branch snagged his jacket. Then he reached Deacon's side and looked up at the grisly sight.

Dolphe Hunsruck was hanging upside down from the tree, with a bloodstained branch protruding from his back.

His upper torso was twisted around on the branch that impaled him so his face was looking down at them.

Hunsruck's face was ruined. But his eyes were still open, glowing in the light of the flashlight beam, showing a horrendous look of surprise and anger, as if he'd realized something freakish had happened to him. Hunsruck was the most shocked dead man Sinclair had ever seen.

"Over here," the newsman called to the rest of his men. "We found our man."

"Poor bastard," one of the approaching men commented.

"Didn't have a chance," someone else added.

"He did it himself the way he was driving," Deacon said. "Practically killed himself."

"No," Sinclair contradicted. "It doesn't make sense. He started out driving just fine, then all of a sudden he just went haywire, like someone pressed a switch in him."

"Or on the truck. Could be someone tinkered with it so it'd go out of control." He looked over the chassis of the wrecked truck, flashing his light on the brake line and the axle. "Can't see anything yet, but if you ask me, he was set up. This is what we heard them planning."

"Yeah, well, we'll have to let the GSG-9 boys figure out what happened for sure," Sinclair said. "Maybe they can find out something from his system. We sure as hell can't learn anything much from him."

"One of our best leads is gone."

The newsman shrugged. "There are others we can follow up on. Same place where we got Hunsruck. I'd say it's time we head back to the garage and move in on the rest of his people."

"Right," Deacon said. "The way our luck's going, they'll all start killing themselves before we get there."

Sinclair spent a few minutes looking around the truck and examining some of the contents of the crates that had cracked open from the impact of the crash.

Automatic weapons. Night scopes. Silencers. Not a big shipment, he thought. But it was enough to implicate Dolphe Hunsruck in gunrunning. Nice and neat. Maybe too neat. He'd been in the game long enough to suspect anything that came all wrapped up in a nice-looking package.

It looked as though Hunsruck had been all wrapped up as a sacrificial goat.

And his altar was a tree in the middle of the Black Forest.

Sinclair shook his head, then looked uphill where the parade of covert cars had assembled at the side of the road.

While one of the men filmed the site with a small video recorder, the others started to move back uphill.

Sinclair was two steps behind Deacon when the driver came to a standstill at the top of the hill.

A piece of his head flew backward in a fountain of blood, bone and gray matter.

Deacon's arms spread out wide, then dropped back to his sides as he toppled over like a falling tree. He slid downhill with a growing red splotch glistening in the middle of his forehead.

The sounds of suppressed autofire filled the woods as muzzle-flashes streaked through the woods like fireworks.

Bullets drilled into the vans and cars parked on the side of the road, sounding like a metal hailstorm.

Windshields cracked and imploded from the relentless assault of automatic fire.

"Get down! Get down!" Sinclair shouted. "Away from the cars." But his words were lost in the chaos that fell upon the men in the woods. And those still capable of hearing had already turned away from the roadside.

As Sinclair dropped to the earth, he heard the hideous sound of lead slicing through the air overhead.

Everywhere he looked he saw men falling.

His men.

He heard the awful impacts of bullets thwacking into flesh, followed by the surprised gasps of the men who'd been hit.

Branches hissed and crashed to the forest floor. Splintered pieces of bark fell like shale when the automatic fire chewed into the forest.

A black shape was silhouetted on the edge of the hill for a moment as one of the men fired down in Sinclair's general direction. The newsman tracked him by reflex and squeezed the trigger of the colt twice, feeling it buck in his hand—and seeing the gunman drop dead back onto the road.

Sinclair fired once more at another shape, hearing a man shout out as he spun around wounded.

From his left and right he saw other flashes of fire shooting toward the road, but not as many as he'd hoped.

Not enough men were left to repulse the attack.

The assault had taken them by such surprise that several crucial seconds passed before any of Sinclair's men could return fire on the ambushers who'd decimated their ranks.

But that brought only an increased response from the attackers, who now could zero in on the scattered men trapped in the gully. Bullets scorched the air in front of them, and a nearly impenetrable forest blocked their retreat.

The hit team was moving in for the kill, swarming across the road and firing from between the cars. From their new vantage point they concentrated their fire on the remnants of Sinclair's surveillance team.

The newsman spotted vehicles speeding down the road and realized reinforcements for the hit team were on the way. More and more cars arrived on the scene, lights out, doors opening and shutting quickly as the gunmen poured out.

Sinclair gave the order to pull back, but he didn't hear any responses.

God! No one was left. Or else they were keeping quiet in hopes that the hit team would pass them by.

How had this happened? he wondered. Had they walked right into the trap? Had he led his people to their deaths?

The thoughts passed away quickly. If Sinclair stayed there much longer and tried to piece it together, he'd be dead.

He stepped back into the woods, trying not to make too much noise as he pushed through the closely grown trees. He held the Colt in front of him, ready to take down the first man to reach him.

The ambushers were moving in unison, dark shapes pressing forward and firing deeper into the forest, then securing the position before they headed out again to repeat the process.

It was a military-style raid, lightning fast with killing results.

Sinclair forced himself into a state of calm that was totally at odds with the situation he found himself in. It was as if this wasn't happening to him, and he was watching the assault from a vantage point high above.

As a cluster of the gunners passed by, their submachine guns searching left and right, Sinclair slowly tracked them with the dull black barrel of the Colt.

They walked past him.

He exhaled quietly and forced his heartbeat to slow. Then he continued backing away from the hunting party.

AXEL ERHARD SURVEYED the battleground as he walked through the tall grass like an exterminator. The sound suppressor on his short-barreled 9 mm Walther MPK nosed from left to right, ready to fire at anything that moved in the small clearing ahead of him.

Four more of his men were spread out on both flanks, scanning the ground with the automatic weapons.

The clearing was hilly with several dips and short drop-offs, and now and then rounded mounds of earth loomed up like burial mounds.

Erhard raised his hand for silence.

They stood for a long minute listening for any sound that might tip them off to their quarry. Then Erhard gave the signal to move forward again.

They'd pushed deep into the Black Forest, each team searching a separate grid. Now and then they'd flushed one of their prey who would run like game through the woods until a stream of autofire brought him down.

But it was dangerous hunting.

Since the first mass rush, Erhard's men had encountered several more of the men who'd been following Hunsruck. They'd followed him right to the grave, but they'd managed to take some of Erhard's men with them.

It was time to cut and run.

If they stayed much longer, they risked being trapped.

"Patrol by fire," Erhard said.

At his signal the hunters opened up and sprayed the field with full-auto bursts.

The silenced weapons burned through the tall grass, kicking up dirt and rock and chomping into the trees at the back of the clearing.

They stepped forward in tandem, changing magazines and squeezing off more full bursts to see what they could beat from the bushes.

SINCLAIR FLATTENED himself on the ground, looking up at the moonlight as lead burned the air around him. The volley of autofire made a continuous whipping and whirring sound.

It was familiar and frightening. The Vampyr gunmen were employing a technique occupation troops often fell back on when hunting guerrillas or resistance fighters—blanket the zone with bullets and you were bound to hit something.

Unfortunately, Sinclair thought, it was an effective method. Sooner or later something was bound to hit him.

The grass and brush broke ranks all around him, sliced by the intense bursts of lead. It sounded like a high-powered scythe chopping through the field, as if the grim reaper were approaching.

Sinclair prepared himself to spring up from the ground and take out the closest one of the bastards. Maybe he'd be lucky and even take down two before they punched his ticket.

He forced himself to lie still, listening to the bullets chop overhead, listening to the sound of other teams sweeping through other zones of the forest.

If any of his men had survived this far, their luck was running out.

The blades cut through the grass as the gunmen drew nearer. Three-round bursts sliced all around him, and now and then someone burned off a full clip.

A silhouette appeared about twenty yards away, standing on top of one of the mounds. The man was visible only for a second before he moved on.

Sinclair could hear him approach on the left.

He looked up at the sky, at the trees forming a circle on the edge of his vision. If this was his last look at the world, it wasn't so bad, he thought.

Not bad at all.

He raised the Colt, then leaned to his left, preparing to push himself straight up and get the drop on his stalker.

Footsteps thrashed closer to him. He saw the man's face. Young. Hard. Feral. Thirty maybe. But he'd spent a lifetime doing this kind of work, and from the look on the man's face, he enjoyed every minute of it.

Time to retire, kid, he thought.

Sinclair settled on a three-count before he would go into action.

One.

The gunman turned his way as if he could hear him thinking.

Two.

Sinclair fixed the man's position in his mind. He'd shoot on the way up, shoot again when he gained his balance, then keep shooting until the field was clear—or he was dead.

Three!

INCANDESCENT MOONS exploded above the treetops one after the other, bathing the woods with an artificial dawn. The ground seemed to glow, the grass painted yellow by the flares that streamed through the sky.

Standing in the middle of the brightness were several easy targets, staring up at the shattered night as if they were thunderstruck, their submachine guns momentarily pointing toward the heavens.

From every direction came the thrumming of black flight choppers, unpainted special-forces choppers that swooped low over the treetops and shook them in rotor wash.

Gus Sinclair was in motion when the sky lit up. He instinctively looked down at the ground, shielding his eyes with his left hand.

Then he changed his mind about the method of his attack. Rather than give himself away to the other gunmen by firing the 9 mm Colt right away, he went in for a quiet kill.

The man with the submachine gun sensed him rather than saw him. He started to turn toward Sinclair—just as the newsman axed his forehead with the gun barrel.

There was a solid thwack, the sound of metal cracking into soft skull. And then the man went down.

He stayed down forever, helped along by a kick to the side of the neck.

The whole thing had taken a couple of seconds, giving Sinclair time to take aim at the next-closest gunman. He fired once, blasting a hole in the man's temple.

The man sank to the ground, as if someone had let the air out of him.

Then Sinclair dived to the ground a split second before Axel Erhard opened up on him.

From the corner of his eye Sinclair had seen the man turn his way. It didn't take too long for his instinct to kick in and he threw himself into the dirt.

The first burst sailed harmlessly overhead.

Sinclair knew he wouldn't be so lucky the next time.

He scrambled to his right and took cover behind a small rise in the tall grass. Then with a two-handed grip he pointed the Colt in the direction he'd last seen Erhard.

He waited for the stalker to show, but there was no sign of the man. At least not in the direction Sinclair had expected.

The blond-haired ex-Stasi killer suddenly appeared off to Sinclair's right, a half smile on his face as he swung the Walther MPK in his direction.

Then the smile disintegrated, along with the side of Erhard's head.

Sinclair heard a silenced 3-round burst, then another. Shouts and screams erupted as the other men in the field were hit from all sides.

He stayed down until he heard a familiar voice call out his name.

It was Belasko.

AFTER A HALF HOUR of searching for the scattered troops of Erhard's strike force, Gus Sinclair emerged from the woods with the Executioner and the rest of the flak-jacketed men who'd rappeled from the silent Nightfox helicopters at the beginning of the firefight.

The choppers that had flown Bolan and a small army of GSG-9 and U.S. "observers" from the Saarbrucken safehouse were scouring the Black Forest from above, angry ravens with heat-seeking sensors that helped them find their prey.

Brognola and his German counterparts had decided to launch an all-out operation against the Roadhouse International crew, sweeping down on them shortly after Sinclair's surveillance team had started tailing Hunsruck.

When faced with the joint task force of German and U.S. special forces, most of the Roadhouse warriors gave up without firing a shot. The ones who resisted were dead. The ones who wanted to live a while longer tipped them off to the approximate location of Axel Erhard's strike force.

And now Bolan stood in the center of a Black Forest battlefield, eerily lit up by road flares and spotlights from the choppers that were hopscotching up and down the road. They were setting up temporary bases for the special-forces units to search for survivors from Sinclair's team, as well as stragglers from Erhard's team.

"We've got to get out of here," Bolan said, leading Sinclair to one of the choppers that sat on the road like a dark metal wasp.

"But Marty's dead—"

"There's nothing we can do for him now. Except maybe go after the man responsible for his death."

"What are you talking about?" Sinclair asked.

"Lorenz," Bolan replied. "We know where he is."

"Where?"

"Munich. Strashmir managed to narrow it down to somewhere in the Schwabing district. Brognola's got some people working on it right now."

Sinclair shook his head. The horror of the death and destruction around him would hit the newsman a lot harder now that the shooting had stopped.

But the war was still on.

CHAPTER TWENTY-THREE

"Pack a suitcase," Konrad Lorenz instructed, poking his head through the doorway of Simona Lascue's bedroom. "We are leaving."

"When?"

"Now."

"But it's almost midnight," she protested. "I was getting ready to go to sleep."

"You can sleep on the way."

"To where?"

Lorenz raised his hand for silence. "Just pack. Make sure you bring only one bag. We're traveling light and fast."

Simona tossed aside the German-language newsweekly she'd been reading. Lately it had been her only way of seeing the world. That and looking out the penthouse window at the street below were her only contact with the night life in Munich, life that was passing her by.

Though she'd been living with a man who controlled untold wealth, he was also one of the most wanted men in the world. The top floor of the Europa-Musikorps Tower had become a prison to her. No matter how plushly her penthouse suite was laid out, it was a prison just the same.

And now the warden was giving her one of his most severe looks. "Do it. You've got five minutes. No more."

"But I've got to know where we're going," she said. "So I know what to bring. I think—"

Lorenz glared at her. "Don't think. Just *pack*. We are running out of time."

Then he was gone, walking down the hallway. She could hear him talking with Christov Gudru, his ever-present bodyguard, in an urgent and hushed voice.

They were taking care of last-minute details: transportation, money, protection—all of the details of a life on the run. They were getting ready to go underground again.

She couldn't bear the thought of another trek with him. His temper was bad enough during good times. When he was under pressure, running for his life, it was even worse.

He would keep her in his sight at all times or entrust her to one of his handlers, the gruff-speaking brutes who followed his commands without thinking.

The same way she was supposed to.

The platinum-haired actress numbly slid off of the bed and began packing. Who would she be next time? she wondered. What alias? What country? What role would he force her to play?

It didn't matter. Konrad Lorenz had spoken and he was not to be denied.

Simona packed one suitcase, then quietly stepped into the hallway. She stopped halfway down the corridor that led to Lorenz's favorite command post, where the bank of television monitors and radio receivers saturated the air with endless bulletins and news reports.

Above the electronic barrage she could hear Konrad and his bodyguard working out the details of their imminent departure.

Christov Gudru sounded animated for the first time ever, like a child who was dreaming of Christmas. The bullnecked bodyguard was discussing their plans as if they were about to go on a holiday.

Or home.

Romania.

Gudru repeated the word several times, as if it were a mantra. There was an almost religious intensity as he talked about the routes they would have to take before they reached their final destination.

Romania. The homeland.

Simona scowled. Anything that could make the bearded and bald-headed troll happy had the opposite effect on her.

Gudru talked about Romania and about a fortress north of Bucharest, near Brasov, where they would be safe.

She saw the future, then. Hiding out in one grim stronghold after another while the Romanian authorities hunted them down. She knew Konrad still had powerful friends in the country but no matter what their positions were, they couldn't openly provide sanctuary to the monstrous Securitate killer.

He would try to bide his time until memories of his crimes faded. Or until witnesses could be reached.

In the meantime, other Romanians would hunt for him. Konrad Lorenz was a prime candidate for hanging, or execution by rifle squad. And anyone with him would get the same treatment.

She remembered the last days of the crumbling Romanian regime. She'd stood among the crowd that filled the palace square in Bucharest when Ceauşescu gave his last speech to throngs of civilians who jeered and laughed him off the podium. The man who'd spent billions of dollars creating monuments to himself had also wasted the treasury on creating summer palaces, winter palaces, country homes and underground bunkers. All this while the rest of Romania went to ruin.

She remembered the laughter and the hatred that had poured from the people when at last they saw the chance to destroy him. It was a universal feeling floating above the square, one still shared by the Romanians.

The people hated Ceauşescu, and they hated Securitate.

Konrad Lorenz was the embodiment of both. He'd help to make the dictator strengthen his position, and he'd excelled at making the Securitate a feared and reviled force.

Going back to the country with Konrad Lorenz was like carrying out her own death sentence.

Suddenly the voices in the next room ceased.

"Simona?" Lorenz called out. "Are you there? Come out where I can see you."

She stepped into the next room and set the suitcase on the floor.

Lorenz and Gudru turned to face her.

The bodyguard studied her with as much regard as if she were another piece of luggage, one more detail that had to be looked after, part of his boss's collection.

"You don't have to eavesdrop any longer," Lorenz said. "You'll know where we're going soon enough."

"I heard," she replied. "Romania."

"Yes."

"Why?"

"We have no choice. Our good friend Axel Erhard did not call in as scheduled. That can mean he is dead. Or worse, it can mean he has gone over to the other side."

The thought of Axel Erhard lying dead somewhere had no effect on her. He was dead from the moment she'd seen him. Dead like all the other creatures in Konrad's net.

"Even if Axel has merely deserted us, we can no longer trust in the sanctity of our operation. Too many people are looking for us and soon they will find us.''

"I don't want to go back.''

"It will be too dangerous if you stay,'' Lorenz said. "They've hit us in London, Vienna. And tonight they hit us much closer to home. Inevitably they will hit us here.''

"I'm not going with you,'' Simona told him.

Lorenz nodded. He seemed amused. "You've never stood up to me before.''

"I'm not going back there,'' she repeated. "Not as a criminal. It won't be any kind of life for me.''

"I see.'' He clapped his hand onto Gudru's shoulder. "Go and get the car ready.''

"You won't need me?''

Lorenz dismissed him with a curt nod.

"So,'' the Vampyr chief said when they were alone. "You wish to stay here?''

Simona nodded.

"I can't change your mind?''

"No.''

He nodded his acceptance, then turned away as if overcome by sadness.

When he turned toward her again there was a gleam in his eye—and a knife in his hand.

It was a small push dagger with the blade protruding from his fingers, the kind designed for easy concealment and rapid deployment.

Simona had just enough time to scream before the blade stabbed into her flesh just below her ribs.

She didn't feel the pain until he yanked the knife up and twisted it in a horrible coring motion. It seemed as if an electric shock were burning through her system and lifting her off the ground in agony.

Lorenz pushed her backward, cutting deeper with the knife.

"In some ways this makes it easier," he said, speaking in a casual voice as he yanked the knife out of her. "One less thing to worry about."

Simona's momentum carried her toward the floor, her hands flapping out like wings as her head knocked heavily onto the carpet.

Her hands curled around her wounds, then fell away coated with blood.

"It's a sad way to end it," he said. Then he smiled. "But I'll live."

A STRANGE QUIETNESS enveloped the room. It was empty of all life.

Almost all life.

Simona crawled across the floor, more dead than alive. She was piloted by willpower rather than strength. Her limbs felt numb, and her breath came in empty, strangling gasps.

Konrad Lorenz was gone, but he wasn't out of her reach.

He'd been too strong and quick for her face-to-face, but she had another weapon to wield.

Knowledge.

Simona moved beneath the bank of television monitors and speakers, their hiss creating an electronic whisper that seemed to urge her on.

Lorenz had spent his whole life gathering information on friends and enemies alike, using that knowledge to build his empire. It seemed only fitting that that information would help bring it to an end.

Simona made it to the phone bank on the table near the leather couch, propping herself up to make a call.

But as she held the receiver to her ear, she realized she wouldn't last much longer. Certainly not long enough to reach the authorities.

But long enough to reach Konrad Lorenz.

She flipped up the lid on the answering machine and pressed a record button, watching the small tape start to move. Then she spoke into the small microphone.

She only said a few words, but they were enough.

"Konrad Lorenz...back to Romania. Fortress. Brasov."

Then she slumped onto the table, still clutching the phone as if it were a direct line from the afterlife.

The pain fell away from her then, as did the sorrow and shame she'd lived with ever since she'd flown into Lorenz's web.

And then a thin smile formed on her lips. She'd struck back at him at last.

CHAPTER TWENTY-FOUR

Hal Brognola paced back and forth across the faded Persian rug that spoke of the former glory of the once-elegant apartment building. Like many of the other stone-facaded buildings in the middle of Bucharest, it had seen better days.

But the big Fed wasn't interested in the decor. He was more concerned with the functioning of the temporary command post that had been set up for him by the Agency's technological services division at the U.S. Embassy a half mile away on Tudor Arghezi.

The TSD crew had provided him with satellite transceivers and scrambler phones that let Brognola communicate with the covert teams he'd deployed in Romania. He kept track of their movements, as well as the suspected movements of Konrad Lorenz, on a large topographic map on the wall behind his desk.

Rather than operate out of the embassy, Brognola preferred to work from this unofficial adjunct, a secluded and secure complex of offices and apartments that the embassy kept on hand for use by visiting dignitaries or for operatives who wanted to keep out of the diplomatic eye.

The head Fed walked over to the floor-to-ceiling windows that looked out on the wide boulevards of the city. The streets below were bustling with activity, looking much like many other European cities. Full of life.

The last time Brognola had been to Bucharest it was a much grayer and bleaker capital, full of death and despair. But now that the shadow of the totalitarian government had been lifted, the atmosphere itself seemed lighter.

The old guard—the Iron Guard—had been finally removed from power. But there were still those waiting in the wings to bring back the old-style regime.

Chief among them was Konrad Lorenz.

He had plenty of sympathizers to call upon—former Securitate operatives who feigned rebellion against Ceauşescu once they realized he was about to fall. Some of them had managed to secure positions for themselves in the new government, although they lived in constant fear of exposure. They did their best to destroy all the evidence that linked them to skeletons in the closet and the underground bunkers.

Of course, if a man like Konrad Lorenz came back to make a bid for power, maybe their true colors would show.

Brognola wanted to make sure things didn't get that far.

The head Fed turned away from the windows and walked over to the map. Using his unlit cigar as a pointer, he tracked the movements of his people, keeping them firmly fixed in mind.

Team One was scouring the Black Sea resorts on the stretch of the Romanian coast near Constanta and Navodari. Several sightings had been made of Konrad Lorenz near the well-known Black Sea resorts. All of their sources, long-term deep-cover agents and officers from the "friendly" Intelligence services, indicated that Lorenz had made the Black Sea crossing from the Turkish coastland. Once on the Romanian side, he'd moved inland.

But Brognola was keeping Team One on the coast just the same. They might either turn up more leads on the whereabouts of Lorenz and his collaborators or they could serve as an emergency port of call for Team Two, the action arm Brognola had sent north. The big Fed was betting on Team Two to make contact with Lorenz's people. And when it happened, most likely it was going to be a *loud* contact, which meant Team Two might have to exfiltrate the country in a hurry once their mission was complete.

The seaside team had a small fleet of powerboats and luxury yachts at their command to handle that scenario.

Of course, there was always the chance that Team Two could hit and run without attracting too much attention. Then they could go back out the same way they'd come in—as tourists and newscasters who'd flown into the Bucharest airport from Germany.

A slim chance.

But he was prepared for anything.

The U.S. Embassy staff had gone the distance for him, providing transport and equipment for his small army of tourists. It helped matters that Brognola had the backing of the Man in D.C. on this one.

Brognola looked at the map again, zeroing in on the foothills of the Carpathian Mountains—where Team Two was heading at this very moment.

Everything pointed to Konrad Lorenz's being holed up there. When the GSG-9 unit broke into the Europa-Musikorps Tower in Munich, they'd found that Konrad Lorenz had been there and gone. But he'd left a woman behind, a brave woman who'd somehow had the courage and the willpower to leave a message for them, a verbal arrow pointing right at the heart of Konrad Lorenz.

Brasov.

Fortress.

At first the clues hadn't made much sense to Brognola and the Intelligence crew. If Lorenz was setting up his covert headquarters in one of the old fortress ruins that surrounded Brasov, he'd be too easy to find. Many of the fortresses that had once guarded the mountain paths were well-known tourist spots.

He'd be an easy target there.

But then someone mentioned the Securitate's idea of a fortress. The Securitate had built mile upon mile of underground tunnels and fortifications throughout Bucharest and the surrounding countryside.

Since Lorenz had been a higher-up in the organization, he'd no doubt had the ability to covertly create underground fortresses wherever he wanted. Their standard method of operation was to build underground, then camouflage the surrounding area to make it look desolate or deserted.

Bolan had seized upon the idea and brought Ion Cusa out of the comfortable safehouse in Frankfurt.

Cusa was reluctant to talk about the fortress near Brasov at first, preferring to keep it a secret.

Brognola remembered Bolan's response. The Executioner told him he could keep his secret—as long as he took it with him to his grave.

A grave that was being dug at that precise moment.

All of a sudden Cusa had felt like sharing his secrets with them once again. He knew of the fortress. As Lorenz's right-hand man, he'd helped to divert the funds and to create a phony paper trail to cover for the units that Lorenz had dragooned for the project.

And just as Konrad Lorenz's slain mistress had said, the fortress was near Brasov. Cusa's memory was weak on the exact location, but he knew the general area.

As an unexpected reward for his honesty, Cusa was promoted from prisoner to guide. He was with Team Two, posing as one more tourist.

Brognola trailed his finger over the wooded Transylvanian terrain. Somewhere out there, Mack Bolan and Team Two were hunting vampires.

CHAPTER TWENTY-FIVE

Bolan drove the Range Rover slowly up the grass-and-clay hillside to avoid kicking up a cloud of dust. He stopped the vehicle just before it reached the crest of the hill so there wouldn't be a large target silhouetted against the horizon.

To his left and right several other British rough-terrain vehicles and campers followed his example, spreading out like a civilian tank corps about to mount an attack over the hill.

The customized vehicles provided for Team Two by the embassy specialists in Bucharest were packed with high-tech surveillance gear and heavy-duty weaponry.

They'd traveled one hundred twenty miles from Bucharest and were now about fifteen miles outside of Brasov. Moving down narrow country lanes and across long grassy stretches and fields, the caravan had moved deep into the wild country of Romania.

Now they'd reached their final destination.

Perhaps.

Ion Cusa was sure this was the right place.

But the Romanian had been sure all day long. He'd found their final destination several times already. It was his guidance that caused the caravan to hopscotch around the valleys and fields surrounded by the Carpathian rim of the Transylvanian Alps.

Acting as interpreter, Gina Salvie was traveling with Cusa and two well-armed handlers in one of the Land Rovers, with Salvie passing Cusa's directions on to the rest of the team. The man's English was fair, but inadequate for the task at hand.

By now some of the men were getting ready to send Cusa to *his* final destination via a well-placed round.

Bolan was almost ready to join them—if this "final" destination wasn't the last one. Cusa said that this time he'd recognized some landmarks that convinced him they were getting close.

So far, they'd passed through a lush land of farms and fallow fields, forests, small villages and lakes. In some places stone walls from Roman days still ran side by side with more recent wood-and-stone fences.

Monasteries had sprung up and fallen across the land like sacred seeds of stone that were sacked and besieged then built up again, over and over through the centuries.

And in the mountain passes were the haunting remnants of castles, every one of which was supposedly *the* last stronghold of Vlad the Impaler, the historical Dracula, who'd been finally run down by the Turkish invaders deep in his own country.

It was a land where a man could easily get lost, Bolan thought. Or hide. But Konrad Lorenz wasn't traveling alone. Several men had reportedly shepherded him ever since he'd come into Romania. They were the old faithful, men who could still be swayed by Lorenz's wealth or wrath.

Such a contingent should be easy to find, if indeed they were looking in the right area.

Beyond the hill was a long and gently sloping incline that led to a sprawling plain bracketed by heavily forested foothills.

Several thick-wooded spearpoints of forest lunged out into the fields. Somewhere in that craggy wilderness was supposed to be the site of the fortress.

Bolan's hand splayed across the lever-studded console between the two front seats of the Rover. At the touch of a button the sunroof slid open, making way for the mast-mounted Jorgen Anderson Ingeniorfirma surveillance camera to rise up through the roof.

When the motorized pan-and-tilt thermal-imaging camera was high enough to look over the horizon, Bolan angled it forward to scan the jagged wall of birch and fir trees at the end of the plain.

Close by the edge of the woods were the shells of a couple of old farmhouses, little more than piles of rotting wood reclaimed by the forest.

While he studied the television monitor hanging in front of the windshield where the rearview mirror normally was, the warrior zoomed in on the larger of the two structures. Most of its roof was gone, and the windows and doors were boarded up and nailed shut.

Tall grass surrounded the house, leaving just a hint of an old path that led to the door.

It looked ninety-nine percent dead.

Hardly fit for a hideout for someone of Konrad Lorenz's stature.

With a slight whirring sound, Bolan levered the motorized periscope to life again and guided the camera across the forest, scanning it for any signs of life.

The imager picked up the heat signatures of small game moving here and there through the woods, but nothing man-size. Bolan adjusted the camera to take in a wide-angle look of the terrain, then hit the Record button and stepped out of the Rover.

To his right Gus Sinclair kept a steady watch through his mast-mounted camera. Sinclair had been somber ever since half of his crew had been wiped out in the Black Forest. Somber but sure. He wanted to ride this one out until the end.

In the long-range reconnaissance Range Rover to Bolan's left, Cass Strashmir calmly sat in the passenger seat with his weapon of choice, the Heckler & Koch PSG-1 sniper rifle, leaning against the roll bar like a fishing pole.

The former Securitate sniper was always watched by a couple of special-forces types who'd been assigned to him ever since they had all rendezvoused back in Germany. But Strashmir had proved himself to Bolan several times over.

The Executioner trusted the man and not just because the guy had everything to lose if he doublecrossed them—his country and his life. Bolan's instinct told him that Strashmir was playing it straight. In fact, he was playing it much the same way Bolan would have played it if he was in the same position.

"This doesn't look like any fortress I ever saw," Bolan said when the Romanian sauntered over.

"That's the idea," Strashmir replied. "It's not supposed to look like anything. These places are always built to blend in with the countryside. In the city, basements are turned into tunnels that lead to lower levels. In the country they choose caves or farmhouses that could provide cover.

"Those shacks might be part of the fortress?"

"I wouldn't walk past them with my back turned," Strashmir told him. "It looks like an outpost. Could be something here. Could be nothing at all. But there are plenty of caves in this area, natural formations that could be turned into Securitate bunkers."

Bolan nodded. "If you're so familiar with the operation, how come you never heard of this one?"

"You must understand the mindset we had in Securitate. It was truly an Alice-in-Wonderland world. More rabbit holes than any one man could keep track of. If Konrad Lorenz wanted to build a refuge for himself out here, he could have done it. And he could trust the people who built it for him to keep quiet. No one wanted to go against him in those days."

"All right," Bolan said. "What's your gut feeling on this? Are we getting close?"

"I think we have found his lair."

"What about Cusa?" Bolan asked. "Why did it take him so long to find this spot?"

Strashmir shrugged. "Take your pick. Maybe he wanted to give Lorenz as much time as possible to learn we are coming and get away. Or his memory really is bad. Maybe he still fears him. And then there's always the chance that Cusa is leading us into a trap."

"Exactly what I've been thinking. That's why when we get down there, Cusa's going to lead the way."

AN HOUR LATER the mast-mounted surveillance cameras picked up some ghost images moving through the forest.

Two man-size images.

As they ran through the dark forest, unaware of the long-distance electronic eyes watching them, the two men headed for the wooden shack.

The boarded-up door opened to admit them.

A few minutes later the door opened again, and two different men headed back toward the forest.

"We've just seen the changing of the guard," Strashmir said. "My guess is there's a lower-level bunker there, with maybe one man watching from the shack, the other man down in the bunker. Or it could be just two men in the shack."

"Let's find out."

A few minutes later a four-man scouting party in night black camos and body armor headed downhill, crouching in the tall grass. Bolan and Strashmir took the left flank while Sinclair and one of his men took the right.

It took about a half hour of running and crawling to reach the exterior of the shack without being seen.

They fanned out on all sides, each man rising from the high grass with a weapon in hand. While the others trained automatic weapons and a flame-thrower on the shack, Bolan stepped forward with a SNPE "Porcupine" rifle that looked straight out of a Buck Rogers movie. A thin hose ran from a cannister of CS gas mounted on top of the rifle to the snoutlike barrel.

Bolan silently nosed the snout of the rifle toward the thin wooden wall and pulled the trigger.

There was a loud thump and hiss when the SNPE dart punched a hole through the wall and flooded the hut with CS gas.

The men inside the ramshackle fortress started to bounce off the walls, coughing and kicking and trying to fight their way out through the choking cloud.

Finally one of the hardmen managed to push his way through the front door, nearly knocking it off its hinges.

As the man tumbled off balance through the open door, Bolan turned slightly and whipped an inside roundhouse kick just beneath the man's breastbone, knocking the wind and the fight out of him at once.

Still trying to shake off the effects of the gas, the man curled up on the ground.

The second guy out was reaching for his holstered weapon when Sinclair smashed the butt of his rifle into the back of the man's head. He went down hard and quiet.

After the gas cleared, the four-man unit searched the shack, finding a hidden room beneath the trap-door, which was equipped with a cot, a few fully loaded magazines and several small arms.

The Executioner fished the slim transceiver out of his combat vest and radioed the mobile team waiting on the hill. "Move in quietly," he instructed, glancing at the two prisoners, who were looking up into the muzzles of a trio of SMGs. "We've secured the shack and have two people who are ready to talk."

By the time Bolan's unit had dragged Lorenz's sentries to the treeline, the Rovers were rolling silently toward the forest to unload their cargo of men and equipment.

Gina Salvie was one of the first to get there and began to question the two captives about Lorenz's stronghold.

They were the talkative kind, figuring the more they said, the longer they would live.

CHAPTER TWENTY-SIX

Jagged spires of rock stood like ancient dolmens at the mouth of the cave, a ravine of rock that wound deep into the mountains. Forest shaded both sides approaching the entrance, but there was a clear swath of land in front.

Dead man's land.

In order to get to the cave, someone would have to approach in plain sight. With the moon shining brightly on the clearing, it was almost suicidal to even consider the maneuver.

It was also suicidal for anyone who walked out of the cave. Automatic rifles, grenade launchers, shotguns and flame throwers were part of the arsenal Bolan's half of the strike team had humped through the woods.

They were spread out in a half circle at the edge of the forest, ready to cast a net of iron if anyone ventured out. Unfortunately the purpose of a bunker was to allow its occupants to stay inside while the attackers were forced to go in after them.

There were signs that someone had been using the cave recently. As well as the thin footpaths running through the woods, several narrow furrows in the tall grass marked the passage of dirt bikes. Some tread marks were visible near the cave itself, though most of them had been swept away.

So far, everything told to them by the sentries captured at the shack had turned out to be true: the location of the caves, the trail bikes used by the couriers and cargo haulers, the bunker mentality of Konrad Lorenz. He was ready to go out in a blaze of glory and take as many people with him as he could in a Hitlerian fugue.

Bolan studied the approach to the cave again. Beyond the mouth, the inner chambers zigged and zagged, giving the defenders plenty of opportunities to ambush anyone trying to penetrate their stronghold.

Cass Strashmir crouched behind the Heckler & Koch sniper rifle, zeroing in on the cave. He moved slightly from left to right, tracking imaginary targets.

"What's our next move?" Strashmir asked. "Wait for him to take a midnight stroll? Or go in like the Light Brigade?"

"I didn't bring the team all this way just to throw their lives away. If we go in, we're going in with everything we have."

"We've got some pretty severe armament here," Strashmir said. "That's overkill, isn't it?"

"No," the Executioner replied. "More like *sure* kill. You know as well as I do there's only one way to fight a war. All out."

Strashmir nodded. "True. But then we risk destroying everything Lorenz has in there. Weapons caches. Plunder. Gold bars. Currency. All the things a man like that needs to stay in power. There might even be sensitive records in there, files that may prove my innocence."

"Your innocence is already proved," Bolan said. "In my eyes. In Brognola's, too. He'll do what he can to help you out. My guess is he's going to be staying behind after all this to smooth things over. He'll be calling in some favors and paying back others. You'll be included in the mix."

"Understood." A moment later the Romanian sniper looked away from his rifle and said, "But if we're going to do it your way, then let's just do it."

Bolan looked at his watch. "Soon. Sinclair's people are almost in position. We have some time. Besides, there is one more alternative."

"What's that? Invite him out?"

"Yeah," the Executioner agreed. "In a manner of speaking."

Strashmir gave him a quizzical look.

"Cusa wants to make a deal," he explained. "He wants to see if he can bring Lorenz out alive. If he manages to do that, we're supposed to drop all charges against Cusa in return. He wants to walk away from this a free man.''

"Do you trust him?"

"No," Bolan said. "Not really. But I'll give him a chance to prove himself one way or the other.''

LIKE A MADMAN HOWLING in the moonlight, Ion Cusa moved closer to the cave, his back watched by the covert strike force gathering in the woods.

"Konraaaad!" he shouted again.

The name bounced off the rocks over and over in a gruff echo. Each time Cusa followed it up with another shout.

Finally a shape appeared at the edge of the cave. The bullnecked man hung back at first, but then as he recognized the voice, he moved out into the open—almost far enough for Strashmir to take him down with a clean shot.

"Who's that?" Bolan asked, studying the man through his hand-held thermal imager. The man was bald and bearded, a Rasputinlike ruffian wielding an automatic rifle.

"Christov Gudru," Strashmir hissed. "I can get him now—"

"No," the Executioner said. "Not yet. First see what Cusa can do.''

"I should shoot Cusa first, then Gudru. Those rotten bastards have been due for a firing squad for thirty years now."

"Just wait. See if Lorenz appears."

KONRAD LORENZ WAITED at the top of the slight incline that led down to the mouth of the cave, staying out of sight until Ion Cusa stood just outside the moon-splashed entrance. Gudru and three other men held their automatic weapons on him.

It was like seeing a ghost.

"Ion," Lorenz shouted. "How can this be? I thought you were dead."

"I made it back," Cusa said. Sweat was pouring down his face despite the chill. "I was on the run all this time."

"But you never checked in," Lorenz said. "That meant that you were dead—"

"I didn't know where to reach you."

"Or you were…" Lorenz left it unsaid. Too much time had passed for Cusa to be wandering around wounded. He could have contacted him through one of their cutout numbers or left a message at the dead drops scattered around Germany. Emergency contact points had been established just for such occasions.

Lorenz thought back to everything that had happened since the failed mission at Koblenz. Shortly after Cusa had dropped out of sight, Lorenz's covert strike teams were hit one by one. Now the man showed up. There could be no other explanation. The Vampyr chief was about to be hit at his last hideout.

Lorenz raised his right arm, leveling the Brigant automatic at the middle of Cusa's head.

"No," Cusa said. "I came back to join you once again. To help you get away—"

The leader of the underground network shook his head. Maybe Cusa really thought he could come back at this point after giving up so much of the network. But the final equation was clear in Lorenz's hard, cold eyes. He pulled the trigger.

The shot echoed through the cave.

Ion Cusa fell dead on his back.

"OPEN FIRE!" Bolan shouted, pulling the trigger of the M-203 grenade launcher and sending a high-explosive round into the cave mouth.

On all sides of him automatic fire scorched through the darkness, chipping off the rocks and ricocheting deep inside the cave. The relentless barrage shook the ground as one explosion after another reverberated through the cave system. Lorenz and his men were forced to retreat.

No one could have lived through that onslaught.

Bolan waved the fire team forward. One man on each side of the cave mouth crept forward as far as possible, angling their flamethrowers to cover both sides. With a whoosh and roar, they torched the interior of the cave, sending long, searing sheets of flame that blackened the walls like dragon fire.

The shotgunners followed, unloading high-explosive shells and smoke and tear-gas grenades in rapid succession.

As the flame and smoke billowed through the cave, Bolan's team flipped down their night-vision goggles and respirators, then moved in like a small army of exterminators.

The team moved methodically inward, securing each chamber of the cave, then moving ahead with more firepower.

During the lulls between the assaults, the cave was lit by lantern light shimmering across the walls. A pathway to the heart of the cave had been marked off by ropes to help secure footing at the most treacherous dips and turns. There were tables laden with radios and coffee cups positioned against the wall where guards had stood their watch.

But the tables were burning now.

So were some of the Vampyr troops who'd been caught by the murderous volleys of flash and flame.

There was still some resistance. Now and then a burst of autofire sang through the cave, chopping at the walls and zigzagging at the feet of the attackers.

KONRAD LORENZ RAN swiftly in the midst of a phalanx of guards racing toward the exit of the underground bunker. Though most of the men were decades younger, he kept up with them with little effort and could have easily passed them.

But he was in no hurry to be the first one out. That was what his underlings were for.

Christov Gudru was in the lead of the armed band when it reached the rear exit of the cave, which looked like a small crevice from the outside until a smooth, sculptured slab of rock was pushed out by someone inside.

Gudru flattened himself against the far wall and pushed with his feet until the slab rolled open. Fresh crisp air poured into the cave, and with it came hope.

The bodyguard patted the man next to him on the shoulder and pushed him outside. He sent two more men right after him, then dispatched a second three-man team.

The first unit ran out into the clearing, followed closely by the second.

Both units had almost made it to the forest when suddenly they were besieged by an inferno of flame and lead.

A half-dozen automatic rifles opened at once, cutting their feet out from under them like a giant lead scythe. All six men were dead before they hit the ground.

From a fallen oak at the edge of the forest, Gus Sinclair slapped a flesh clip into his Colt and triggered a burst at the narrow opening in the cave, drilling one more Vampyr trooper who'd been about to turn back.

As the slain gunmen fell, one of Sinclair's men ran forward with an M-203 grenade launcher and thumped a round of choke smoke into the cave. At the same time the rest of Sinclair's team kept up a steady barrage while they advanced toward the crevice.

Then, like lethal bookends matching the team on the other end of the cave, Sinclair's men donned respirators and goggles, then hit the cave with flame, smoke and gas.

To KONRAD LORENZ, it must have seemed like hell.

Everywhere he looked, smoke billowed to the scorched roof of the cave and sheets of flame licked at its walls.

Grenades went off round every bend, generating a deadly cascade of rock and gravel.

There were only a handful of survivors to follow his retreat toward the cave mouth.

Gudru took the lead as they charged ahead like dead men on borrowed time. The man's SMG strafed around each corner, now and then hitting one of the attackers. His example gave confidence to the others, who were now propelled by fury and madness as they struck back at the invaders who'd brought death to their last retreat. There were few sharpshooters among them now, just trapped soldiers who were showing their teeth with every clip they fired.

The suicidal counterattack worked, forcing the invaders to pull back all the way to the mouth of the cave. They'd spent most of their grenades and flamethrowers in the first part of the assault, and had to regroup in the woods.

Lorenz made it intact back to the mouth of the cave.

But it was a shallow victory.

The invaders who'd breached the rear exit were coming up behind him. He had about another minute until they were here.

In front of him was a small but veteran strike force who'd in effect sealed off the mouth of the cave when they retreated to the woods. One step out of the cave would be his last.

And at his feet was Christov Gudru.

Gudru had been caught point-blank by a full-auto burst from one of the last of the invaders to retreat. He was lying dead in the dirt, his blank eyes staring up at the roof of the cave. There wasn't much left of his chest.

Nor was there much left of Konrad Lorenz's empire.

The men around him who'd been fearless ber-
serkers a moment earlier, now stood facing the gap-
ing mouth of the cave. They looked to him for
command.

But Lorenz had nothing left to say to them. They
could do what they wished. Live or die. His fate had
already been decided.

BOLAN'S TEAM had temporarily moved back to let
the force of the Vampyr charge spend itself as it
swept through the cave. Now that his team had a
chance to fall back and reload, they were going back
in to finish the sweep.

The Executioner slapped a fresh clip into his Beretta 93-R, preferring the accuracy of the machine
pistol to the destruction of the grenade launcher.

From here on in they had to be more precise in
their tactics. Sinclair's people would be hard on the
heels of Lorenz's Vampyr remnants, and the last
thing Bolan wanted were casualties caused by
friendly fire.

The warrior was about to give the order to ad-
vance when Konrad Lorenz appeared before them.

"Hold your fire," Bolan ordered.

The man looked as if he'd walked right out of the
mouth of hell. His skin was blackened from smoke
and fire, and countless cuts marred his skin. His

blood and the blood of his comrades had painted his scorched shirt red.

But Lorenz was still moving on his own power, inexorably stalking toward the woods. The look in his eyes was totally mad—as though he were the one with the superior numbers and had won the war.

He appeared to be unarmed.

At first.

But as he drew nearer to the woods, it was clear that the hand held close to his side carried an automatic.

He walked like a robot, with no sign of stopping or shooting.

Yet.

"Take him!" Bolan shouted, reading the look in Lorenz's eye just before the Vampyr chief raised his automatic.

Strashmir fired, the round from the PSG-1 drilling a round through the middle of Lorenz's forehead.

The Brigant automatic fell out of the man's hand before he could raise it high enough to shoot at anyone.

When Lorenz fell, Bolan stepped forward and looked at the mouth of the cave, where Gus Sinclair and the rest of the team were herding the hardmen who had surrendered rather than follow Konrad Lorenz's lead.

A cloud passed overhead, momentarily blocking the moonlight, as if the darkness was claiming one of its own.

The Executioner glanced down for one last look at the corpse that was the embodiment of evil.

The nightmare was over. Here was one Vampyr that would never rise again.

ATTENTION ALL ACTION ADVENTURE FANS!

In 1994, the Gold Eagle team will unveil a new action-packed publishing program, giving readers even more of what they want! Starting in February, get in on even *more* SuperBolan, Stony Man and DEATHLANDS titles!

The Lineup:

- MACK BOLAN—THE EXECUTIONER will continue with one explosive book per month.

- In addition, Gold Eagle will bring you alternating months of longer-length SuperBolan and Stony Man titles—always a surefire hit!

- Rounding out every month's action is a *second* longer-length title—experience the top-notch excitement that such series as DEATHLANDS, EARTHBLOOD and JAKE STRAIT all deliver!

Post-holocaust, paramilitary, future fiction— Gold Eagle delivers it all! And now with two longer-length titles each and every month, there's even more action-packed adventure for readers to enjoy!

CATCH THE FIRE OF GOLD EAGLE ACTION IN 1994!

GOLD EAGLE ®

NEW

**A HARROWING JOURNEY
IN A TREACHEROUS NEW WORLD**

by JAMES AXLER

The popular author of DEATHLANDS® brings you more
of the action-packed adventure he is famous for, in
DEEP TREK, Book 2 of this postapocalyptic survival
trilogy. The surviving crew members of the *Aquila* reunite
after harrowing journeys to find family and friends. They
are determined to fight and defend their place in what's left
of a world gripped by madness.

In this ravaged new world, no one knows who is friend or
foe…and their quest will test the limits of endurance and
the will to live.

The thrills come cheap...so does death.

JAKE STRAIT BOGEYMAN

by FRANK RICH

In the ruthless, manic world of cheap pleasures and easy death, professional bogeyman Jake Strait has stayed alive the hard way, and like everything else, he's available for a price.

In Book 4: **TWIST OF CAIN,** Jake Strait is hired by one of the rich and powerful to find an elusive serial killer called Cain—a collector of body parts who is handy with a nail gun. In this action-packed fourth and final book, Jake Strait wanders into the playground of the rich, only to find that he has been set up from the start.

Bolan delivers a death warrant to a conspiracy of blood and hatred in

DON PENDLETON'S
MACK BOLAN.

DEATH'S HEAD

While in Berlin on a Mafia search-and-destroy, Bolan uncovers a covert cadre of Soviets working with German neo-Nazis and other right-wing nationalists. With the clock ticking, Bolan hunts rogue Spetsnaz shock troops and skinheads out for blood…uncertain that his own people won't shoot him in the back.

Don't miss out on the action in these titles featuring
THE EXECUTIONER, ABLE TEAM and PHOENIX FORCE!

The Freedom Trilogy

Features Mack Bolan along with ABLE TEAM and
PHOENIX FORCE as they face off against a communist
dictator who is trying to gain control of the troubled
Baltic State and whose ultimate goal is world supremacy.

The Executioner #61174	BATTLE PLAN	$3.50	☐
The Executioner #61175	BATTLE GROUND	$3.50	☐
SuperBolan #61432	BATTLE FORCE	$4.99	☐

The Executioner ®

With nonstop action, Mack Bolan represents ultimate
justice, within or beyond the law.

| #61178 | BLACK HAND | $3.50 | ☐ |
| #61179 | WAR HAMMER | $3.50 | ☐ |

(limited quantities available on certain titles)

TOTAL AMOUNT	$	
POSTAGE & HANDLING	$	
($1.00 for one book, 50¢ for each additional)		
APPLICABLE TAXES*	$ _____	
TOTAL PAYABLE	$ _____	
(check or money order—please do not send cash)		

To order, complete this form and send it, along with a check or money order for the
total above, payable to Gold Eagle Books, to: **In the U.S.:** 3010 Walden Avenue,
P.O. Box 9077, Buffalo, NY 14269-9077; **In Canada:** P.O. Box 636, Fort Erie, Ontario,
L2A 5X3.

Name: _____

Address: _____ City: _____

State/Prov.: _____ Zip/Postal Code: _____

*New York residents remit applicable sales taxes.
 Canadian residents remit applicable GST and provincial taxes.

GEBACK5